Selling Out

Selling Out

AMANDA LEES

PAN BOOKS

First published 2000 by Macmillan

This edition published 2001 by Pan Books
an imprint of Pan Macmillan Ltd
Pan Macmillan, 20 New Warf Road, London N1 9RR
Basingstoke and Oxford
Associated companies throughout the world
www.panmacmillan.com

ISBN 0 330 39235 2

5 7 9 8 6 4

A CIP catalogue record for this book is available from
the British Library.

Typeset by SetSystems Ltd, Saffron Walden, Essex
Printed and bound in Great Britain by
Mackays of Chatham plc, Chatham, Kent

For everyone I love;
you ought to know by now who you are.

ACKNOWLEDGEMENTS

Unlimited thanks to Luigi, Amanda, Arabella, Clare, Jeremy, Neil, Nadya, Caroline, Becky and Emilie: an author's dream team and a great bunch of people to boot. And to everyone, especially Julia, who was generous both with encouragement and the occasional fiver. I am delighted that your faith was so spectacularly justified.

ONE

One more minute and she'd walk away. Back down the hushed corridor, past all the anonymous doors behind which a sad collection of travelling businessmen sweated it out in front of the porn channel or reached for the phone to order up a girl like her. She'd made it past the front desk unscathed and had swished along to room 537 exuding a great deal of attitude, changing her sensible flats for soaring stilettos in the lift and whipping off the glasses she wore as part of her respectable disguise. Having got this far she wasn't too happy to find a door that stayed firmly shut despite her increasingly less discreet knocks. OK, enough. She'd just have to write off the taxi fare and the hour spent slapping on her classy harlot look.

In a way she was almost relieved. An evening spent with a good book and a large glass of wine would be infinitely preferable to several hours' massaging some ageing ego. Well, this was one boring old buffer who would have to entertain himself whenever he decided to reappear. Alex reached for her mobile, her heart sinking at the prospect of dealing with the rapacious Swede who was her current procuress and who hated nothing more than to lose out on hard cash. She had barely dug it out from the depths of her bag when the door suddenly swung open in front of her. Hastily assuming her professional persona, Alex looked up and froze.

'Alex?'

'Nick!'

There was a short, stunned silence as the two of them gaped at each other. Nick was the first to recover. 'You'd better come in, before someone comes along.'

Opening the door a little wider, he ushered her in and solicitously took the coat she had draped over her arm. Alex's mind was racing almost as fast as her heart and she could feel a surge of heat flushing her whitened cheeks. Her worst nightmare had been exceeded. Bad enough that it was someone she knew. Much worse that it was someone she talked about incessantly with her very best friend. And in the most lusting and adoring of terms. Yes, it would seem that her best friend's man was not what he seemed. And now he knew that neither was she.

Nervously, they both started to speak at once. Nick graciously gave way, allowing Alex to blurt out the first and slightly tactless thought she had.

'Does Simon know you're here?'

'Of course not.'

No, of course he wouldn't. For a man who had half the models in London practically begging to service him, Simon could be a remarkable prude. Just wait until he heard about this: there would be no stopping the flow of disapproval.

There was an excruciating pause as they both cast around for something appropriate either to do or say.

'Um . . . drink?'

Alex nodded gratefully as Nick grabbed the handily

placed bottle of fizz and rather inexpertly poured most of it on to the table. Interestingly enough, his hands seemed to be shaking almost as much as hers. Alex took a deep breath and a frantic gulp from her glass and tried very hard to take control, not an easy feat through the paroxysm of coughing that had resulted from her unwise haste.

'So now you know,' she declared, in as dignified a fashion as streaming eyes would allow.

'Know what?' Nick looked at her in what appeared to be genuine bewilderment.

An impatient trill from her mobile interrupted Alex's sigh of exasperation. It was her latest madam, the bossy Swede, berating her for forgetting the drill. Always, always phone ten minutes after you get there. Make sure he's not an axe-murderer then conduct the transaction. Crucified with embarrassment, Alex aimed unsuccessfully for professional dispassion. 'She wants to know that everything's OK and that you are happy to pay the fee.' She could barely look at him.

Mercifully, Nick seemed to be expecting this part. 'Oh, yeah . . . of course . . .'

Numbly, Alex watched as he counted out the cash in front of her and tactfully placed it on the table at her elbow. Good old Nick, always sensitive to a situation. Through stiffened lips she reassured her boss that everything was now in order and that she would let her know when she was leaving.

'Sorry about that . . . I'm a bit like a taxi – you know, meter running and . . . um . . .' Alex gazed desperately at the floor for inspiration. A refilled glass of champagne was thrust into her trembling hand.

She glanced up gratefully and was rather disconcerted to find Nick grinning at her.

'You bastard. This is not funny.' Horrified, Alex heard herself choke on the lump that had risen out of nowhere to block her throat.

'Shit, Alex, I'm sorry. I was only trying to lighten things up a bit.'

'Well, don't.'

He tried again. 'Look, why don't we just pretend that this is just one of your normal . . . er . . . dates.'

'Oh, great.'

Still furiously trying to maintain some semblance of dignity, she could only mutter very short sentences for fear that the wobble in her voice would give way to a howl of humiliation. It was all right for him: he was paying for this débâcle and therefore, theoretically at least, the one in control. Oh, God, he was paying and she could only cringe at the thought of what he expected for his money. A sudden thought cut across her inner turmoil. 'Nick, how on earth did you get the number of the agency?'

This was heading into murkier waters and Nick knew he would have to play it carefully.

'Well, I didn't stand sweating in one of those phone boxes, if that's what you're thinking. Honest to God, it was pure coincidence. I was in a cab the other day on the way to a shoot and picked up this card someone had left on the back seat. I thought it was for the mini-cab firm or something but when I looked at it more closely it wasn't. Actually, it wasn't too clear what it was for so I dialled the number out of sheer curiosity.'

Alex didn't know whether to feel relieved or

intrigued. 'So you had no idea what you were doing when you called the agency?'

'Absolutely none. And I put the phone down pretty quickly, I can tell you. But then I got to thinking . . . And, well, here we are. I suppose I must have described you perfectly when she asked me what I was looking for. Unconsciously, of course.'

There was a meaningful silence and Nick prayed that his explanation had done the trick. She favoured him with a coolly appraising look, before nodding in apparent satisfaction at his story which, like all the best lies, was based partially on the truth. Alex would have been horrified if she had known she had dropped the card right where he could find it during one of her handbag scrambles. As for describing her perfectly, well, he had. It had not been too difficult to visualize someone who seemed to be occupying a large proportion of his waking thoughts. Now all he had to do was wine, dine and win her over.

He looked at her hopefully. 'Are you hungry? I've booked a table for eight thirty.'

'To be honest, I've completely lost my appetite. Look, Nick, you can't afford this – I mean, me and all of this other stuff . . .' Alex caught sight of his guarded expression and her attempt at kindly concern died on her lips. She could have kicked herself for so obviously hurting his pride. Averting his eyes he plonked himself down on a small sofa and gestured to her to follow suit. 'That's my problem, but I'm not too fussed about eating either so maybe we could just stay here and talk.'

The prospect was even more unsettling but the man had paid for her time and, besides, curiosity was winning out over mortification. What the hell was Nick doing this for? To prove something to himself? To try something new? Well, if that was the way he wanted to play things she was more than capable of assuming her all-too-familiar part. Alex seated herself opposite him and declared, 'OK, let's talk,' in as professional a manner as she could muster.

Silence replaced defiance as she tried hard to think of something appropriate to say. When she finally managed to speak, it was again at exactly the same moment as Nick chose to break the deadlock.

'Nick, I really think—'

'Look, why don't we—'

His grin softened the knot of nerves still resting at the pit of her stomach. 'Go ahead, Alex. Ladies first.'

'Still think I'm a lady, do you?' Her self-mocking smile signalled the fragile return of her streetwise attitude, but Nick was not fooled for a nano-second.

When he replied it was with gentle but absolute sincerity. 'Sweetheart, I always think of you as a lady. Now, what did you want to say?'

Taken aback by his kindness, Alex launched headlong into the big question. 'Nick, are you going to tell Simon about this?'

He seemed positively astounded at the suggestion. 'Of course not. It's none of his business, is it?'

'Isn't it?'

She had fixed him with her steadiest look but Nick was not to be fazed. His flatmate might be the perfect landlord and a bloody good boss but he was also the biggest control freak outside of a uniform, especially when it came to Alex. Simon seemed to assume that because he had grown up with her he had surrogate big-brotherhood and treated her accordingly.

'Alex! This has nothing to do with him. Simon need never know. I'm certainly not going to tell him, although I think you owe me a few answers.'

Alex's eyes glinted in defiant indignation. 'Bollocks to that. I don't owe you anything right now apart from a few hours of my time. I could just sit here and say nothing until ten o'clock and you'd still have had what you paid for.'

'Is that how you treat all your . . . customers?'

'If you must know, it is. All they are entitled to is the pleasure of my company and I make damn sure that's all they ever get.' Alex stared at him defensively over the purposely dignified tilt to her chin. She wouldn't swear to it, but for some unaccountable reason he suddenly looked vastly relieved.

Still, he pressed on, unwilling to let her off the hook until he had got to the bottom of things. 'But why on earth are you doing this? I mean, a girl like you . . . you have a job. You earn money to pay the bills and stuff so why this?' He tried to keep any judgemental note out of his voice. She was defensive enough as it was.

Alex gave a bitter little laugh. 'Oh, yeah, I have a job all right. One that pays a pittance and does my head in. I want to earn enough to give it up, afford some time to write the great novel or whatever. I want to be able to buy my own freedom and this was the only way I could think of to do it. After all, how many jobs can you think of that would pay an arts graduate this well?'

He had to concede she had a point but another part of the jigsaw had to slot into place before he got the whole picture. 'And what about whatsisname, y'know, that merchant wanker type you've been seeing? Can't he help you out? I'm sure he could afford to set you up and so on.' Much as Nick would hate to see that happen, he had to find out how the ground lay.

'Isn't that just another version of what I'm already doing? At least this way is more honest. I'm hurting no one but myself. It's my money, I've earned it. And worked bloody hard for it, I can tell you.'

'I can imagine . . .'

She rounded on him, intellectual argument abandoned in the flood of her visceral response. 'No, Nick, you can't. You really cannot imagine what it's like to sit there for hour after hour as some wrinkled old fool flatters himself that someone like me would actually want to hang on to his every word or gaze up at him like a lovesick sheep. That's what they pay me for – the pretence that they don't have to. That and the fact that they can kid themselves I might one day succumb to their charms if not their cash.'

'Are you trying to tell me you don't actually sleep with any of these guys? Oh, come on, Alex, this is the nineties, you know.'

'Precisely. And because it's the nineties I tell them it's my choice, imply that I need to know and trust someone before taking things any further. They can't complain. All they have technically paid for is my time and anything else is up to me. That's why I try to go only for the old boys. They're delighted that I actually want to spend more time getting to know them and they're old-fashioned enough to hate anything that seems too hard-nosed and commercial. I just make damn sure I never see the same person twice. It's a doddle.'

Not totally convinced, Nick pressed on. 'And they fall for this?'

'Swear to God. I've finally learned the art of batting my eyelashes. The silly old bastards go for it time after time.'

She might think she had it all under control but Nick couldn't mask his growing concern. 'You want to be careful, Alex. You're dealing with some dodgy people. They can't be too happy if you keep ducking out on your clients. Not that I'm suggesting you should sleep with them. Christ, no! But you really are playing with fire.'

Alex was growing impatient at this rather too searching interrogation. 'Look, they always ask to see me again, which keeps the agency happy. So long as they get their money they couldn't care less what I do. I just have to make sure the client is also happy. And they are, they're always trying for another date in the hope that they can get in there.'

'It must be very tempting, all that money and attention.' His tone was drier than a perfect martini.

'You should know. All those rich fashion types you mix with day after day. Must be hard to resist some of the offers you get. I know, Simon's told me many a hairy tale. We're both in the business of peddling illusion, Nick, it's just that I make sure I never promise more than I'm willing to deliver. Can you honestly say the same?'

Her barbed comments seemed to have hit home, although he was apparently more puzzled than pained by her attack. Still, she had to award him full marks for self-control as he kept his temper in check and pressed on in an admirably reasonable manner.

'Yes, but there must come a point where they lose their patience. It is, after all, what they expect for their money.'

She tried not to wince at this last comment and to match him for businesslike restraint. 'But by then I've moved on. The *Yellow Pages* are full of these agencies and when I want to leave I always tell them I'm getting married to an old boyfriend and giving up the business. It's amazing how sentimental some of these tough old bags can be. They usually wish me luck and in the same breath ask to see me again if and when it all falls apart.'

Having made her point, Alex held out her glass for another top-up, looking for all the world like a precociously clever child who has outfoxed the grown-ups. Gazing at her, Nick's accusatory stare softened and his shoulders sagged. He believed her: in her current frame of mind Alex had no reason to lie. If anything, after three glasses of champagne she was inclined to tell the truth with often breathtaking brutality.

'Anyway, now you know what I'm up to, what the bloody hell are you doing here?' she asked.

Caught on the hop, Nick tried to cover himself with ambiguity. 'Well, let's say I've got something to prove.'

'Thought so!'

Ignoring her triumph he ploughed on desperately,

improvising wildly. 'Alex, this is between you and me. Promise? This is really hard for me, especially as it's you of all people who knocked on that door. Swear you won't tell a soul.'

Looking at her expression of sympathetic curiosity, Nick knew he'd struck the right chord. Not too far under that glossy urban exterior there lurked a streak of ready, if occasionally misdirected, compassion.

'Alex, I don't quite know how to say this but, well, I've had some doubts. For some time now. About, you know, erm . . .'

Horribly fascinated by what she was about to hear, Alex nodded in what she hoped was encouraging empathy. Her heart lurched as he dropped his beautiful head and knotted his fingers in what she could only assume to be an agony of inarticulate embarrassment.

'Come on, Nick, I think you can tell me . . . whatever it is. Come on. Try.' At this soft encouragement he seemed to rally slightly. If truth be told, he was desperate to get it right. Too much and he would lose her for ever. Too little and she might think he was trying merely to get into her knickers for one night of experimentation.

'OK, here goes. I'm not sure I can do it properly any more. You know – sex. That is.'

Alex was trying hard to believe what she had just heard. Here was this gorgeous, kind, funny man who represented Adonis and then some to Simon and not a few others, and he was telling her that he needed to find out if he was any good in the sack. Her mind boggled at the possibilities.

'Nick, this might be a dumb question, but why are

AMANDA LEES

you talking to me? Why not Simon or . . . someone else,' she finished, rather lamely. This was all most bizarre. Surely he couldn't be confused about his sexuality? It had certainly never been an issue with any of the other gorgeous creatures Simon had snared. Not many could resist him, if they were at all that way inclined. What he wanted he got, in the most charming of ways, and he wanted Nick badly. But for once, maybe, things were not going as well as Simon made out.

He looked at her oddly. 'Surely I'd get a better idea from a woman.' Nick knew that Alex and Simon were close friends, but did she have to bring him into everything? He always found it vaguely irritating that she assumed Simon had all the answers. Simon, of all people, would be the least suitable person to give advice to any straight male about his sex life, prone as he was to single-minded pursuit of the prettiest male flesh on offer.

Alex shrugged and conceded this point. 'Well, I suppose so. We're easier to talk to and all that.'

'And all that.'

Nick lifted his head and for rather longer than a heartbeat their eyes locked. Alex broke the dangerous moment to swill back the contents of her glass and reached for reinforcements. 'Shit. The bottle's empty.'

He smiled at her anxiety and reached for the room phone. 'Not to worry. I'll order up another.'

'Nick, I know you can't possibly afford—'

The look he threw her cut her off in mid-stride. Whatever he was out to prove, it included an inaccurate assessment of his own bank balance. Still, she had to admire the aplomb with which he handled room service. She had forgotten how well travelled Nick was. His modelling days must have taken him to more than a few four-star hotels. All this was quite revelatory and she found this sophisticated side to Nick oddly attractive.

She must have been staring for a second too long, because Nick shifted under her gaze and demanded, 'Alex, why are you looking at me like that?'

The embarrassment of it, caught with her tongue hanging out like a lovesick teenager! Desperate to regain some semblance of cool, she leaped a little unsteadily from her chair and made for the bathroom. 'Like what? Erm . . . I really must go to the loo. 'Scuse me.'

Safely locked away behind the bathroom door she allowed herself a small sigh of relief. Catching sight of her dishevelled, bright-eyed appearance in the mirror above the basin, Alex decided that what she needed was a good talking-to.

'You silly cow, he's probably just trying to talk to you as a friend. You are not to do this. Not that anything is going to happen. Simon would kill you if he found out.'

'You all right in there?' Nick's voice made her jump and she called back brightly. 'Oh, ah, yes. Just coming.'

She hoped fervently that her muttering to herself had not filtered through the bathroom door. An unnecessary flush of the loo and a last meaningful glare at herself in the mirror and Alex emerged, a slightly hysterical grin plastered across her face. Almost immediately there was a discreet tap on the door.

The thought of being rumbled by room service

usually sent her clients into a fluster but Nick seemed entirely unperturbed. She affected nonchalance as a uniformed waiter swept in and discreetly ignored her presence. A handsome little tip passed hands and they were again left alone to untangle their situation.

Nick cracked open the bottle and, having topped up her glass rather more than his own, began again to dig for details. 'I presume you haven't told Richard about your sideline?'

She grinned at the sheer impossibility of the idea. 'What do you think? He'd probably collapse face forward into his *Daily Telegraph*.'

That, he had to concede, was a very real possibility. What little Nick had seen of Richard had only confirmed Simon's expressed opinion of him as a man pompous before his time.

Alex shrugged, as if to dismiss Richard, and smiled, a little too brightly. 'So I guess we're both here under false pretences.'

Nick caught his breath. 'Why do you say that?'

'Well, you know, we've got an equally guilty secret. It's just that you're on one end of things and I'm on the other. This isn't really my scene and I'm pretty sure it's not yours. It's just . . . bizarre.'

He played for time. 'Which bit of it? The situation or the fact that it's you and me?'

'Well, both, I suppose. But it is strange that it's you and me here, yes.'

'Why?' It seemed as if they were getting down to the nitty-gritty and Nick's voice sounded half strangled, so hard was he struggling to suppress a mixture of anticipation and apprehension.

'Well . . . because.'

'Because the idea of you and me is totally ridiculous?' There, he'd said it. Nick looked at her face and watched the feelings flit over it, crossing his metaphorical fingers with all the hope and despair of a gambler who has played his last card.

Unaware of the significance of the moment, Alex wondered where he was taking this. She was trying hard not to shatter what little confidence in himself he seemed to have left. 'I just think you're a little confused about things right now, Nick.'

He had never been clearer-minded in his life, his only source of confusion trying to work out whether it was guilt bringing a flush to his cheeks or a surge of excitement as he crept ever closer to his ultimate goal. 'It's pretty clear to me, Alex. I think you're gorgeous, really beautiful. And far too good for that boyfriend of yours.'

So that was his tack! A dull glow of anger began to form in the pit of her stomach. God, men were so transparent. This was yet another attempt to make her see sense on the Richard issue, albeit the most elaborate one yet. No doubt Simon had put him up to this charade, had probably even financed it with his gold card. Just for that Alex gulped back yet another glass of fizz and resolved to drink his plastic dry. 'I see.'

He had hoped for a more enthusiastic response but pressed on regardless. 'And what about me?'

'What about you?'

Funny, but she seemed almost to be toying with him now. Bravely, he persisted, 'What do you think of me?' With a sinking heart he realized that the surge of excitement had been a touch premature. She seemed to have retreated behind a sudden wariness and he couldn't for the life of him work out why.

'Oh, I think you're absolutely lovely, Nick. And I'm sure that this . . . problem of yours is purely temporary.' Alex took another sip from her glass and fixed him with the iciest of social smiles.

There was no mistaking the definite drip of sarcasm. Something had spooked her and she had withdrawn all the earlier sympathy that had built up his hopes to fever pitch. Bewildered by her reaction, he spoke from the heart. 'You don't believe me, Alex. I don't know why but you seem to think I'm making all of this up. What kind of sick bastard do you think I am?'

Dejection and desperation added just the right edge. Snapped back from the lofty heights of her moral superiority by the genuine catch in his voice, Alex leaned forward and grabbed one of his hands in hers. 'No, no, of course I don't. I'm sorry, Nick, I just had this ridiculous idea that Simon put you up to all this and . . .'

Now he stared at her as if she really had lost the plot. 'Simon? Are you nuts? I told you, he knows nothing about this and if he found out I'm sure he'd be banging on that door demanding to know exactly what was going on.'

'I'm sure he would.' Alex gazed at him sorrowfully, all too aware of the warmth of his hands between her own.

His nerve-endings tingling at her touch, Nick risked the introduction of another tricky subject. 'And as for Richard . . .'

'Oh, I wouldn't worry about him. He'd probably just bash us both over the head with the newspaper or something. Not that we're doing anything wrong.'

At least, he mentally amended, not yet. 'Of course we're not, but some people might think otherwise. You know what they're like.'

'Let them. Pass your glass. I think you could do with a splash more, Nick. You're awfully slow tonight.'

And with good reason. He hadn't come this far to fall at the last hurdle, a victim of his own excesses. When the moment came he wanted everything to be perfect, and that included his own performance. Snatching the glass away before it overflowed, Nick noted that her cheeks were glowing and her eyes brighter than ever. Alex had always been fairly good at holding her drink, the only obvious sign an endearing increase in affection as with each glass the layers of reticence were sloughed away. That, at least, was what he had been banking on.

'Anyway, the boring bastard's gone off to some conference in Geneva. Something to do with shuffling bits of paper around to make even bigger piles of cash.'

Nick could just imagine Richard cutting his deals, not a flicker of emotion disturbing those smugly sanguine features. 'Must be great, having all that dosh.' Although it was a shame about the lack of personality. For the life of him he couldn't understand what Alex was doing with a man who made insurance salesmen seem sexy by comparison.

'I don't think he even notices, far too busy making it to have fun with it. Although, to be fair, he's always really generous,' she amended hastily, recalling Richard's ostentatious attempts to win her over.

Rattled by this kindly comment, Nick sloshed yet more champagne into her glass in the hope of blotting out all thoughts of his rival.

The pleasant fog forming over Alex's brain did not prevent her from noticing that Nick was far more generous with her glass than with his own. Half-heartedly, she protested, 'Trying to have your wicked way with me?'

Even to her own ears that sounded unbearably coy but Nick took it straight on the chin. 'That would be nice.'

His tone had been light and his half-smile was almost reassuring. Almost. Alex was finding it increasingly difficult to concentrate, never mind work out whether he was being serious.

Clinking his glass against hers, Nick privately toasted the absence of any other distractions. 'There you go, Richard's not the only one who can ply you with champagne. Bet you've never spent an evening like this with him.'

'This is certainly different. I mean, of all the people to open that door . . .' Alex's shoulders began to shake as the ludicrousness of the situation hit home.

Nick didn't know whether to be affronted or amused. 'And what is that supposed to mean?'

'You, me, this . . .' she spluttered, waving a helpless hand as she gave in to infectious laughter.

Succumbing to his own sense of the ridiculous, Nick felt incongruously happy. Finally they had both begun to relax, something he had been afraid would never happen, given the circumstances. Seizing the moment, he reached out to her with his free hand. 'Alex, come over here. No, don't look at me like that. I'm not going to leap on you. It's just easier to talk when there isn't that stupid table between us.'

Inexplicably disappointed, she plonked herself beside him, kicking off the hated stilettos and curling her legs beneath her in a way that threatened Nick with mild asphyxia. At this rate he would expire from sheer shortness of breath before he got to first base.

Unsettled by his proximity, Alex went for one last attempt at conscience-pricking. 'Not too bothered by fidelity as a concept, then?'

He looked at her with utter seriousness before replying, 'As a matter of fact, I am. And you can't talk, you're the one with a steady boyfriend.'

That reminder of her own culpability distracted her, or Alex would have thought harder about his last remark. 'Richard's very big on it. Probably because he's convinced that half the time I'm off playing whilst he's chained to a hot stock market.'

'And he'd be right, wouldn't he?'

Her cheeks flushed with indignation. 'That's not fair. I told you, I never actually do anything. Not so much as a snog. If there's one thing going out with Richard has taught me, it's self-control.'

'God knows why you stay with him, Alex, you could have anyone.'

At this her shoulders drooped. 'Yeah, right. All I've got to offer is a whole heap of unfulfilled potential.'

'I know how you feel.'

It was his turn to look crestfallen and Alex rounded on him with justifiable indignation. 'That's bullshit,

Nick. Your photos are bloody good. Anyone knows that all you need is that one break and you've made it. Ask Simon. It took him ages to get there but now look at him. Loads of money, great flat, great flatmate . . .'

She couldn't quite keep the meaningful edge out of her voice but Nick appeared oblivious. Like a Rottweiler on heat, there was no diverting him from his ultimate goal. He would do anything, argue any corner and break any rule if it would make Alex see the truth about a man who considered ludicrous ties to be the epitome of self-expression. Richard would simply have to find someone else to admire his Windsor knots.

'Stop trying to change the subject and listen to me. You don't have to sell out, Alex. You don't have to compromise for someone like Richard just because he'll make sure all the bills are paid. I mean, how could you even think about settling for a man who colour codes his socks, for goodness' sake?'

She glanced at him in admiring astonishment. 'How do you know he does that?'

'I can tell. And you're trying to sidetrack me again. What about what you want from life? What about your own talent? Simon often talks about your writing, says it's bloody good. And you tell me not to give up on my dreams. What about yours if you settle for the easy way out? Somehow I can't see you as the perfect corporate wife, never mind mother to Richard's little pink offspring. Just think, a few years down the line and you'll be driving the Volvo down to the country at weekends.'

'Enough about me and Richard! You can't tell me your love life isn't complicated. Otherwise you wouldn't be here.' Alex silenced him with her most forbidding glare, and another awkward silence descended upon them. Determined not to be the one to rush in and fill it, she gazed off into the middle distance and let her mind fill with one of the great imponderables. Why was it, she wondered, that the good guys always had some fatal flaw? Take Nick – and, boy, how she wished she could. Good-looking, talented, kind, adorable . . . and gay. So unfair, but Simon had never yet been proved wrong. It was enough to turn the most red-blooded of women into a raving fag-hag.

Nick's quiet response to her assertion interrupted her agonizing over the unfairness of it all. 'Actually, it's very simple. I don't really have one. At least, not in the way you mean.'

Trying delicately to clarify matters, she enquired, 'But what about Simon?'

What about him? Simon might be friendly and generous with his attentions, but Nick put it down merely to his artistic temperament. He had the broadest of minds and the sunniest of natures but there might well have been blood on the minimalist floorboards, had Simon forgotten himself so far as to show his hand, never mind any other part of his anatomy.

'I'm not sure what you're getting at, Alex, but if you really want to know—'

'No!'

Even she was startled by the vehemence of her response but, faced with the prospect of the ghastly details, Alex could not bear to listen. Whatever it was they got up to, she would rather leave it to the darker depths of her imagination.

'I was only going to tell you that—'

By now she was practically burying her head in the sofa cushions. 'No, really, Nick, I'm sorry I asked. It's none of my business.'

'And my sex life is? Look, I wasn't going to tell you this but the truth is that I don't . . . you know . . .'

This brought her out from her upholstered safety-net. 'You mean you don't . . . do it?' She could hardly sputter out her words. Someone, somewhere was taking artistic licence with the truth and she would bet it wasn't the unMachiavellian Nick. Or, rather, she very much hoped it wasn't.

'Haven't since I lived in the Far East. You know, all that once bitten, twice shy stuff. I thought it was going to last for ever but it all ended badly – a real mess. And I'm not into one-night stands so I've just been kind of licking my wounds ever since. Or acting like a total coward, one or the other. I sometimes feel like all the confidence has been knocked out of me.'

'I'm sure that's not true. You just haven't met the right person yet, that's all.' Alex's heart went out to him whilst simultaneously sinking at the thought of Simon's reaction. Knowing him, it would only stiffen what could be euphemistically referred to as his resolve.

'Bet you think I'm a dead loss, eh, Alex?'

A sad loss to womankind, maybe, but one glance at his shy smile and Alex had to stop her heart from performing back-flips. She was sure her bosom was practically heaving in time-honoured fashion and she was amazed that a puddle had not yet formed around her feet from the palpable melting of her heart. Here was most definitely a man in need of help; at any rate, that is what Alex chose to tell herself, whilst ignoring the real reason for her inability to breathe evenly.

'Nick, you must have at least dabbled your toes in the water since then. You know, the odd . . . um, kiss or something.'

Dolefully, he shook his head. 'Oh, God, this is so embarrassing! I can't believe I'm telling you all this. No, Alex, the truth is that I haven't so much as pecked anyone on the cheek for the best part of two years and if you want to know why it's because my ex informed me as a parting shot that a Labrador puppy slobbers less than I do, and I quote. As for my prowess in the sack—'

To her horror, Alex thought she caught a glimmer of unshed tears in his clear blue eyes. They were certainly shining very brightly and he was staring fixedly at nothing in the way that people do when they are trying very hard not to embarrass themselves.

Lifting his head in response to the soft little hand that had been placed upon his arm, Nick's heart lurched at her expression. The sassy urbanite was gone, replaced by a woman with a mission and a gleam in her eye to signal its presence.

'Nick, I'm sure that was said in the heat of the moment. I bet you're a great kisser. Look, I know I'm not the right person or anything but why don't we try to just . . .'

'Well, if you're sure . . .'

Fighting his eagerness to seize the moment before she could change her mind, Nick slowly bent his head to meet the soft mouth held so trustingly up to his. Unbelievably delicious, it sent shivers down his spine and he was sure that he could feel Alex trembling under his touch. To touch her at last was sheer bliss but he had to force himself to tear his mouth from hers, anxious not to appear too adept. The look of trepidation on his face was perfect, and he had done his best to appear as inept as he could. It had not been the most technically perfect experience but the sense of unfulfilled passion was tantalizingly apparent.

'I think . . . erm . . .'

'What are you thinking?' When it comes to the crunch, go for a cliché. Nick was not proud of himself but these were difficult circumstances.

She looked suitably disgusted at the crassness of his question. 'I hate being asked that. Always makes me want to lie instantly.'

Nick was desperate now to hear the truth. 'Don't. Just tell me exactly what you're thinking right this very minute.'

'I was thinking that there is nowhere else in the world I would rather be right now.'

'Except perhaps in bed?'

She attempted a quip to defuse the unbearably heightened tension. 'With my mug of cocoa?'

'Not exactly.'

Disconcerted by his directness, Alex cast around for a diversion. Her eyes lit upon the bottle of champagne and she strove valiantly to cover her increasing nervousness by brandishing it with what she hoped was abandoned gaiety. 'Top-up?'

Manfully suppressing his frustration, Nick held out his glass. 'Thanks— Now come back here. There, isn't this nice?' Glasses refilled, he pulled her gently back down beside him and dropped a casual arm around her.

Alex felt as if a million bolts of electricity were shooting through her shoulders and she strove in vain to emulate his relaxed insouciance. With unforced naturalness he began idly to stroke her hair and, lulled by the languorous motion, she began slowly to relax. She loved the feel of his gently raking fingers. It made her feel like a pampered Persian cat, all boneless sensuality. Unconsciously she arched against him and turned her face up, a beatific smile betraying her delight. She was floating away on an intoxicated cloud of pleasure, limbs all heavy and thoughts drifting somewhere way above the clouds.

And then he kissed her.

Just like that, no warning, no hesitation. This time no games were being played and no points being proven. She kissed him right back as if it were the most natural thing in the world. Which it was, far more than it had been before. No awkward clashing of teeth or cricks in the neck. No embarrassed desire to keep babbling on even with someone else's mouth firmly covering her own. No, this was real and honest and totally divine, and she could hardly bear it when he eventually pulled away. 'Stay with me, Alex. Please.'

'I'm not going anywhere.'

'No, I mean stay the night. With me.'

For a long, long moment she stared straight into his eyes and, for the first time in her life, understood the real meaning of intimacy. She could look at Nick for ever and not feel a need to cover up her emotions with some clever little line. There was none of that familiar need to defuse the almost palpable tension between them with a joke or a self-deprecating little remark. She didn't want to keep this man at bay. Far from it: Alex was having to restrain herself from lying at his feet and begging him to do anything he liked, anything so long as it was right here and now and would go on and on and on. Not that there was any need to go that far. When he stood up from the sofa and held out his hand to her she took it unhesitatingly and allowed herself to be led over to the king-size bed, which had loomed in the background throughout the evening.

Pulling her down beside him, Nick had just begun a thorough exploration of her dress fastenings when, faintly and insistently, her mobile again began to trill. Somewhere in the fogged recesses of her mind Alex recognized its tone and a sudden thought caused her to sit bolt upright.

'Shit! It's that bloody woman. It can't be ten o'clock already.' But it was, and now she would have to convince Ulla that her date was over or there would be hell and a lot more money to pay.

'Ulla, hi. Yeah . . . actually I'm in the loo.' This whilst backing frantically into the bathroom and turning on a convenient tap. 'No, it's OK. I can talk. Yes . . . we're just leaving the restaurant. Yes, very pleasant. No, that was literally all he wanted. Um . . . well, to tell you the truth I think he's a bit nervous. Probably a good candidate for another date. I think he likes to get to know someone first and all that stuff. Yes, sure, I'll drop the money by tomorrow. Yes, I'm signing off now. Think I've eaten far too much. Saturday? I'll have to, uh, check my diary and let you know. Great, OK, see you tomorrow.'

Emerging from the bathroom now coldly sober, Alex met Nick's enquiring look with a guilty one of her own. 'I'd completely forgotten about all of that. I'm supposed to call her and let her know if I'm leaving or staying and sort out the money stuff if there's any more to be paid.'

'You're staying.'

Nick's unequivocal arm had again pulled her down beside him and his mouth effectively silenced any more need to explain. Amazingly enough, she began to relax again almost immediately. It felt so right to be pressed up against him with his hands gently roaming over her and his gorgeous mouth promising her a whole new world of delight. Tentatively, she reached out her own fingers and ran them down his spine. She had just begun on his shirt buttons when her little black number dramatically gave way as he mastered the zip that ran the length of it and pulled it down over her hips. Wholly absorbed in her task and relishing the feel of her bare flesh against his, Alex forgot to suck in her stomach or worry about an attractive angle for her thighs. And as his hands slid down to make light work of her knickers, she forgot about anything and everything in the world save this incredible moment.

He trailed kisses across and along her body, exploring and arousing as he went. She shivered as he pressed lower and lower, the white heat of her desire blanking out any residual shyness. The faint scratching of his chin against her soft flesh felt brazenly masculine, the softness of his touch belying the seriousness of his intent. He was an astonishing lover, both tender and light-hearted at the same time. There were no awkward pauses or fumbles and absolutely no need to impress.

Alex could, and often did, put in a technically brilliant performance in bed. Sometimes she almost enjoyed herself. But this, this was something else. Above all, it was amazingly honest. Inspired by his own lack of pretence, she grabbed his hand, guiding it where she wanted it and he returned the compliment. They moved beautifully together, at times playfully, at others with blinding intensity. Just the two of them, for a brief time completely at one. And with no thought of anyone but each other, no hint of guilt or remorse to diffuse their passion. They were, quite simply, meant to be.

Driven half mad by the mounting urgency of her need, Alex grew desperate to feel him inside of her, to claim him as her own. She pulled him hard against her, at the same time answering his unspoken question with a demanding, desperate kiss. Lifting her hips towards him he entered her in one clean thrust and for a moment there was absolute stillness in their souls. Their eyes met and locked in a gaze of such transparent love that no words were necessary and no awkwardness permitted. In response to the almost unconscious grind of her hips he began to move inside her, as slowly as he could at first and then with uncontainable abandon. They descended together into a red haze of lust, the sweat slicking their bodies as their passion burned higher and faster. At one point he gazed at her through half-shut eyes and marvelled at the beauty of the body joined to his own, the dim light outlining every curve and sinew as she reared back and then fell frantically against him once more. Theirs was a lovemaking made more abandoned by the depth of their feeling for each other, emotions which, in those few short hours, were unconstrained by reason or convention. They spent themselves in unrestrained expression of their need for each other and cried aloud for the blinding ecstasy of finally coming together.

Afterwards, as she curled against him and felt that same slow caress across her back and around her shoulders, Alex drifted off into a warm, distant place where it would always be like this, just the two of them suffused in mutual bliss. She would never have believed how perfect it could be. Richard made love as if from a great and impenetrable distance, an affliction common to many an Englishman. Nick, on the other hand, had no fear of emotion or of intimacy. His openness had taken her beyond her hesitation and half-felt shame to a place of trust and relaxation. A place where she could giggle with her lover and not be afraid of a dented ego and where the flatness of her stomach bore absolutely no relevance to her capacity to please and arouse. Alex had never felt so accepted and desired in her entire life. She was totally and completely satisfied, a languid heap now sleeping the sleep of the happily exhausted. And next to her Nick lay alone with his thoughts and prayed harder than he had ever done in his life.

TWO

Another day spent hunched behind her flickering PC, brain rapidly rotting as she churned out the odd item of Lydia's correspondence. For a financial PR, Lydia seemed to spend an awful lot of time fobbing off her creditors. Alex had lost count of the times she had lied fluently down the telephone whilst obeying the frantic gestures of her spendthrift boss. She could only attribute it to Lydia's messy divorce and subsequent dependency on retail therapy, something in which Alex would love to indulge more often if only she could drum up the same elasticity of plastic.

Only three more hours to go and she was free to schlep home to a nice glass of red, a takeaway and an evening camped out on the sofa in front of a couple of videos. Richard was away on one of his regular jaunts Stateside, leaving her free to indulge in pure slobbery and the odd inebriated supper with Simon and his flatmate Nick. She wondered how that was going. Simon's heartfelt phone calls to the office had dwindled, a sure sign that things were proceeding nicely. Alex could chart the progress of Simon's relationships in direction proportion to the amount of time he spent bending her ear in his best suffering romantic fashion. She couldn't begin to remember the number of times he had finally, irrevocably, been in love for ever and ever until his boredom threshold kicked in and eternity became a matter of weeks, or days if the new squeeze was really unlucky. Not that he was ever unkind. Far from it: he was one of the most generous and charming creatures most of these pretty young men could ever hope to meet. Unfortunately for them, he was also possessed of a rapier-sharp mind that demanded more fuel than the conversation of the average aspirational male bimbo.

Alex smirked as she remembered one spectacular specimen who devoured action movies as if they were the word of God and viewed art films with singular suspicion. Simon had confided that he thought Chad's aversion to subtitles might well be related to an inability to read more than the odd tabloid headline and, reluctantly, Alex had had to agree. Such a waste: a perfect physique occupied by a man with all the depth of an amoeba. Even Simon had found it hard to tear himself away from what was becoming a physical addiction but, fortuitously, a shoot in Antigua had presented itself and by the time he got back it was to find Chad more suitably ensconced with the session hairdresser from hell.

And now there was Nick. Beautiful mind to match breathtaking good looks and a sweet soul to boot. Alex had to damp down the odd twinge of envy whenever she visited their apartment. Funny that, thinking of it already as their place. Nick had been there barely three months but Simon already hovered proprietorially over him, referring whenever possible to the pair of them in the plural. She could hardly blame him: why was it that the good guys invariably turned out to be either taken or gay?

A shrilling phone brought her back from her musings but it was only some pal of Lydia's setting up yet another fashionable little lunch. God knows how she ever made a profit. Actually, it wasn't too difficult to work that one out, given that Lydia seemed surprisingly successful at her job and was held in great regard by the old buffers who headed up their largest client companies. Far be it from her to slag off a fellow female but Alex was sure that the coquettish manner and slightly too tight outfits did little harm to Lydia's professional achievements. As far as Lydia was concerned you did what you could as a woman to get ahead of the pack, whatever those glossy articles bleated about the caring, sharing nineties. Alex snorted derisively at the thought of any thrusting young urbanite caring enough to share the spoils of success with anyone and flicked over the pages of the magazine secreted behind a large pile of files on her desk. With Lydia still out for the last hour of her usual three-hour lunch, Alex could catch up on her daily dose of dream therapy.

A beautifully lit photograph arrested her eye. There was one thing that always made her stop and salivate: a particularly gorgeous pair of shoes would do it for Alex every time, and these loafers were stunning. The perfect colour, the perfect shape and a price tag to match. Alex wondered why the hell she did this to herself. Escapism was one thing but only if reality occasionally matched up to bridge the gulf. Sometimes she wished she had the guts to get up and walk out; go off and pursue those dreams of hers. Trouble was, she was none too sure what they were or whether she could afford them. Her talents were not amongst the most saleable, much as she loved travel literature and her occasional bursts of 'creative' writing. Suburbia and babies did not do it for her either, although she was pretty sure that Richard would be in clover in such a set-up.

Richard. Now there was an option. Guaranteed freedom from bank letters for life and, no doubt, a Harvey Nicks charge-card to boot. She supposed she should be jumping at the chance but some inner voice still shrieked no. It was not just the lack of electricity whenever he attempted one of his clumsy fumbles – she could learn to live with that; according to most of the articles she devoured, that was par for the course. She could even, at a pinch, put up with the fact that he lived, breathed and worshipped his status as pinstripe *extraordinaire*. The thing she could not ignore was the hollow, sinking feeling in her gut whenever she contemplated a future with him, spent living down to his narrow viewpoint whilst she withered away in some comfortable little corner.

No, there had to be another way to use an active mind before it sank totally beneath the weight of banality. Other women managed to earn pots of money, often for far less effort than she put in at her desk each day and without having to endure the capriciousness of the unlovely Lydia. In that lay her clue: perhaps if she adopted the attitudes of divadom then success would follow. Somehow Alex could not envisage herself sweeping majestically through the hottest restaurants in town clad in the latest label, but she would quite enjoy throwing the odd tantrum in the office or even just spending half the day schmoozing important clients. On the other hand, perhaps not. She had dealt with said clients and could imagine what half of them would be like with a good bottle of wine or three under their straining belts.

Turning back to a safer sort of fantasy, she flipped over a few more glossy pages until another stunning image made her pause and read on. Now, here was a woman who was doing well for herself. Even in half-profile she looked incredible and judging by the screaming headline she was making a ton of money at the age of twenty-five. Well-educated, well-spoken . . . and a high-class hooker operating at the top end of the market. Alex read on in growing fascination. Of course she knew how lucrative life as a call-girl could be, she had seen and read enough to know that it was not always a poverty-stricken lifestyle. But she had always imagined it took a somewhat, well, different type of girl to be working in the field. And yet here was this university-educated young woman, who had been brought up not a million miles from Alex's own home and who had been sent to a private school that easily outshone hers in terms of kudos. Not only that, she was proud of her success in her chosen profession. Not proud enough, admittedly, to have revealed her real name or enough of her features to be identified but still prepared to come clean and announce to a journalist that she enjoyed what she did for a very good living.

Alex was intrigued, and even more so when she read that this glamorous creature never actually had sex with her clients. Instead of being just your average call-girl, she indulged them in whatever whips and chains fantasy they preferred, even getting free housework from some sad specimens who were happy to pay for the joy of scrubbing out her loo. The article went on to compare her working lifestyle with that of more conventional call-girls, all of whom ended up as dessert for the wealthy clients who wined, dined and fondled them, and expected the inevitable for their money. None of them seemed to have the confidence and control of that first girl, to say nothing of her higher earnings and self-esteem. She had even registered for PAYE, albeit under an assumed profession. Alex only hoped that she had an accountant with a fertile enough imagination to translate her more exotic deductions into something that would get past the Inland Revenue.

Alex could imagine nothing worse than having some middle-aged executive cringing at her feet, with perhaps one or two notable exceptions amongst whom she counted her bank manager, and didn't really see herself decked out in head to toe PVC. Somewhere in there, however, was an interesting solution to at least one of her problems, and the tiny seed of the idea that had been planted began to germinate. What if she could somehow be an escort to these guys in the most literal sense of the word? It was clear from the article that that was not what they really wanted when they called up one of these agencies, but there had to be a way to earn that sort of money without having to take things any further than a few hours' conversation and company. Without being vain she knew that she was attractive, could hold her own in conversation and, thanks to her fusty private academy for young ladies, could dredge up the loveliest of manners when she put her mind to it. Some of these assets were employed with varying success when dealing with the irascible old sods who stomped up to her desk on their way to a rendezvous with Lydia, although she had noticed that they positively melted when subjected to her boss's fluttering girlie routine.

That was it! Her clue, her angle on the oldest profession. Target the old boys, play up to their vanity in the way Lydia did and flirt sweetly. Just enough to keep them interested but not enough to encourage them on to encounters of a closer and far more intimate kind. Alex was sure that she could handle the dirtiest of old men: a schoolmarmish air assumed when necessary and they'd be putty in your hands. It was so simple yet could be so effective. Alex wondered if she would have the nerve even to attempt to pull it off. Well, there was only one way to find out.

Delving into the deepest recesses under her desk she came up with a dog-eared copy of the *Yellow Pages* and flicked through it with nervous fingers. She was astonished to find an entire section devoted to escort agencies and unnerved when she realized just how extensive a section it was. Four pages, all advertising the siren-like delights of an intimidating array of exotic beauties. One or two had vaguely arty line-drawings to get their message across even more explicitly and almost all promised new young flesh to satisfy the most jaded customer. Well, with all that fresh flesh on offer there must be a supply to fill the demand but Alex was still not convinced that she could go through with it.

'Darling! What a nightmare!'

Alex barely had time to let her fingers do some very fast walking to a more innocuous section before Lydia was at her shoulder, wailing about some wretched client who had had the temerity to mistake this week for next, thereby missing their monthly *tête à tête* over lightly tossed salad leaves at some exclusive eaterie.

'It was *so* embarrassing but Alfredo could not have been sweeter. Well, he knows me, darling. I mean, I practically *live* in the place. I used to wonder if he thought I was some high-class tart or something, the number of times I've been in there with various men. But this was the first time I've been stood up, as it were. God! Wretched man. If he wasn't the majority shareholder I'm sure they'd have got rid of him by now. I've thought for a while that he's been losing his touch, getting a wee bit vague. I mean, he forgot my name the last time we met – kept calling me Lavinia or something. And now this!'

Stiff with guilt from her narrow escape, Alex let the familiar tirade wash over her and adhered her sweetest smile to somewhat frozen lips. 'You poor thing. Let me get you a coffee. Then you can show me whatever it is you've bought.'

Lydia smiled at her with suitable gratitude and allowed her clutch of glossy carrier bags to slide to the floor. 'How sweet of you. Of course, I'm absolutely starving but there was no way I could possibly eat a thing sitting at the very best table all on my lonesome. No, the only thing to do was dose myself up with a spot of retail therapy.'

As far as Alex could tell she barely ate at the best

of times, preferring to sip from her own glass whilst energetically plying her client with whatever expensive wine he had chosen. As the kettle boiled, Alex sagged against the stainless-steel worktop, grateful that Lydia had appeared when she did. Another few seconds and Alex might have succumbed to that particular moment of madness and dialled one of those numbers. And then . . . who knows? As a token of her rather misplaced gratitude she used the cafetière of which Lydia was so fond, although over months of experimentation she had discovered that her boss never noticed the difference between that and the instant stuff Alex usually put in front of her. And a few biscuits for Lydia to refuse prettily, that should keep her happy.

'How kind! Oh, no, Alex, I shouldn't. You have them or I'll never fit into my bikini for St Bart's.'

There, she'd even given her the opportunity to mention her precious trip to some media megastar's holiday haven. Now she knew that the afternoon would pass in honeyed calm without being punctuated by the peevish demands that usually emitted from a thwarted Lydia. She just wished she could fill that calm with something more creative than diary management and constant ego-stroking. A tedious day at the office, and then a sometimes even more demanding evening entertaining one or other of Richard's unspeakable contacts, left precious little energy for any other form of achievement. She had never considered herself a natural diplomat, which made it twice as hard to bite her tongue in the face of attitudes she felt sure should have disappeared with the Ark. Doubtless it was that fortitude that had made her think, God forbid, that she would be the perfect companion for a stream of temporary sugar daddies.

Thankfully Lydia chose to occupy herself in her favourite position with phone clamped to ear and the occasional finger poised to dial, leaving Alex to shuffle the odd bit of paper and get on with reading her magazine. Boring it might be but she preferred times like this to those frantic evenings when she bashed away at some press release until one in the morning.

A happy half-hour passed before Lydia thrust her head out of the inner sanctum to ask Alex to run out to the bank for her. 'Silly me, in all the upset I quite forgot to deposit a couple of cheques. Would you be an absolute darling and . . . ?'

At least it gave her a chance for some fresh air and the opportunity to gaze longingly in the windows of several shops on the way. Only the most stratospheric salaries could cope with such purchases, although as no price tags were on display it was purely an envious and educated guess. Alex thought, rather guiltily, that she ought to check her own bank balance: two telling white envelopes had arrived in the past couple of days and she had not been able to bring herself to open them. Another small fortune in bank charges to add on to her ever looming overdraft.

Having deposited Lydia's cheques with only a brief consideration of the possibility of changing the payee's name on them, Alex resolved to bite the bullet. After all, how bad could it be? No, she didn't want to answer that. She went for the printout option at the cashpoint and squinted at the machine through half-closed eyes whilst simultaneously praying and holding her breath.

A few churning and grinding noises, a small piece of white paper was spat out at her and then it happened. Her precious card was swiftly swallowed into the bowels of the machine. Alex would have howled in anguish on the spot had she been able to work her jaw muscles, but instead she swallowed hard to contend with the dryness of her throat.

She could hardly bear to look at the bit of paper scrunched up in her hand and when she did so it was to ever deepening panic. Not only did the mini-statement display a final balance way in excess of the outermost limits of the bank's patience, but she could see quite clearly that her recent rent cheque had not yet gone through. And at this rate was unlikely to do so. Trying hard to remain calm and adult, Alex approached a young woman sitting at the misnamed customer service desk. It felt unnervingly like some far-off encounter with the headmistress at school.

She was greeted with a glossily insincere smile. 'How can I help?' The voice was professionally polite but something about the woman suggested that Impersonal Banker might have been a more accurate moniker.

'Um . . . I seem to have a problem with my account and the machine just swallowed my card. The thing is, I need it. I cannot possibly do anything without it so I really need it back. Today.' Alex tried to act cool and confident but a swarm of butterflies was playing havoc with her innards.

'I see. Can I just take your account details?' Another condescending smile as the woman looked at her, fingers poised over the keyboard which gave her access to the ignominious details of Alex's finances.

Fighting a strong sense of doom, Alex gave her the necessary information and watched her perfectly manicured nails tap away until the extent of her fiscal ineptitude was displayed on screen for the woman's scrutiny. She was probably about the same age as Alex but a vast gulf of responsibility and uniformed respectability yawned between them.

After several moments of frowning and more tapping, she looked up at Alex with a slightly more glacial smile. 'As you are probably aware, you are somewhat in excess of your overdraft arrangement and I see here that we have just returned a substantial cheque marked refer to drawer. We have written to you in the last few days to ask you not to pay out any more sums until you have sufficient funds to cover the excess amount. In the circumstances, I cannot authorize the return of your card.'

Valiantly resisting an urge to throttle the smug cow, Alex took several deep breaths. There had to be a way out of this. Banks were always trying to throw money at you. There had to be *something* she could do to rescue the piece of plastic that was her lifeline.

'What about a loan? I could pay it off in regular amounts.'

The woman looked at her with amused pity. 'I don't think that in your current financial position you would meet our loan criteria. Our records show that you consistently exceed your income with your outgoings on a monthly basis. You could not possibly afford loan repayments on top of that. I'm sorry.'

Like hell she was.

'But I just cannot exist without my card. I need it!

I pay money into my account each month – OK, I spend some too. You can't just take away my card and expect me to starve. I mean, this is just outrageous!' Alex's voice had risen from a whimper to an outright cry of indignation. Several customers turned from the nearby queue to observe in fascinated empathy. Alex felt rather like the victim of a car crash. Everyone was staring now, her face was red with humiliation and this unmoving bank official had turned seemingly to stone in front of her.

'Please, Ms Hunter, do try and calm down. Of course the bank will not leave you to starve, as you put it. We can work out a repayment plan that will allow you a reasonable sum of money each week to live on, which you can collect over the counter at this branch.'

Oh, the shame of it. Forced like a naughty child to stand in line and ask for her pocket money each week.

'And what do you consider to be a reasonable sum?'

'Well, we can look at your regular outgoings, rent and suchlike, and work out a figure. But I warn you it will have to be considerably pared down from your normal spending pattern.' The woman just had to perform bikini-waxes in her spare time, such was her sadistic delight in another's suffering.

'Rent. Oh, God, that cheque you've bounced. That's my rent cheque. That simply has to go through, it just has to.' She tried hard not to wail but it was an impossibility in the face of such indifference to her plight.

'I'm sorry but it has already been returned. There is nothing I can do about it at this stage.' She looked about as sorry as a mechanic producing a bill for some supposedly minor defect.

'Well, what if I write another one? Will you honour that? I mean, it's my rent cheque. If it doesn't get paid I'll get kicked out and have nowhere to live and then probably no job and absolutely no way of paying off my overdraft.' Alex's cheeks grew pinker and her voice rose higher as the desperate reality of her straitened circumstances hit home. People were staring even harder now and Alex noted with satisfaction that her rising hysteria had had the desired effect on marble woman.

'Ms Hunter, please. I will just go and have a word with our lending manager and see if something can be done. If you could just sit there for a moment.' And shut up, no doubt, so as not to disturb the hallowed walls of her high street bank.

Alex watched as the woman scurried off to consult a higher power and silently seethed. Shame it was a woman, really, or she could have turned on the tears as a final and effective resort. This was not Alex's first run-in with a bank but it had never before got to this stage. As she sat slumped and praying silently in the aquamarine surroundings she sourly reflected that all this colour co-ordination had probably cost five hundred times her overdraft and then some. Oh, good, Frozen Features was returning, in as dignified a manner as her court shoes and matching aqua outfit would permit.

'I have had a word with Mr Cartwright and he has agreed that, on this occasion only, you may write out another cheque for your rent and the bank will honour it. Further rent cheques will have to come out of your budgeted sum.'

At least that was one victory, one less nightmare to

contend with. Unfortunately there was more to come as she proceeded to put Alex's spending habits under the most detailed and tortuous scrutiny, finally coming up with a figure on which a celibate nun would find it hard to exist. Her authorized overdraft had been increased alarmingly for a frighteningly short space of time and her card held until such time as she could prove her financial reliability. Alex reflected gloomily that rehab might be considerably less painful to undertake.

Finally allowed to shuffle away, her pride in tatters, Alex got back to the office over an hour late, to be greeted by an icy Lydia. Here, however, was one trauma with which Lydia could only empathize and Alex laid it on with several trowels until her boss had thawed out sufficiently to make her a soothing cup of tea and promised to have a think about an increase in salary, although she did not hold out much hope. Neither did Alex. Lydia might indulge herself wildly but always fobbed off any such request with vague promises of future bonuses and veiled insinuations that there were a million other candidates who would happily do Alex's job for pocket money and the occasional pat on the head. Alex had her doubts about that: any glamour factor the job might have promised was firmly Lydia's province. Even now she was slapping on the warpaint before dashing off to drinkies and her place in some corporate box at the opera. She did, however, pause whilst arranging her pashmina to deliver a few last words of encouragement: '*Nil desperandum*, sweetie, don't let the bastards get you down. They should all be razed to the ground, wretched banks. Must dash, see you in the morning.' And with many an air-kiss she was gone.

It was all right for Lydia to come out with her platitudes: Alex wondered how on earth she would cope if her access to cash disappeared overnight. None too calmly, of that she was sure. And now she had to make the dreaded phone call to her landlady, reassure her that her next cheque would be good, that it was all due to some mythical mistake on the part of the bank. This was one task she did not relish and, sure enough, she was put through the hoops before being let off the hook.

'So long as I get that cheque Thursday at the latest.' The old cow was as condescending as could be, but Alex had to bite her tongue and effuse her gratitude. Ringing off in a flurry of more apologies and promises she took a shuddering breath and buried her face in her hands. At least that was out of the way, however unpleasant. She supposed that she had better bung the cheque in the post tonight before sloping off to Safeway and stocking up on whatever she could get before her pathetic food budget dribbled away to nothing. Forget the takeaway and videos and scale down the Chablis to a bottle of plonk. No more glossy mags, no little presents to cheer herself up, and most definitely no expeditions to the shops whenever things went marginally wrong. These were going to be the most boring few months of her life, punctuated only by the odd free meal on Richard's expense account, an ordeal she could almost bear if it meant a taste of luxury.

There was no way in hell, however, that she would let Richard get wind of her financial plight. His smugness would be insufferable and it would only confirm his firm belief that she, like every other woman, was incapable of running her life without male guidance. He would also, to be fair, offer to help her out, something Alex would not countenance. She would never, as long as she could scrape by, be beholden to someone who might threaten her precious freedom. She knew it drove him mad and secretly she enjoyed the fact, almost as much as she enjoyed the way it made him try ever harder to pin her down. Some small part of herself despised the game she was caught up in, but the trouble was that Alex really did not know what she wanted, although she suspected it was not what Richard had to offer.

Only another fifteen minutes to go and she could pack up her desk, a task she usually enjoyed a little more than she did tonight. Oh, the joys of pasta, the telly and that glass of something cheap and cheerless. With so little to look forward to, she could hardly muster up a trace of enthusiasm, shuffling bits of paper into some semblance of order in a particularly vicious manner and punching the off button on her computer with no little spite. She was in the middle of heaving the *Yellow Pages* back to its usual dusty spot by her feet when a tiny fragment of her discarded plan popped teasingly into her disillusioned mind. Not daring to stop and think, she flicked through the tissue-thin pages until once again the purple prose of the adverts was staring her in the face. So many of them, all promising the classiest, most beautiful, most interesting of companions, and most of them with a discreet postscript asking for interested 'escorts' to get in touch. In her current frame of mind Alex was less convinced that she could match up to the glorious descriptions on offer. Then again, she had little dignity left to lose.

Before allowing herself to think any harder, she picked a number at random and dialled it. After two or three rings a husky voice answered, with disconcerting anonymity, 'Hello?'

'Oh, ah, hello. I'm ringing about your advert. For new escorts, that is.' Better add that hastily before the woman on the end of the phone had any other ideas.

'Have you ever done this kind of work before?' She sounded as if she were reeling through a well-worn checklist.

'No.'

A disappointed pause.

'But I do have a good education, a degree, and I'm, well, everyone says I'm attractive and I work in PR so I'm good at dealing with people, clients and so on. And I'm . . . twenty-five.' Give or take two or three years. Alex vaguely remembered reading that twenty-five was the cut-off point to start in the oldest profession, something she would later come to realize was erroneous.

This elicited a more interested response. 'OK, and do you have your own flat where clients could visit you, preferably somewhere central?'

This Alex was ready for, having remembered a detail from the article she had read, which now seemed like aeons ago. 'I'm only interested in out calls at the moment. My home situation is a bit . . . difficult.'

God forbid that Richard would stumble across some sordid scenario, having decided to avail himself of the key she had given him in a moment of foolishness.

Besides, the thought of some stranger in her home was so sickening that she knew there was no hope of her plan succeeding on anything other than neutral turf.

The woman on the other end of the phone was sounding more amenable by the second. 'I see. Well, I could always do with a new face, if it's the right sort. Why don't you come and meet me and we'll take it from there? I usually see new girls in the coffee shop of the Montgomery. Do you know it?'

She and Richard had collected one of his clients from there for dinner only the other week. Oh, well, it was an anonymous enough hotel and not too much of a trek.

'Sure. Um . . . When were you thinking of?' Alex wondered just how you interviewed someone for such a sensitive post: the possibilities were truly mind-boggling.

'Tomorrow at six-ish?'

'Fine, yes, fine.' That gave her a good twenty-four hours to chicken out.

Now her prospective employer was all brisk and businesslike. 'And your name is?'

'Angela.'

Alex wondered if it was her imagination or if there really was a hint of knowing disbelief in the woman's voice. She remained, however, polite and brisk. 'OK, Angela, I will be sitting at the back of the coffee shop next to the conservatory area. I'll have a brown briefcase with me.'

This was getting to be more like a blind date by the minute. 'Oh, fine. Well, I've got long dark hair and, um, I'll probably be carrying quite a large black bag.'

With enough junk in it to kit out the average Everest expedition. There was a distinct feeling of unreality about this whole scenario, but in an odd way Alex found it intriguing, a bit like being a character in some bad Bond rip-off movie.

'Any problems, please call me on this number. It diverts to my mobile so you can always reach me. I'll look forward to meeting you tomorrow, Angela.'

As Alex put the receiver down her whole body exhaled with relief. She could hardly believe what she had just done and could almost discount it as some bizarre aberration. She could easily get away with not turning up tomorrow: the woman had no idea of her real identity and all the work phones withheld the outgoing number so she had no way of reaching her if Alex decided to stand her up. And yet she was not so sure that she would, or even that she wanted to. In a way Alex felt liberated by the craziness of the situation and by her own daring. Her drubbing at the hands of the bank had only served to stoke her frustration, to make her want to kick back in whatever way she could. This was one way to get back a sense of control when everything seemed to be spiralling dangerously away from her. Or was it? Was this a step forward or a step over the edge? Well, she had twenty-four hours of penny-pinching to find out.

In the event, Monique turned out to be surprisingly normal. Of course, that was probably not her real name but Alex was in no position to comment. A pleasant-looking woman in her late thirties, she had been easy to spot and had graciously offered a cup of tea to her nervous interviewee. Alex carried it off with admirable bravado but couldn't quite disguise the tension in her voice or her rather too-eager smile.

Monique, naturally, had seen it all before but something about this young woman intrigued her. She was clearly intelligent, eager to please and, most importantly, very pretty in a particularly English way, which would prove highly attractive to many of her clients. Most fortunately of all, here she was declaring that she would prefer to see the more mature clients, a sensible attitude that Monique had tried in vain to instil in some of her other girls. Some were more than a little vacuous but this one had an indefinable spark. Monique was sure that she would do well, with only a little grooming.

'So you realize, Angela, that I have to be able to contact you at all times. Do you have a mobile?'

Thank goodness, Richard had insisted on giving her one for Christmas.

'And a good wardrobe? Smart suits and suchlike?'

That could prove a tad more difficult but she was sure that one or two of her store cards still held some elasticity. More importantly, she needed to know just how much could be made in this unfamiliar line of business.

With impressive insouciance, she leaned forward and cut to the chase. 'What rates do you charge, exactly, Monique?'

The older woman's voice dropped discreetly. 'The gentlemen book you for your time, which is charged at two hundred pounds for the first hour and one hundred pounds for each hour thereafter. All of my clients are very high-class. Each booking is for a minimum of three hours to include dinner, conversation and . . . your time.'

Alex got the message. What she did with her time was up to her but if the clients were not kept happy then Monique would be down on her as fast as that steely glint in her eye promised. Still, she was pretty sure that she could get away with it, with a great deal of flattery and charm and not a little deviousness. And she would relish the challenge: it had been quite a while since her keen mind had been put to work and there was nothing Alex enjoyed more than a spot of intrigue. In a funny sort of way she could hardly wait to get started, whilst at the same time her stomach lurched with dread at the thought of fending off some ageing Lothario. She made herself think of the money, lots and lots of it, and more than enough to shut the bank up for good. It was not to be for ever, just long enough to get her out of this hole and on her feet on her own terms. And she was determined that she wasn't going to end up on her back to do it, not for one of those so-called high-class clients and certainly not by lying down and giving in to the equally questionable lure of Richard's lucre.

With numbers exchanged and an exhortation to phone in each day to check on her availability, Alex floated out of the hotel in a daze. She had been hired, she was now officially an 'escort' to the rich and dubious, whatever that meant. The promise of easy riches sang in her relieved ears and, giving in to an increasing sense of recklessness, she swept confidently into one of the black cabs waiting in front of the hotel. Sod the bank: Alex was on the way back up and she would do it in her own inimitable style. In glorious defiance, she sat back, enjoyed the ride and counted her chickens all the way home.

THREE

There was nothing Simon enjoyed more than a pert bottom and a pretty pout but sometimes the price of such perfection was too high even for his smooth patience. Sebastian needed a throat-gaggingly high amount of ego-stroking as he sulked and preened before the camera, resolutely refusing to give it every last ounce until he had been reassured of his desirability a dozen times or more. The average six-year-old would have been easier to coax into a semblance of sunny exuberance and Simon felt drained as the session neared its conclusion. At his elbow the stylist flapped and fussed whilst the client lurked unhelpfully in the shadows at the back of the studio. Sebastian had been her choice, her untutored eye seeing only the floppy blond hair and Colgate grin, and failing to notice the petulance that informed those glorious cheekbones. Thanks to Simon and his ability to charm candy from a cobra, she had her precious campaign in the bag, but it had been a long, stressful day and he was in dire need of a cold beer and some peace and designer quiet.

An enticing vision of his cool empty apartment had kept Simon going through the endless afternoon but a sudden thought punctured his notion of a solitary evening of pure self-indulgence. The stylish little supper faded into a renewed sense of irritation as he remembered that he had quite forgotten his promise to Charles to put up his hippie son for a couple of nights, some sort of crusty type who'd been bumming around South East Asia for the best part of two years. Simon's laser-like ambition had never permitted such frivolity; the nearest he had ever come to dropping out was his blunt refusal to follow his father into the family business. And he was careful to preserve the majority of his parents' illusions: outside his circle of Soho sophisticates Simon was still a scion of solid ex-Army stock and the son and heir of a man who viewed pink shirts with singular suspicion.

Oh, well, he supposed he had better show willing and throw some food together for this wretched boy. Charles Bell was one of his father's oldest chums and, more importantly, one of his best business contacts. The imminent return of his son to the smoke had been mentioned over lunch several Sundays ago and Simon had found himself offering a billet under the meaningful eye of his father, a suggestion that had been taken up with grateful alacrity by Charles and his faded but still lovely wife. Looking at Charles, Simon could only assume that Vivienne had married him for reasons other than his looks and he was not so sure that personality ranked amongst them. He hoped for the son's sake that he took after his mother in both appearance and temperament, the rather bucolic Charles being a difficult companion at the best of times. He and Simon's father seemed to get along famously, probably as a result of their shared military background, but Simon preferred more restful company. Still, he would do his duty and act the perfect host and hopefully the boy would slope off to a squat or something after a couple of days. Somehow Simon could not imagine a happy hippie traveller enjoying the streamlined sophistication of his urban lifestyle.

Simon stuck his head around the door of the dressing room to be confronted by a butt-naked Sebastian wriggling into a pair of jeans that would pay tight homage to his greatest assets. Simon normally found it hard to resist such a peachy pair of buttocks but in this case he was prepared to make an exception. Sebastian's ability to perform only to maximum reassurance would doubtless extend as far as and beyond the bedroom. Simon was more than a little tired of massaging monstrous egos whilst having to contend with conversation that engaged perhaps three of his brain cells at most. His jaded gaze was met with an insolent stare and a knowing smirk as Sebastian hoicked the jeans up over his hips and fastened the button fly with elaborate care.

'Feel like a drink?' he asked, with an infuriatingly knowing expression conveying what he obviously assumed was deep meaning.

Simon shook his head, delighted to dent his cocksure self-confidence. 'Can't, I'm afraid. I have a guest.'

'Oh?' Sebastian drew out the syllable to its zenith and signalled his gossipy interest with widened eyes. This was unwelcome news: Simon represented the key to a golden door and he was not going to give up lightly. 'Anyone I know?' He pouted with feigned indifference.

'I doubt it.' Simon's reply was dismissive.

Simon was weary of Golden Boy. A great model he might be, but Sebastian Snow had a long way to go in the personality stakes and the haughty toss of his bleached blond crop did little to endear him to a man who could make his nascent career soar to a stratum way above that of his current, somewhat ironic role as the housewives' choice.

Simon was wholly confident in his well-deserved role of fashion hotshot and, as one glossy had recently cooed, 'the by-line to beg for'. Finally shooing the yapping team of crimpers and preeners out of his studio, he bade goodnight to his admirably calm assistant and headed for home. As if there wasn't already enough on his plate, he had heard only that morning of Jürgen's plans to return home to exploit his invaluable experience across the fashion pages of Europe and beyond. Simon had always expected him to take off and do his own thing but was reluctant to let him go quite so soon. As well as possessing an acute sense of what would appeal in the street, Jürgen had been a soothing influence on more than one fraught occasion, his reassuring bulk at odds with his gentle manner and almost preternatural politeness. Still, if he wanted to fly off and try his wings Simon would not stand in his way. It just meant that he had to go through the whole tedious business of wading through the hordes of arrogant young hopefuls who considered the menial tasks of an assistant to be demeaning and believed that they could go straight from their degree shows to a serious spread in one of the upmarket fashion maga-zines. Coffee-making and model manipulation were not high on their list of priorities, only the brightest amongst them coming to realize that people skills were 90 per cent of the game.

Simon himself could have put Machiavelli to shame. A cunning combination of lethal charm and carefully concealed intelligence fooled most of the fashion cognoscenti into underestimating how brilliant a businessman he was and more than one editor rued the day she had denied him some small but essential detail. To Simon it was all part of the game, one that he played consummately. As his rates soared and his demands grew, so his popularity and notoriety ensured that his name came up first for the big advertising work and the lucrative campaigns. Models, both male and female, fought for a place in front of his camera as his reputation on the cutting edge grew, the more rapacious females retreating in disappointment from his charming indifference to their blatant flirtation. One or two he had even taken home to meet his parents, silently amused at their attempts to win them over whilst trying hard not to break any fingernails. He would never forget the look on the face of one gorgeous young thing who had been dragged off on the customary Sunday-afternoon walk and had hobbled over hill and dale in the most impractical sandals he had ever seen, her vanity forcing her to refuse the offer of a pair of wellies. If only she had known that her efforts were wasted on a man who preferred bulges below rather than above the waist. His mother was beginning to despair that he would ever do the decent thing and spawn gorgeous grandchildren with one of these flawless creatures but he considered blissful ignorance to be much the wisest approach in a family where the word 'homosexual' still conjured up visions of a court-martial.

Held up still further by horrendous traffic, it was a

decidedly pissed-off Simon who stomped through his front door and poured himself a stiff drink. He had barely time to take one gulp before the doorbell summoned him, cursing, back down the corridor to admit the prodigal hippie son. Simon flung open the door and the snarl of welcome died on his lips as he grasped the firm hand stretched out towards him. His first instinct was to keep on grasping whatever he could but he rapidly recovered himself as he realized that a pair of azure-blue eyes were regarding him with justifiable bewilderment.

Finding his voice, he stood aside and ushered in his suddenly welcome visitor. 'Hello, hello. You must be Nick. Do come on in, come through, let me help you with that.'

Even to his own ears Simon sounded like a parody of a jovial host but he was doing his level best to cover up his astonishment at the sight of his guest. Forget shaggy hippie, this was more like six foot of unadulterated, smoothly tanned Nirvana. Granted he was wearing a ripped and faded pair of jeans and carrying the ubiquitous rucksack but that was as far as the traveller image went. The leather friendship bracelet knotted around one sinewy wrist only underlined his radiant masculinity, and when he smiled, half the cosmetic dentists in Harley Street would have wept. A strong nose matched with the most lethal pair of cheekbones he had ever seen outside a Russian ballet troupe lent strength to a full, sensitive mouth, which at the moment hovered somewhere around a shy smile of greeting. Simon wanted to scream in ecstasy and dive for his camera, but had to content himself with offering a beer and a shower – although he was not sure how he would cope with the knowledge of a naked Nick bare inches away through the bathroom door. Luckily for him his guest was happy to settle for a beer and a seat on the sofa with a shower and a shave an attractive but less urgent requirement.

Simon sat down gingerly on the opposite sofa and assumed anew his attitude of benign bonhomie. 'So, Nick, good journey?' he enquired of his disturbingly attractive guest.

'Yeah, great. Bit odd having to wear a sweater again after all this time. When I flew out of Bangkok it was in the nineties.'

Said sweater was obscuring the finer details of Nick's admirable physique, but Simon had always found mystery irresistibly attractive and he couldn't wait to unravel this one. 'What were you doing out in the Far East?' he asked innocuously, his focus riveted by Nick's quite remarkable eyes.

Nick answered him with an easy smile, apparently unaware of the effect of his startling good looks. 'Oh, bumming around, travelling, the usual trail. I started doing some modelling and acting in Japan and Thailand. They go crazy for fair hair and blue eyes out there so I did quite well and I'd go off and travel on the proceeds. Bloody easy money if you ask me.'

Now this was familiar and promising territory. Simon's finely tuned antennae could pick out a straight man at a hundred paces but his experience also told him that options could be widened if it meant the offer of a career leg up. Wishful thinking took care of the rest and as Nick chatted easily about his travels his imagination went into overdrive. Sod Sebastian Snow! This young man possessed far greater appeal and visions of a glorious career guided by Simon's astute and self-interested patronage floated in front of his seemingly guileless gaze, only to be rudely punctured by Nick's next assertion.

'Of course, I got really pissed off with prancing around in front of the camera. The money was great, couldn't knock it, but what I really got into was the technical stuff. Good equipment is cheap out there and I found some decent kit and started taking pictures of my own. Scenery and stuff but also lots of shots of the locals, although I made sure I always asked them first. Can't stand those tourists who barge in and just click away without any respect for people's beliefs although the city folk seem to have got charging for it down to a fine art.'

Ever adaptable, Simon revised his vision and rewrote his mentor status. Jürgen's sudden defection now seemed like a glorious opportunity and he offered diffidently to look over Nick's work.

Nick seized on the suggestion with alacrity. 'That would be great. But are you sure? I mean, tell me if you think they're crap. I've seen a lot of your stuff around and it's fantastic. This is real beginner stuff in comparison.'

Brushing aside his unfeigned modesty, Simon took the proffered portfolio and silently flicked through the pages. He could quibble over one or two technical points but other than that they showed real talent and a wonderful eye, something that could never be taught. Nick's work would wipe the floor with half the graduates from those prestigious art schools who sauntered so self-confidently through his studio doors. Raw energy combined with a sensitivity to atmosphere and expression lent his pictures a rare quality. Simon had a sudden vision of a master plan. 'These are good, Nick, very good indeed.' Nick's beam of gratitude and relief was reward enough for what he was about to offer.

Taking a deep breath, Simon launched into Plan A. 'Look, my assistant announced today that he's leaving me to go back to Germany. He feels he's learned all he can and wants to set up on his own and I'm very happy for him, although I had hoped to hold on to him for a bit longer. It takes time to build up a good working relationship and we work well together. And I think you and I could do the same. Fancy a go as my new assistant? I warn you, it's not glamorous but you'll learn a lot and I can give you some great contacts.'

Nick was gobsmacked by his good fortune. He was barely through the door and already one part of his future seemed to have fallen into place. Whilst fashion and advertising photography was not really his area it would be a fantastic break and give him the opportunity to learn on the job, something Simon was very much counting on. 'Simon, that's great. But are you sure? Look, just because of my dad and so on please don't feel that you have to—'

Simon cut him off in mid-effusion. 'It's got nothing to do with that. Trust me, I never do anything unless it's in my best possible interests. It doesn't pay that well and often you'll hate my guts but I think you'd get a lot out of it. As would I.'

Quite overwhelmed, Nick stuttered out his gratitude.

'Well, I can't thank you enough. Four hours back in London and I've already landed myself a job. I'll start the flat hunt in the morning. I don't want to impose on you and I know my parents probably bullied you into having me. I would have gone to stay with a mate but they're all abroad or living in the Outer Hebrides farming sheep and things.'

Better and better. Suddenly, Simon's jealously guarded solitude seemed to lose its attraction and a further dimension to his grand plan presented itself. With an air of innocent benevolence he offered reassurance. 'Oh, don't worry about that. There's loads of space here and if you were imposing I would tell you. In fact, stay as long as you like. I would enjoy the company.'

If Simon's little coterie could have heard him they would not have been able to believe their ears. Simon, the most monastic of people, offering up his precious space to a virtual stranger and one with whom he would be working to boot. It wouldn't make any sense to most of them until they clapped eyes on Nick and then it would be the cat-fight of the century as they scratched and spat in their attempts to win him over. No easy task, of that Simon was sure. Equally, though, he was sure of his ability to charm the most reluctant of débutantes, especially those who needed a break, something he very fairly and unusually gave them in exchange for their favours. It was that very sureness that blinded him to the reality that sat not two feet away, happily slugging back his beer and congratulating himself on his luck.

Beautiful he might have been, and sensitive and creative, but Nick preferred his pleasure to be of the more curvaceous kind. Strictly a sucker for a female face, he gravitated to those whose figures gave more hope of sensual delight than the stick insects with whom he had worked on many an occasion. Hipbones looked great in bikini shots but Nick was of the firm belief that a healthy appetite for food announced an appreciation of all forms of hedonistic happiness, and he was by no means averse to a woman who could hold her own at the bar and still have enough energy in reserve for a night of unbridled lust. The fineness of his features and quietness of his manner had fooled many into underestimating the appetites hinted at by the wicked fullness of his lower lip. Amongst whose number Simon could now be counted.

Businesslike now that things had been organized to his satisfaction, Simon stood up and headed for the phone. 'So, that's settled, then. Why don't you make yourself at home whilst I order in some food? Thai OK for you?'

'Yeah. Great.' Nick still seemed a little stunned by the whirlwind way in which he had landed on his feet and was not about to argue over a takeaway.

Simon clapped his hand to his forehead in mock theatricality. 'Christ, how stupid of me. You must be sick to death of the stuff. Pizza, then?'

This eagerness to please was quite uncharacteristic but Nick had not been around long enough to experience Simon's intractability. He was more than happy to hand decision-making over to someone who had not spent the last sixteen hours in transit and assented with an easy-going 'Great, whatever. I'm easy.'

The little smile that accompanied these words fired

a beacon of hope in Simon's groin, the epicentre of his emotional universe. Clapping his hands together in a quite uncharacteristic gesture, Simon nodded enthusiastically. 'Good, good. Well, let me show you to your room and then I'll order up the food. It's just along here . . .'

Nick gathered together his meagre possessions, and followed him down the corridor to the spare bedroom. He nodded in appreciation, noting the carefully composed minimalism. He preferred a more classical approach but the rough-hewn furniture looked perfectly serviceable, if a little unfinished, and he was delighted at the prospect of a comfortable bed, never mind that it was a miracle of orthopaedic design. A little disappointed at the lack of the customary cries of enthusiasm, Simon slunk off to order sustenance and Nick busied himself with chucking a large pile of T-shirts into a drawer and putting his far more precious photos and diaries into a safe place. He could vaguely hear Simon talking in tones of hushed excitement but it would never have crossed his mind to question the length of his conversation with a take-out service.

For his part, Simon was trying hard to appear nonchalant as he murmured down the phone to Alex. He was fooling no one and she snorted with derision at his protestations of Good Samaritanship. She had known Simon all her life and almost all of his, and in all that time his good deeds had contained a healthy dollop of self-interest mixed with a great deal of manipulation and machination. Much as she adored him, she gave little for this handsome newcomer's chances, once

Simon stopped protesting too much. For now he was in full flood.

'Really, darling, how could you say such a thing? I am merely fulfilling a promise to look after some lost soul until he finds his feet in the big city.'

Alex was not fooled for an instant. 'Finds his feet under your duvet more like. God, Simon, you are incorrigible. How do you know he's even up for it?'

At this he chuckled. 'Oh, I know. I can always tell, it's in the eyes. And what a pair of eyes! Ah . . . Look, darling, must go. Supper's here, talk to you soon. Lots of love.'

The doorbell had indeed interrupted this sly little conversation but a bigger inducement to put down the receiver was the reappearance of Nick, hair still wet from the shower and large bottle of whisky in hand.

'Got you this in Duty Free.'

'Oh, marvellous, you really shouldn't have. Here we go, two large Quattro Stagioni.'

Simon normally watched his weight with the vigilance of a National Hunt jockey but he had correctly deduced that Nick would require more man-sized portions. Or, rather, he very much hoped he would. And Simon, along with a large proportion of men alive on the planet, both gay and straight, had no doubts about his ability to fulfil the most gargantuan of appetites. He fussed around with pepper grinders and bowls of freshly grated Parmesan as his guest tucked in contentedly to his pizza and beer, pausing occasionally to make polite conversation about Simon's work and family news. A satisfying couple of hours passed and they had just retired to a post-prandial whisky on the sofa, where

Simon was stealthily planning a careful campaign of slow seduction, when the telephone rang. Suppressing a sigh of intense irritation, he answered it, and wasn't too surprised to hear a slightly drunk and hysterical Alex on the other end of the telephone.

'That bastard, Simon. He's a shit, a total shit!'

This was not exactly news to Simon but he murmured the right things as Alex unleashed her torrent of grievances.

'He's only gone and forgotten our Valentine's dinner tonight because of some stupid client person he has to entertain. I sat here like a total lemon until ten o'clock, then left a message on his mobile. I'd drunk most of his sodding Château Whatever by the time he called me back. Bastard!'

This last was spat out with some venom and it was Simon's turn to experience a sense of *déjà vu*. Whilst Alex could chart the course of his latest affair by the frequency of his phone calls he could plot the familiar pattern of hers with Richard by the lateness of the hour and the level of vituperation. This ranked as reasonably serious. Heroically putting aside self-interest with only the merest sense of irritation, Simon talked soothingly into the telephone. 'Come on, Alex, it's not that bad. I'd completely forgotten it was Valentine's Day myself. Men do, we're not so great at that kind of thing.'

This was only a partial untruth as the one garish card that had landed that morning on his doormat had been unceremoniously dumped in the bin for fear that its mawkish sentiment would diminish the tastefulness of his surroundings. He had a sneaky suspicion that Sebastian had sent it, hence the sulks for most of the day, but there was no way in hell he would respond to that kind of childish blandishment. Unfortunately for Simon, his soothing words had little effect and Alex's self-pitying sniffles only increased in volume and frequency. Abandoning all hope, he ordered her to get in a cab and come over to be administered to in best surrogate-brotherly manner. That, he ruefully reflected, should at least guarantee him a place in purgatory if not quite past the pearly gates.

She thanked him profusely, and promising further supplies plundered from Richard's wine racks, she rang off, leaving Simon to explain the situation to a mildly interested Nick.

He had just about got through the finer points of Richard's character flaws when there was a knock at the front door. A red-eyed but defiant Alex stood on the doorstep, the bulging carrier-bag betraying the liberation of a few choice items from Richard's prized wine collection. Stomping ahead of a solicitous Simon, she chucked her jacket on the back of one pristine cream armchair and managed a vague 'hello' in Nick's direction. This had to be serious: Alex would never display less than total curiosity unless things were really amiss.

It was barely a moment before she launched back into her tale of woe, brandishing the clinking carrier-bag at them as she spoke. 'Lucky for us I was left stewing in his flat rather than mine. I made sure I took all the really good stuff, the dusty ones he's kept for ages and ages. That'll teach him. Bastard!'

Brave words but her eyes were glittering dangerously and that last expletive sounded distinctly wobbly.

'How about a nice cup of coffee, darling?'

Simon was doing his best to handle things whilst Nick looked on in intrigued amusement. It struck him that her eyes, although pink, were huge and their dampness only added to her air of vulnerability. This boyfriend of hers, whoever he was, was obviously even more of a moron than Simon had given him credit for.

'Don't patronize me, Simon! I'm not half as drunk as I could be, I'm just a bit tired. Now get the bloody corkscrew.'

She dived into her precious carrier-bag and pulled out a gratifyingly expensive-looking bottle. Simon knew better than to argue and dutifully presented her with the corkscrew whilst keeping the glasses at a safe distance.

'Bugger! Now the sodding cork's broken.'

Unable to bear watching her push a cork down into a bottle of vintage claret, Nick took it from her and salvaged the situation. A few particles remained but they each took an appreciative sip or, in Alex's case, several.

'Come on, sweetie, it's not that bad. After all, it's not exactly an unfamiliar situation.' Simon's dislike of Richard had never been well concealed.

'That's my whole point. I know he's a thoughtless pig. I told him so only the other week and he promised to make much more of an effort. Now this. I spent ages on that stupid dinner and I put on a dress for once and I even bought a pair of those horrible stay-up stockings he likes so much. See.'

Her sudden flash of thigh had an immediate and profound effect on Nick's heart-rate. On this one he was in silent agreement with the missing boyfriend: she really did have extraordinarily smooth thighs and there was something about that little gap of flesh that did it for him and half the male population of the Western world. This inebriated damsel in distress was becoming more interesting by the second.

'Yes, my love. But his idea of an effort is to call you more frequently from his mobile and tell you how late the meeting is going to run.' Simon's words, kindly meant, had a dispiriting effect.

She sighed in pained agreement. 'I know, I know. I have to face it. He's more into the rise and fall of the sodding stock market than any similar movement under the sheets.'

She gazed morosely into the depths of her drink, failing to notice the embarrassed pause that greeted her words. Simon threw a meaningful look at Nick but his attention was firmly fixed on the hunched figure sitting opposite. Simon tried to brush aside his renewed irritation but couldn't help feeling rather miffed. Alex was not the only one whose romantic plans had been thwarted.

'At least he's got good taste.' Nick's gentle words punctuated the silence and were thankfully taken at face value. Alex beamed at him in grateful malevolence. 'Hasn't he just? Took him ages to build up that collection and there's plenty more where that came from. Top-up, anyone?'

Shrugging his shoulders, Nick accepted this unexpected bounty, leaving Simon no option but to give in gracefully and follow suit. It would not do at this early stage of acquaintance to seem a boring old party pooper and, besides, Nick seemed quite happy to get stuck in for the duration.

With glasses refilled all round, Alex took a gulp and threw back her head melodramatically, rather enjoying the sensation of spinning that resulted from this unwise action. 'God, you boys are lucky. You don't shit on each other in quite the same way.'

Surprisingly, it was Nick who chose to respond to this observation. 'Oh, I don't know. Men are incredibly competitive with each other.'

'Yes, but not when it comes to relationships. You'd never catch a man doing this to another man – he wouldn't get away with it.'

'I suppose not.' He seemed bemused but noncommittal.

Simon decided it was time to change the subject. 'Nick has just returned from living in the Far East,' he announced brightly.

Alex took the bait but bodged her response. 'So you said.'

Simon's glare failed to remind her that their earlier conversation had been supposedly confidential and she carried on in blissful ignorance of his ire.

'So, Nick, what were you doing out in sunny old Singapore?' she asked in a friendly fashion.

'It was mainly Thailand and I was bumming around for a good deal of the time.'

Alex snorted derisively. 'On Daddy's credit card, I suppose?'

His reply was saintly in its patience. She was, after all, under a good deal of stress as well as the influence of quantities of booze. 'Nope. I financed most of my travelling by doing some modelling in Japan and Hong

Kong and it ended up taking me to Thailand. I liked it so much I stayed for about eighteen months.'

This was getting interesting and Alex determined to dig deeper. 'What on earth brought you back to boring old England?'

His response seemed a little more guarded. 'Oh, it was time to move on. Had a bit of a bad experience and decided it was time to come home and get a proper job. Well, have a go at becoming a photographer at any rate.'

He seemed to have got away with that one but his hesitant manner had caught Simon's attention and he began to wonder just what had driven Nick out of Thailand. Probably a bad time with some rich older expat lover: Simon had met plenty of guys who had lived the high life until said lover had grown bored and moved on to younger, more compliant flesh. No doubt Nick's fresh-faced appeal had worn thin when compared to the latest shipment off the plane. In a place like Thailand there was always a new and pretty face with whom to fill the empty hours far from home.

The wine had hit that liberational spot and Alex was touched. 'Good for you. Should always try and follow your dream and all that stuff.'

She was solemnly conveying her approval whilst waving her half-full glass around in a wayward manner. Simon, fearful of the upholstery, took it from her despite some protest. She rounded on him but it was only to cajole in her best interfering manner. There was nothing Alex liked better than to lend a helping, if somewhat unsteady, hand. 'Simon, you could help Nick out. You know tons of the right people.'

He smiled benevolently at her. 'Already done. Nick is to be my new assistant.'

She peered at him in astonishment. 'Blimey, that was quick. What about the closet Kraut?'

'Jürgen has decided to go back to Germany. And the closet stays shut, although there's no doubt about that one. I can always tell.' This last was said with a loaded glance at Nick, who affected not to notice. Assuming shyness on his part, Simon carried on, 'Personally, I think he's more into his camera than anything else.'

Alex sighed theatrically. 'Just like Richard and his bloody bank. I know the feeling. But that's great, Nick, really good. You've got to watch Simon, though. He can be a right demanding drama queen.'

Nick grinned at her. 'I'm sure that's not true. And it is a great opportunity. About time I settled down to what I really want. I can't drift around for ever, not at my age.'

Never one for tact, Alex bounced this undiplomatically back at him. 'Oh, come on. You've got plenty of time to go for what you want. Anyway, how old are you? Twenty-three? Twenty-four?'

This was also roughly where Simon would have pegged him and his reply surprised them both. 'Very flattering but I'll be twenty-nine in five days' time.'

This was getting better and better. A man of twenty-nine was a far more interesting prospect than an unformed boy and Simon perked up considerably. He had grown bored of liaisons with cute young things like Sebastian, whose physical development belied their continuing emotional adolescence. A relationship of equals would be a new and much more satisfying experience.

'Well, you don't look it,' Alex declared bluntly.

Her look of frank appreciation rattled Simon and he seized his chance a few moments later when Nick excused himself to go to the loo. 'Nice, isn't he?'

Alex was not fooled by his studied nonchalance: she knew Simon rather too well to be convinced by an offhand remark when confronted with a vision like Nick. 'Very. Cute, too. Looks a bit like that bloke you brought to the Boom Bar – whatsisname with the cheekbones and attitude problem.'

Simon knew just who she meant: it was, after all, a perfect description. He felt honour bound, however, to defend his taste if nothing else. 'Oh, come on, Alex, Sebastian had been working very hard that week. But, yes, there is a resemblance, although I have to say I find Nick has slightly more . . . edge.'

That and a whole lot more substance, but Simon was going to play this one very cool. He would rather die than admit it but there was the tiniest nagging sense of doubt in his bones. It might not be the easy slide to seduction that it usually was and he really wasn't clear as to which side of the fence Nick stood. Right now he seemed to be straddling it, and Simon didn't like the way he had been looking at Alex with open appreciation.

'Of course, Nick modelled too, out in Japan and places. Between you and me I think some bust-up with a lover sent him scurrying home.' Simon spoke authoritatively, marking out his territory as friend and mentor to someone in obvious need of his own particular type of guidance.

Alex could have sworn that the frisson she had felt earlier had signalled some interest in her direction but in her inebriated state she wasn't going to argue with Simon. In fact, she would never question his judgement when it came to ascertaining someone's sexuality. As an authority on closet cases he was second to none, and more than one disappointment had been averted by his wise counsel. She could remember only too well the time she had been besotted with a moody young musician only to be informed that he had been living with his very male manager for the best part of a year. She was never quite sure if half the guys she met through Simon were completely attracted to their own sex or whether it was a convenient addition to their career repertoire but, whatever the case, she could not compete when it came to connections. She had none, simple as that.

'I see. And you're hoping to console him, are you, Simon?' Whatever his status as sexuality spotter, she was not going to allow him the high ground without a dig or two.

A faint noise spooked Simon into frantic hushing motions. 'Ssh. I can hear the bathroom door . . . but if you must know, I'm doing this as a favour to his father. We're just old family friends.'

'Yeah, right.'

Altruism did not sit well on Simon's shoulders but if he wanted to delude himself then who was she to stop him? In the same way, he was not going to stop the little demon in her from weaselling out a few more tasty details about the life and loves of Simon's fascinating new flatmate.

As Nick entered the room she bombarded him with her most winning smile. 'So, Nick, what kind of photography are you into? Can I have a look at your stuff?' There might even be a few giveaway clues in his portfolio. Alex, ever the sniffer hound, was now hot on his trail.

Nick smiled at her. 'I'm into travel pictures and environmental photography. I'd love to specialize in it eventually but, of course, any break is a welcome one.' He flashed a grateful look at Simon who inclined his head graciously.

Eager to see his work, she pressed on, 'Fantastic. And *do* you have anything I can look at?'

'Loads, a lot of which I sent back to my parents' place. But I have a portfolio of sorts with me which is in my . . . um . . . room. Want to take a look?'

Simon interjected hastily, not relishing the prospect of a tipsy Alex being closeted with Nick in the confines of the guest room, 'Bring it out, Nick. I'd love to take another look – didn't really take in all the detail the first time.'

Alex chimed in, 'Yes, go on, Nick. Really. I'd love to see your work.'

He smiled at her flushed, eager face, the consumption of yet more costly claret having lent it a not unattractive rosy glow.

Her colour seemed to deepen as she leafed through the pages of the portfolio he had fetched. She gazed at the pictures in sincere appreciation. 'Oh, Nick, these are beautiful. I love this one – look at her gorgeous little face.'

Touched by her obvious interest, he nodded in agreement. 'She is lovely, isn't she? Her family live in a remote northern hill village and I was very careful to ask permission before taking her picture. Some people still believe that it can literally steal their soul.'

Struck by such an oddly romantic notion, she looked up from the picture and mused, 'How weird. Although I suppose it's not that strange, really, when you think that's you frozen in time for ever.' Drink always made her eloquent, although the danger of slurring her words increased in proportion to the broadening of her vocabulary.

Nick appeared not to notice the eliding of the consonants. 'That's just what some of them believe. That you've robbed them of that moment in time.'

This was all getting a little too lyrical for Simon's taste and he flicked over several more pages until they were all looking at safe but still stunning images of paddy-fields at dawn and hilltops silhouetted by the glow of the evening sun. A few pages on and Simon's impatient fingers hesitated over a photograph of a Western woman, her savagely beautiful face in stark contrast to the gentle loveliness of the native women standing alongside.

'Who's this?' Alex was peering at it too, her curiosity sparked. She wondered how and why this sophisticated woman came to be amongst a collection of unstudied images.

'Oh, that's someone I used to work with out there.' His neutral tone belied the flash of pain in his eyes but the mood was abruptly broken by the shrill ringing of the telephone and Alex lost her chance to press him further.

Simon answered and handed over the receiver. 'It's for you. It's Richard.'

He had mouthed this last piece of information and Alex's heart sank. There was no way she could get out of speaking to him and she had often bitterly regretted ever having given him Simon's number. Still, the damage was done and there was nothing for it but to sound as noncommittal as humanly possible, a difficult thing to achieve after countless glasses of wine and an evening spent inventing fresh epithets to hurl on his unwitting head.

'Hello.' She aimed for frosty and ended up with feisty, her tone a blatant invitation to a fight. Simon sighed and waited for the blood to flow.

'No, I can't bloody come over and cook for you. In case you hadn't noticed, I have already cooked. It's the cold, stiff stuff in the oven.'

Richard, it would seem, was incapable of learning his lesson. It wasn't as if he was intentionally thought-less, just a typical male suit with aspirations way beyond his perfectly nice and entirely mediocre origins. Alex had gone ominously quiet, her shoulders stiffening as she listened to his placating voice. Simon met Nick's eye and they shared a wry grin, a moment of male empathy that did not go unnoticed by Alex. Shooting a scorching look at the pair of them, she silenced Richard's far too reasonable and adult attempts at dis-cussion with a satisfyingly childish gesture, slamming down the phone and sitting herself back down beside

Simon with an air of triumph. 'Well, you should have heard him. Pompous sod, he kept trying to tell me that they needed him there to seal the deal and that in any case Valentine's Day is merely an excuse for card manufacturers and flower sellers to up their profits. And merchant bankers, of course.' This last was pronounced with appropriate disdain and she settled back, inordinately pleased with herself.

Never one for kitsch cuteness, Simon felt that Richard had a point but wisely refrained from saying so. Instead, he chose to adopt his familiar fraternal air. 'So what are you going to do? Obviously you haven't eaten and you can't keep throwing back that wine on an empty stomach. You'll make yourself sick. I think there's some Camembert in the fridge and some other leftover stuff. Come on, we'll take a look.'

She followed him obediently into the kitchen and peered expectantly into the fridge as Simon rummaged around. He assembled a few choice items on a plate for her and added some extra cheese and biscuits for general consumption, directing Alex to wash a bunch of tiny seedless grapes as the finishing touch. Whilst she was dangling them under the cold tap Simon's next words floated oh-so-casually over her head.

'So, any thoughts on your boyfriend situation?' His tone was deliberately artless.

She shook the grapes with some malevolence and roundly declared, 'I think he's a total pig.'

'Yes, well, we know that. But what are you going to *do* about it?'

'Nothing, I suppose.'

'Nothing? Again?'

'Well, what can I do? He's always so bloody reason-able with his excuses and so damn adult the whole time that I end up feeling like a six-year-old . . .'

Her voice rose on a wail, unfortunately only lending credence to her words. Feeling another reluctant spark of sympathy for Richard, Simon decided then and there to change the subject. Piling plates into her hands, he ushered her out of the kitchen and back to the far more enticing prospect of Nick and, hopefully, more tales of his travels. Or of one particular sojourn at least.

They had barely begun to dig into the gloriously melting Camembert when an insistent peal of the door-bell disturbed them. The crumbs dried in Alex's throat when Simon returned from answering it with a clearly angry but always civilized Richard in tow. Refusing Simon's bland offers of a seat, wine and cheese in that order, he walked over to Alex and removed the plate from her hand. 'Alex, I think it's time to go. We need to talk.' There was no room for argument: Richard was employing his most definite and intractable tone.

Flabbergasted by his proprietorial attitude and furious at being deprived simultaneously of much-needed nourishment, she could only gape at him in embarrassed astonishment. Unwilling to make a scene and ruin the evening for everyone concerned, she had already risen from her seat when Nick unexpectedly and quietly came to her rescue. 'Alex, you haven't finished what you're eating.' His rock-steady tone brooked no contradiction but where people and atmos-pheres were concerned Richard lost his analytical skills.

'She can eat at my place. Plenty of food there and I'm sure we don't want to impose on you any longer,

Simon. We'll just get her jacket then leave you in peace.' His attitude might have been impressive in the boardroom but it went down like a falling FTSE index in the company of those with a social conscience.

For once not knowing quite what to do, Simon hovered between annoyance at Richard's attitude and relief that he would be left on his own with Nick.

Well aware of this, Alex spoke through gritted teeth whilst silently seething. 'No, really, Simon, it's time I went. Thanks for everything and, Nick, it was lovely to meet you. See you soon.'

He looked up at her and said with direct sincerity, 'I shall look forward to it.'

For a split second he smiled right into her eyes, then managed a curt nod in Richard's direction. With many hugs and effusive thanks she was gone and Simon returned to his guest, a sense of heightened anticipation winning out over fraternal guilt at his lack of assertiveness in the face of Richard's appalling behaviour.

Nick was looking thoughtfully into his glass but almost as soon as Simon sat down he spat out, 'That guy is a total jerk.'

He found Nick's vehemence somewhat surprising but could only agree. 'So we've all noticed. He must have some redeeming features or she wouldn't have stayed with him this long but so far they remain well hidden. A bit like his sense of humour. Anyway, enough of that. Another drink?'

To his intense disappointment, Nick stretched, yawned and announced himself absolutely whacked. 'No thanks, mate. I think I'll head for bed. It's beginning to catch up with me.'

Casting around for something, anything, to prolong the evening, Simon seized upon Nick's portfolio. 'Would you just show me those village pictures again? I love the idea of using it in a fashion shoot. The locals would make a wonderful backdrop.'

Nick was unwilling to refuse his extremely hospitable host but the idea of using the gentle villagers in this way struck him as ludicrous, if not downright repellent. He obligingly flipped through the photos until he found the appropriate section and handed it over to the hovering Simon. 'I prefer to think of them as fascinating subjects in their own right,' was all he said, but Simon, instantly chastened, cursed himself for his tactlessness.

'Of course. I just meant that their serenity would provide a perfect foil for the superficiality of fashion. You know, the sublime and the ridiculous.' Even to his own ears he was struggling, but he was doing his best to create empathy, if that's what you could call it.

Nick seemed mollified by this revised approach and Simon's confidence grew. He glanced at a couple more pictures before pausing over one of a village child laughing up at the camera, his unselfconscious expression a tribute to Nick's own empathetic skills. Turning to Nick, he spoke in the sort of tones generally used when confronted with objects of sacred and almost supernatural beauty. 'His eyes. It's true what they believe. You really have captured his soul.' By now patently gushing with more force than a rampant geyser, Simon was out of control. The scent of what he thought was victory and Nick's overwhelming proximity had had a disastrous effect on his generally good judgement.

He looked straight at Nick with perfectly sincere admiration and declared, 'You have an incredible eye. Well, eyes, actually. Ha ha.'

The glove had been thrown down between them, the handkerchief dropped, and Nick failed to get the point. Stifling another yawn he grinned his appreciation, stood up and stretched, clearly a man on his last jet-lagged legs. Simon felt like someone who had peered over an abyss and been pulled back at the final, fatal second. Horrified at his uncustomary obviousness, he could only be grateful that Nick seemed remarkably obtuse. He rose as well and took Nick's empty glass from his hand. Of course, the poor guy was exhausted and desperate for a bed only as a place to sleep off the hours of travelling. He could wait: there would be plenty of time to get to know him on a more intimate basis and to build on the mutual attraction he was sure lingered enticingly between them.

Hotting up his role as the unthreatening host, at least for the moment, Simon fluttered anxiously but was reassured that Nick had everything he needed and would be grateful for a shout in the morning. 'Off you go, then, Nick. Leave those. I'll pile them up for the cleaner in the morning. Sleep well. I'll knock on your door about sevenish.'

'OK, thanks. See you in the morning.'

Not quite a declaration of undying passion but Simon was content with the little smile that had accompanied the gentle pat on his shoulder as Nick stumbled off towards his longed-for bed. In fact, it kept him awake for quite some time as he lay in the dark and tried to puzzle out the strange warm feeling somewhere in the region of his chest. Uncomfortably aware that it might constitute genuine affection, he dozed off, only to dream restlessly of future nights of hot ecstasy spent in Nick's arms.

FOUR

A steady thumping penetrated the fog of sleep and Alex was brought slowly back to consciousness by the insistent beating of someone's heart. She moved her head experimentally and winced slightly. The pounding of her head equalled that in her left ear, and the inside of her mouth seemed to have turned to blotting paper. The weight and warmth of the arm around her waist were unfamiliar, as was the scent of the skin and the breadth of the chest on which her head was resting. And then a familiar silver ring caught her bleary eye. Dimly realizing that something was not quite as it usually was, Alex raised her head gingerly and blinked at Nick in sleepy bewilderment. Nervously, she licked away some of the dryness around her lips and managed an interrogatory sound. His look of confusion confirmed its unintelligibility and she tried again. 'Wha' . . . wha' happened?'

Not the most intelligent question, the situation being self-evident. It was followed swiftly by another pained grimace as the words seemed to reverberate through her skull. That's what came of drinking the house champagne instead of the vintage stuff, something to which she had unfortunately grown accustomed during her brief flirtation with a life of petty vice.

'Everything.'

His rather terse reply confirmed her worst and best suspicions. 'Ah.'

She lay still for a moment and tried hard to conjure up a clear thought through the crescendo in her skull. And then, in one glorious wave of recognition, it all came flooding back. She could feel a dull ache in her stomach and her inner thighs had that satisfyingly stretched feeling. If she cared to look hard enough there would probably be a few trophy bruises to match the tell-tale blue circles under her eyes and if all else failed the Cheshire grin would be evidence enough. There was no doubt about it: she and Nick had had sensational sex. No, more than that. They had made love all night long until exhaustion had forced her finally to beg him for mercy, or at least a couple of hours' respite. Not that it had been anything but the most unimaginably ecstatic experience but there comes a point when even the most willing back can arch no more and a parched throat can barely croak out a breath, never mind a cry of delight. She seemed to remember, however, sleepily placating him with the promise of a dawn chorus of an entirely sensual kind and she was more than happy to live up to her word. Extending one arm lazily across his chest she stretched, yawning like a well-fed cat.

Nick took this as his cue to come up with some sort of suitable response. Trouble was, he hadn't yet worked that one out. What he wanted to do was somehow fathom how she was thinking and feeling before proceeding cautiously to the next stage, whatever that was. He could not allow himself to believe that the culmination of many of his hopes and fantasies would turn out to be nothing more than a one-night stand but he had to admit that the evidence weighed heavily towards just such a scenario. The spectre of Richard loomed large and had gained in significance the more his thoughts had wrestled with the conundrum. He would have to tread carefully if he was to fulfil his ultimate fantasy and wrest her from the arms of a minor public-school success story with only a fat bank account to distinguish him from a hundred other born-again nerds. And that was going to prove difficult without a clear set of signposts from Alex, something that in his current frame of mind he was all too likely to misread. Aiming for a neutral sort of question to test the lie of the land, he again managed to hit the bull's eye of banality and sound like a boarding-house landlady to boot.

'Sleep well?'

Alex, her head tucked somewhere near his armpit, heard the tension in his voice and concluded that his sudden stiffness was not quite the kind she had been looking for. She raised a cautious head and smiled at him hesitantly. His answering smile seemed distinctly guarded. Unfortunately not privy to his innermost thoughts, she sank back to her earlier position, a puzzled frown marring what had up until then been a face marked only by an irrepressible little smirk.

Her muted reaction to his question immediately stirred up in Nick those latent little nuggets of negativity that had punctuated his long, sleepless vigil. Lying awake, with Alex a deadweight in his arms, Nick had done a lot of thinking and hardly any sleeping. The conclusions he had drawn were not the happiest. He had listened to her even breathing and felt unbearably lonely as the darkness turned inexorably to daylight and failed to banish the 4 a.m. demons that had kept sleep at bay.

Still half asleep, and with the encroaching hangover from hell, Alex knew nothing of his agitation. There it was again, a definite flinching away from her touch. He was making it more than clear that her presence was no longer as welcome as it had been and that the flesh which had previously melted to her touch now seemed to have a permanent case of frostbite. One more squirm, and he turned away from her gently reaching fingers.

'Don't do that. It tickles,' he gasped, with a distinct lack of tact.

The truth was that he did not trust himself not to leap on her and do his worst until she had yet again to beg for mercy, something that had done his ego the power of good. And he wanted to have that important chat before things again got out of hand and they both had to rush off with things unsaid and everything still in limbo. Her touch was sending him into sensory orbit and it was only by turning away that he could hide the evidence of his pressing desire to pounce on her and relieve the growing tension in a definite and probably more satisfying way. Determined to behave in an adult fashion, his well-meant wrigglings signalled something entirely different from the object of his long-term plans.

She gazed at him with the stunned expression of an accident victim and waited for some form of no doubt embarrassing enlightenment. When none came she muttered an insincere and faintly humiliated apology. 'Sorry.'

It was proving rather difficult to keep her head up on the end of her neck and she laid it delicately back down, this time choosing the safety of a pillow rather than the exotic territory of Nick's chest. A long silence ensued, during which she could still faintly hear the echo of his heartbeat, which seemed to have gained in pace. Or maybe it was her thoughts whirring around her head in hopeless confusion. An insistent growl from her stomach broke the mounting tension and Nick started in response. 'You're hungry,' he pronounced.

This was evidently the morning for stating the obvious. The thought of food was not the most attractive prospect but coffee might be a good idea and a soggy slice or two of toast would help mop up the alcohol, which seemed to have soaked through every cell of her body. Grateful that someone was taking charge, she grunted in assent, reticence seeming to be the order of things. She could feel the shift of his body as he reached for the telephone, which brought back all sorts of recent memories, and a hot flush surged through her. It was all she could do not to dive beneath the duvet covers and whimper aloud. Instead, she swiped a surreptitious finger under her eyes to wipe away any lingeringly unattractive smears of mascara and breathed as unobtrusively as possible into a cupped hand, the better to ascertain the state of her kissability. The rampant passion of the previous night had not allowed for such niceties as tooth-brushing and makeup-removing and she was damned if smeary cheeks and a lack of minty-fresh breath would make her feel any less attractive than she already did. The easy confidence she had so recently felt in his presence was being rapidly eroded by his continuing aloofness, and self-consciousness was replacing that gorgeous sense of gay abandon. Now, there was a thought; and one she suppressed the minute it reared its unwelcome head. She would so hate to be the one to confirm for ever his predilection for members of the same sex; the humiliation would be more than she could bear. Best to suck in that stomach and keep hope alive.

She smiled brightly up at him. 'So, how are you this morning?'

He was half sitting up against the pillows, a stern expression forbidding intrusion as he gazed off into inner space. Still, her words got through and he flicked a glance at her. 'Fine. Breakfast is on its way.'

He didn't seem prepared to enter into more expansive conversation so she uttered a bright 'Oh, good,' before lapsing into her previously prone position, the seed of doubt sprouting at an alarming rate.

The pounding passion of the previous night seemed to have dissolved into an unholy mess of self-recrimination and all of a sudden Alex wanted to weep in frustration and disappointment. Summoning up her last reserves of unquenchable optimism, and unable to believe that it could all have vanished overnight in a cloud of doubt, she decided to come up to his level. Gently easing herself up the pillows, she inched towards him until skin was touching skin. Nick glanced down again and swiftly averted his eyes. Following his gaze, she noticed that the duvet had slipped and hastily hauled it up again to cover herself. The breasts he had lingered over so lovingly not a few hours before seemed to have acquired a frightening significance and she began to feel like the most brazen of hussies. At least he had not flinched from bodily contact, although he was holding himself so rigidly that she wondered if he was in fact still breathing. She looked to him for some reaction but he seemed entirely oblivious to her, still staring off into the middle distance.

A tap at the door brought welcome relief from the agonizing tension and Nick bounded from the bed, taking care to wrap a towel around himself before he opened the door to room service. As she stared longingly at the exposed length of his taut thighs, Alex reflected dismally that he had been only too happy for the waiter to see her the night before. The cold light of day must expose her as an embarrassment, rather than the erotic icon she had thought she had become. Maybe that was it; maybe, having got what he wanted, he was going the way of an unfortunate number of men the world over. A small part of her rejected the idea out of hand but she knew only too well what good liars some men could be. She had met them time and time again in a professional capacity, men who regularly cheated on wives and girlfriends whilst whispering well-practised sweet nothings into her own disbelieving ear. The trouble was, they really believed their endearments were true. At the time.

Nick brought the breakfast tray back to the bed and handed her a cup of coffee, unconsciously pouring it just the way she liked it, exactly as he had on many occasions at Simon's flat. She smiled her thanks and hoped that perhaps a caffeine injection might loosen his tongue. He had never before appeared to have a problem with mornings but he might, perhaps, be suffering from an equally sore head and fur-laden mouth. She sincerely hoped so: anything would prove a welcome excuse. Although she had to admit that even the best of men had the potential to transmogrify into that well-known beast, the Lying Bastard.

Breakfast was good, and Alex found she was exceptionally hungry, a result no doubt of the night spent in unending enjoyment. Unending, that is, until dawn broke and with it what must have been some sort of insane spell. A covert look at Nick confirmed that he was still examining the molecules of dust in the air whilst munching thoughtfully on a slice of toast. He had sprawled across the top of the covers, a careful distance from her, with the towel still firmly in place. The signals could not have been louder or clearer.

As for Nick, a night spent far too deep in thought had dulled his normally sharp perceptions to near opaque levels. All sorts of things had whirled and churned through his mind, chief amongst them a miserable realization that in the solvency stakes he trailed at the back of the race. It was going to prove enormously difficult to act the white knight on a budget that ranked somewhere alongside Richard's petty cash expenditure. Whichever way he looked at it, Alex was selling herself short, and he could hardly offer to rescue her without so much as a debit card to his name. To add to his self-imposed confusion, sometime in the early hours a new, unwelcome thought had popped up to torment him: she might not want rescuing at all; might well, in fact, be perfectly happy with her lot. He couldn't imagine Alex enjoying her little sideline, and preferred not to think about it, but the Richard safety-net was always there to catch her in creditworthy comfort.

Or maybe she got a kick out of stringing these old guys along. Maybe she loved the fact that it gave her freedom from bank managers and massaged her own ego to boot. Impossible, surely, that some fat-bellied businessman could make her feel good about herself but, then again, she had failed to notice the effect she had on most men and on him in particular. Something that had to indicate a severe dearth of self-esteem. From the way she had acted it was pretty obvious that the thought had never entered her head, which up until now he had been placed firmly in the box marked 'Platonic'. That much was clear from many an evening spent over a few glasses back at the flat. He had sometimes felt like a guest at a hen party as she and Simon bitched and giggled and he did his best to listen in and learn. And very enlightening it was too. In fact, some of the information he had gleaned had come in very useful when it came to the crunch and she had succumbed, finally and blissfully, to his thoughtful ministrations. Knowing how insecure she was about herself, he had been at pains to make her feel at ease, and he treasured the fact that she had positively blossomed in his arms. Then again, it might well have been the fizz that had worked its magic rather than his own less intoxicating charms.

Whilst Nick ruminated in impenetrable silence Alex was hard at work puzzling out this all too familiar display of male illogicality. The previous night he had been practically worshipping at her feet; this morning she doubted if she could get him to tread on her toenails never mind suck them. She thought long and hard over the sequence of events, trying to pinpoint the moment when the balance of power seesawed back into his unresponsive lap. And came to the conclusion that, whenever it was, she must have slept through it. Which, ironically, was not too far from the truth. She raked over the conversation that had led up to that incredible meeting of flesh and a sudden, shaming thought struck her. Wondering how on earth she could have been so obtuse, and trying very hard for the correct dose of compassion, she wriggled a little closer to Nick and tentatively took one of his hands in her own. This was going to require all her diminishing reserves of tact. Anxious to reassure him over his performance, she was gushingly flippant. 'Nick, I am so sorry . . . I feel such an idiot. How was it? I mean, was it OK for you? Because you really have nothing to worry about. In bed, I mean. Keep on practising and you'll soon have the hang of it. Ha ha.'

He stared at her as if she had taken leave of her senses. The cold light of dawn had driven all thoughts of his little white lie out of his mind and he had no idea what she was talking about. Alex tried again. 'I just wanted you to know that everything's . . . fine. With you, I mean.' She could not fathom why he was looking at her in such a peculiar way and the rest of her soothing speech dried in her throat. His careful withdrawal of his hand served only to compound her growing sense of humiliation. Whatever she had done, she was obviously no longer the woman he had whispered to so tenderly in the dark.

He spluttered, 'Thanks. Thanks very much,' before lapsing back into brooding thoughtfulness.

So that was it. It was all coming back to him now and it was clear to him what her intention had been. Ever the saviour of the underdog, Alex had evidently looked on the whole thing as some kind of exercise in sex therapy, with him as the patient. And there he had been thinking that all barriers had been broken down, that she really had given herself to him heart and soul. The thought that she had somehow endured his lovemaking out of misplaced pity was more than he could bear. God knows, perhaps he even did kiss like a dribbling dog. She was well practised in pulling the wool over the baggy eyes of supposedly sharp businessmen so what chance did he have? For all he knew she could have been pulling off the performance of the century.

Yet whilst he was thinking all this Nick knew in his heart of hearts that Alex had not been acting. Fake orgasms were, to him, like reproduction furniture, and Nick had a good eye for real quality. It was, however, enormously convenient to latch on to this rather than admit to the far more real fear of being beaten by a banker with a nice line in bombastic behaviour. Pride, however, won over prudence, and the sardonic edge in his voice had sharpened noticeably as he turned to her and announced, with dignity, 'Well, it's nice to know I passed the test. But I think I'm quite happy to carry on as I was, in blissful ignorance.'

Alex's heart sank. It was far, far worse than she had

feared. The sheer ignominy of it rendered her speechless. How could she ever live with the knowledge that she had once and for all confirmed that boys together really did have more fun, something Simon had been telling her for years? It was bad enough that she had even tried to prove her point, but to have failed so miserably didn't bear thinking about. The hag that drove him back to the fags – she could see the headlines now writ large across her heart. Feeling sullied by the whole affair, it was her turn to leap out of bed, somewhat hampered by the sheet she tried unsuccessfully to drape around herself. Muttering something about taking a shower she managed to get safely behind the locked bathroom door before hot, angry tears started coursing down her cheeks.

Left to his own devices, Nick's own confidence plummeted to an unimaginable low. Her precipitous departure for the bathroom could only signify an undignified haste on her part to get the hell out of his presence. He had been hoping they might linger a while over breakfast and perhaps set a few things straight but it was obviously not to be. Her locking of the bathroom door had clearly indicated that she did not wish to be disturbed so he chewed his toast in solitary discomfort and wondered where the hell it had all gone so wrong.

With the poundingly hot shower washing away the tears on her upturned face, Alex was wondering exactly the same thing. He had obviously not wanted to join her in a mutual session of back-scrubbing or he would no doubt have hammered on the bathroom door. If she had learned anything from last night it was that Nick was not at all shy when it came to expressing his desires.

And now, evidently, those desires lay elsewhere. Soaping every inch of herself, Alex tried to erase any trace of his presence but only succeeded in conjuring up visions of his hands touching in her in precisely the same places and with a lot more tenderness and love. Love: she could have sworn that was what he had whispered more than once in her ear but perhaps his concept of it was a little more fluid than hers. Certainly, it was a lot more flexible, although maybe convenient was a better word. Whatever, she seemed to have served her purpose and now the best thing she could do was exit with as much dignity as humanly possible. Although how she was going to do that with eyes that were pinker than her grandmother's lipstick and with a bad case of heartache to match was not altogether clear.

Realizing that she could not stay for ever behind the bolted bathroom door, Alex marched forth in her towelling robe, teeth cleaned and face splashed to hide the evidence. She felt more together after her shower, certainly now that she had something more than a sheet to cover her modesty. Noticing that Nick was still propped in the same position against his pillows, and still gazing patiently at his dust motes, she surmised that he had been waiting for his turn in the bathroom. Well, he could wait a bit longer. Hastily gathering up her clothes from various points around the bed, she scurried back to the safety of a closed door and tugged them on, all the while cursing the fact that she had ever knocked on this particular hotel-room door.

Taken aback by her hasty retreat, Nick swallowed the speech he had been about to make and cast around for his own gear. If that was the way it was going to be then he wasn't going to be the one left defenceless in his underwear.

Emerging yet again from her sanctuary, this time clad incongruously in her little black number, Alex was greeted by a partly dressed and upright Nick. He was hovering nervously beside the sofa and Alex assumed that he was by now anxious to get away, back to less confusing, more masculine company. She decided to take the bull by the horns and looked him straight in the eye.

'Going somewhere?'

It sounded like an accusation and Nick was startled at her venom. 'No. Although I do have to be out of here by eleven thirty. Work thing, of course.'

His directness was his undoing. Arching an eyebrow and managing a look of great disdain, Alex practically hissed her response. 'Of course.'

A moment of emphatic silence whilst Nick floundered around for something to say. Gesturing vaguely towards the sofa, he sat down in one corner and looked up at her still standing over him. He tried for a placatory tone as he almost begged, 'Alex, why don't you sit down a second? There's something I want to . . .'

Still looking at him with that infuriating raised eyebrow and her defences on full alert, Alex shrugged her shoulders and sank gracelessly into the opposite corner. With the most polite and frigid of little smiles masking her terror at what she was about to hear, she waited for him to finish his sentence.

Bravely, if foolishly, he tried again. 'Um, there's something I want to ask you.'

His eyes were pleading with her now to give him a

chance but the knot of tension rising in Alex's stomach seemed to blind her to the fact. The blood pounding in her ears deafened her to all but the inevitable and her scalp prickled alarmingly as she waited for him to pronounce sentence. She knew what he was going to say, could feel it in every rigidly held bone and fibre of her body and nothing would convince her otherwise.

And he knew, sure as she did, that if he didn't take this one chance then he might lose her for ever to the land of Volvos and Montessori nursery schools. Still he hesitated, scared witless by the enormity of his task. With a life decision facing him and both their futures resting in his hands, Nick took a deep breath and asked the question. 'Alex . . . I . . . I wondered . . . if you would, if we could . . . erm, look, are you doing anything later?'

She could hardly believe her ears. She had been poised for the guillotine to drop, excise her dreams, cut away her heart and all he could think of to ask was that. Forget the profound insights into their thrillingly complex situation or the meaningful questions about their future. He had fudged big-time. Struck dumb by his lack of imagination, she glared at him in profound disappointment. By now an expert at speaking through clenched teeth, she managed to reply, without screaming aloud, 'Richard's coming back some time this afternoon. I said I'd meet him.'

It was Nick's turn to feel a sick lurch in his stomach. He knew that he had blown it but couldn't for the life of him work out how. Or, indeed, why she was staring at him with an expression of abject betrayal on her face. As for the inevitable return of Richard, he had been hoping that by now she would have seen the light and renounced all notions of a constant cash-flow in return for a lifetime of passion-fuelled penury. The bravado that had carried him thus far evaporated and he looked glumly at his bare feet and muttered a telling little 'Oh.'

Pleased with the impact of her announcement, Alex was also vastly relieved that the axe had not quite fallen. Not yet, anyway.

'Well, I'd better get moving. I said I'd meet Simon back at the flat by eleven.' He spoke lightly, unaware of the impact of his words.

This time there was barely a pause before her lips again formed that dangerous smile. With all this recent practice, she was getting rather good at concealing her true feelings behind a veneer of polite friendliness. 'And we wouldn't want to keep him waiting, would we?' she breathed.

He really couldn't fail to spot the vinegar beneath the honey in her voice but chose to ignore it in true uncomprehending masculine fashion. Practical matters had to be dealt with and Nick's unusual sensitivity did not extend to miraculous levels. He glanced at his watch and calculated that, with a shower thrown in, they should still have time for a serious chat before he had to leave. And that would give her a chance to get over whatever it was that seemed to be bothering her.

'I think I'll just grab a quick shower so why don't you have some more coffee or something? I'll only be a few minutes, then maybe we can decide what we're going to do.'

Her impossible hopes reared up again, only to be squashed firmly back into oblivion by his next remark.

'You know, it might be nice to meet up later for lunch or something.'

Or something. Like a long-winded explanation of how, whilst she was a very nice girl and he liked her enormously, it had all been a hideous mistake and he now knew where his real sympathies lay. Alex could picture it all only too clearly: Nick's unmoving earnestness and her own feeble attempts to laugh it all off as some sort of ridiculous aberration that had been doomed from the start. A bit like her relationship with Richard, although after this little episode time spent in his predictable company would prove soothingly normal. If crashingly dull.

That polite smile was proving extremely adaptable and Nick seemed to take it as some form of assent. Alex watched him covertly as he gathered his things together for his shower and found it rather unsettling when he chose to leave the bathroom door open. Illogically averting her eyes from the familiar but now forbidden sight of an undressed Nick, she waited a few seconds until she could hear the water running, then hastily began her hunt. She didn't have too far to look: on top of the bureau she found exactly what she was looking for and sat down again to carry out her task.

It seemed the best, most face-saving thing to do but she had to wrestle the right words out of her head and on to the page. Several screwed-up attempts were secreted in her handbag until she came up with the winning formula, all the while keeping an anxious ear cocked for silence from the shower. Thankfully, he seemed to be performing his ablutions with conscientious thoroughness – no doubt, she reflected sourly, washing away all the evidence before his rendezvous with Simon. This sudden stab of bitterness found its way on to the page and it was with some satisfaction that she surveyed the end result.

'Dear Nick . . .' The form of address had taken precious seconds of agonizing as she rejected 'Darling' as too affectionate, if delightfully sarcastic, and 'My Dear' as too motherly, a role she was not having thrust upon her no matter what his problems. Keeping it simple and fairly neutral had been of the utmost importance: it would never do for Nick to know how badly he had wounded her and she wanted to convey an impression of sophisticated understanding mixed with a tiny dose of reproval and a dash of vitriol for her own self-esteem. After all, she would have to see the guy again and Simon would pick up on any leftover awkwardness in less time than it took him normally to remove a tight T-shirt from a chiselled chest. Best to aim for knowing normality and leave him thinking that she had well and truly got his number. And, most importantly of all, that she wished him well and was unaffected by what had been merely an interesting encounter on the path of twentieth-century urban sophistication. That should get him right where it hurt, somewhere between his balls and his ego.

So her note continued, in its pleasant yet pointed, and carefully casual without being flippant, manner.

Dear Nick,

   Thank you so much for a very pleasant and enlightening evening. It is always nice to share a few thoughts with you over a glass or twelve, especially when that glass contains my favourite fizz. Very thoughtful.

Nice touch, that, making it quite clear that she had recognized his well-worn tactics whilst retaining a sense of wit and levity. It went on, the whole laced most lethally with that faint trace of sarcasm.

   Sorry I have to dash off like this but I suddenly remembered that Richard is taking the earlier flight and I thought it would be nice to be at the airport to meet him.

She had thought no such thing and always relied on Richard to phone her from the chauffeured car, so efficiently organized by his nanny-like PA. That usually gave her time to throw on something a bit smarter than her customary street-wise look and meet him at whatever venue he had chosen for his latest spot of entertaining. She could count on one hand the number of times they had dined alone and had long ago lost track of the number and variety of contacts and clients he had to schmooze and cosset. But it looked good on paper, making her out to be a devoted girlfriend who wouldn't let a little slip-up like the previous evening get in the way of her primary relationship.

   Hope you and Simon have a successful and rewarding day and give him my love.

As well as your own. That bit brought an unexpected lump to her throat and she brushed at her eyes angrily, forcibly reminding herself that she was in control of her emotions and that the best thing to do was walk away in a calm, dignified manner. Then she could weep, safe in the knowledge that by the time she next saw Nick she would be fine and well on the way to forgetting the whole sorry episode. Although even Alex had to admit that she was probably kidding herself over that one.

She signed off with a defiant flourish, hesitating before omitting to add any kisses. She was sure he could get a decent supply elsewhere, no doubt in a hot darkroom as he and Simon worked on their latest masterpieces. The sounds of splashing were still emanating from the bathroom as Alex slipped on her coat and slung her bag over her shoulder. With one last, regretful look at the bed she spun on her heel and marched out of the room, closing the door with a quiet but definite click and not daring to breathe again until she was out of the lift and into the lobby. For once she did not care what the reception staff thought and held her head high as she strode past, a firm clamp on her lip keeping the tears at bay. It was only once she had given the cab driver her address that she felt able to rest her head on the window and stare blindly at the traffic, her vision blurred by a feeling of devastating loss.

Emerging from his shower just a few minutes later, Nick could not at first work out where she had gone. It had taken him quite a while to plan what he was going to say but under the guise of scrubbing and singing he had come up with what he considered the perfect speech. It took a few seconds of blank astonishment before he noticed the note lying on the bed, meaningfully placed on the pillows he had so recently propped himself against. He had to read it twice through before its full impact sank in. He sat on the edge of the bed staring at it in incomprehension, unable to believe that he had misjudged things so badly.

All the while in the shower he had been trying to work out how to tell her how he felt about her and how to convince her that true love would win out over all obstacles. Even one as large as his overdraft. Some great lines had been tried and discarded, the noise of the shower successfully masking his muted attempts. He had finally settled on simplicity for its age-old effectiveness and had come up with a pithy but piquant speech. He was going to ask her to marry him. No more pussyfooting around, no more half-hearted attempts at playing it cool. This time he was going to bite that bullet, fling fear to the wind and drop to one knee if that was what it took. And so, having braced himself, taken a deep breath and girded his loins, whatever that meant, he had strode forth from the bathroom to plight his troth.

His heroic bubble punctured and all poetic thoughts crushed by the content of her note, Nick sat and wondered what to do next. He had gone to the absolute outer limits of his imagination on this one, not to mention his credit rating, and now he was stumped. He had hoped that the fancy hotel suite and limitless champagne might convince her of some mythical cash-flow but she had instantly seen through it. His current lowly status and label-free gear did rather give it away.

For a free spirit he was rather hung up on his fiscal inadequacy, a sad hangover from his last romantic fiasco. Sex had never been the problem: it had been his inability to keep her in aspirational heaven that had caused Louisa to hurl insults in his face. He could picture only too clearly the look of derision on his ex-girlfriend's lovely face as he had announced his intention to make it as a photographer. She had never been able to understand how he could give up a lucrative modelling career for certain struggle and that had been the end of that. Goodbye, Asia, hello, London, and the beginning of a whole new life, which he had hoped this time would be the right one for him. It had certainly brought him the right girl, although she didn't seem to be in total agreement.

Well, in that case, he would just have to convince Alex. Underneath his gentle exterior lurked a core of pure intractability. It had got him to the Far East against all the wishes of his formidable father and it had brought him as far as Simon's doorstep and the beginnings of what he was sure in his bones would be a successful career. And he was equally sure that Alex was the woman for him, would bet his prized Nikon and his entire portfolio on it. All he had to do was win her back, for he was certain that for a few short hours she had been entirely his. As she would be again – somehow he would make sure of that.

With a renewed sense of purpose and a lighter feeling around his heart, he threw his things together and stuffed his wallet in his back pocket, grimly reflecting that the bill would no doubt have a similarly lightening effect on his pocketbook. A final glance around before leaving the scene and something on the pillow caught his eye. Striding over to the bed he picked it up. It was a strand of Alex's hair. Glad that no one was there to see him, he pulled a tissue from the bedside box and wrapped it with infinite care. It would be his talisman; a symbol of his quest to make her his own. Strangely comforted, Nick let himself out of the room and set off to catch his bus, the white charger being unavailable to a man who had just emptied his bank account in the name of love.

FIVE

❦

'I thought we might pop down to Joe's later. A few people are meeting up for lunch.' Richard spoke from the depths of his Sunday paper. He was buried in the business section and only occasionally surfaced for refills of coffee and croissants. The last time he had done so he had noticed that Alex seemed unusually quiet but decided that it must be some form of recurrent female trouble and had retreated behind his rustling broadsheet. After all, she had even rejected his amorous advances the previous night, muttering something about a stomach-ache with a headache thrown in for good measure. When he got no answer to this latest attempt at conversation he peered over the headlines and repeated himself patiently. She seemed absorbed in the wallpaper, her expression vacant although some would have recognised it as dreamy.

A loud throat-clearing from Richard brought her back with a start, and she looked at him for an instant as if he were a total stranger. 'What did you say?' she asked, in an infinitely weary voice.

'I said, Jules and the gang are meeting up later at Joe's Café and I thought we could join them.' His voice was still mild but a tinge of impatience was beginning to permeate through the well-modulated vowels. She had been like this since he had got back the day before and he could only assume that it was a virulent case of PMT. For once his conscience was clear: he had racked his brains to think of some imagined or real misdemeanour but could come up with nothing recent. He had been on his best behaviour ever since the Valentine's Day disaster after which she had refused to speak to him for a fortnight, and he had tried his damnedest at least to phone and let her know when he would be late and occasionally when he would not be showing up at all.

The trouble with Alex was her inability to be totally supportive when it came to his career. For some bizarre reason she simply could not comprehend that her desires and needs, such as they were, would inevitably take second place to the huge demands on his time. It wasn't as if he didn't take her to the nicest restaurants, ply her with good wines and, as an added bonus, expose her to some of the finest minds in finance, truly fascinating men, all of them movers and shakers in their fields. And all she had to do in return was smile, look pretty and make the right number of polite noises. Hardly an awful lot to ask. She had often accused him of being a selfish workaholic but it wasn't that simple. As far as he was concerned he was doing it for both of them, building that secure future in which he was certain she would play an important part. Alex had class, breeding and a style that, once tamed, would prove an enormous asset. He only wished that she could show a little more enthusiasm for his clients. Just the other week she had refused point blank to join him and a couple of American bankers for dinner, claiming that she could not spend another minute in the company of people who thought that Anthony Robbins epitomized literary genius.

'Whatever.' Her response to his suggestion reflected the inertia that seemed to have damped down all her natural spark. Clearly something was more wrong than usual. Sighing to himself at the impenetrability of the female psyche, Richard retreated back to his stocks and shares and thanked God that he had been born a man.

This gave Alex the chance to fall back into her daydream, in which Nick swept her up in his arms and took her away from all of this to a place where complications were miraculously swept aside in the name of true love. He hadn't called, not even on some lame pretext, and she could hardly blame him. Her note had not exactly encouraged further intimacy, which was clearly not what he wanted. Even now he was probably laughing over some story in one of the scandal rags whilst Simon fed him freshly squeezed orange juice and brioches for breakfast. It really did not bear thinking about but her imagination insisted on playing havoc with her emotions. She hadn't slept properly the previous night, kept awake not so much by Richard's snoring as by recurrent images of the night before. It had been bad enough fending off Richard's feeble attempts at foreplay without having then to be haunted by memories of a much more exciting lover. And try as she might to put them aside in the name of sanity, the thoughts just kept bouncing back to taunt her.

She had also had to deal with the insistent Swedish madam, convincing her first of all that some awful form of gastric flu had struck her down. The very thought of a date with one of her sad little clients was more than she could stomach. In fact, the thought of being touched by anyone but Nick was repugnant. She didn't know how long she could hold Richard off but, too bad, he would just have to lump it. She looked over at him, or at least at the two stubby pink hands gripping the sides of his paper, and wondered how on earth she could ever have contemplated him as a long-term prospect. Or even as a boyfriend at all. As if to prove her point, one hand disappeared as he licked a finger in that incredibly irritating way and used it to turn the flimsy page. It always set her teeth on edge, that and his habit of clearing his throat every three minutes or so. No, this would never do. She had to get a grip. Nick was gone, convinced that a muscled chest and designer stubble beat soft curves any night of the week. She would just have to make the best of it, although she was not too sure that the man hidden behind several inches of newsprint was any sort of alternative.

As if sensing her thoughts, Richard chose that moment to emerge from his hiding-place and favour her with his attentions. He had digested all the facts and figures he needed and now felt that it was time perhaps for another sort of figure to fill a few pleasant hours on a Sunday morning. It might even cheer her up, make her feel that even at those delicate times of the month she was still a desirable woman. Richard knew his stuff: he had taken many a surreptitious peek at Alex's magazine collection and considered himself the epitome of the sensitive New Man. He always thought of the pair of them as a team, working towards the common goal of his success backed up by her loving support, and would have been more than happy to allow her to pursue her dabblings in creative writing, if only she were not too proud to accept financial help. He knew that it was important to take her feelings into consideration and often consulted her on important issues such as holiday destinations and the colour of his new duvet cover.

He was even open-minded enough to accept her peculiar collection of friends and to understand their exotic tendencies. He supposed that that was what came of being artistic, which he had never been, and although he still shuddered privately at the thought he was quite prepared to take on board Simon's homosexuality. Richard was still inclined to chortle with his mates and mutter darkly about shirt-lifters and bum-bandits and the necessity of keeping one's back to the wall. He might have viewed the more outlandish New Age concepts of male bonding and sweat lodges with singular suspicion, but all in all Richard considered himself a thoroughly hip and modern sort of bloke and, most importantly of all, a true red-blooded male, as was evidenced by his frequent muddy appearances on the rugby pitch. He had never yet persuaded Alex to wash his kit for him, unlike some of the other team girl-friends, and had instead to leave it for the cleaning lady to do. Still, she had other redeeming qualities, one of which was her irresistibly sexy body. Tossing his paper to one side and pushing himself up from the armchair, he sidled over to Alex and draped his arms over her shoulders, burying his face in her neck as he nuzzled and groped around the top of her breasts.

Alex shook him off and stomped towards the kitchen, leaving a decidedly miffed Richard in her wake.

He followed her through and watched as she banged kettle and mugs around before placing a restraining hand on her arm.

Alex glared up at him. 'Yes?' she practically spat in his face before turning her attention again to the destruction of the top of a new packet of coffee.

'Alex, what on earth is your problem?' He was angry now, more at the rejection than at her often illogical behaviour.

'What's yours?' she demanded, still with her back to him and digging away at the foil wrapper with a fork in the absence of a sharp knife, for which Richard should have been grateful.

'Well, if you must know I don't like being ignored. Or treated as if I smell or something.'

God, he could be so childish at times. 'I have no idea what you mean.' She pushed past him and headed for the sanctity of the bathroom, which was rapidly becoming her refuge of choice. She flung down the lid of the loo seat and plonked herself on it, burying her face in her hands and letting out a despairing groan. This was going to be a lot harder than she had thought. She couldn't eat, found it hard to sleep, never mind the background noises, and could think of nothing but Nick. As she rocked herself back and forth and ran her fingers distractedly through her hair, she came to the inevitable conclusion. She was in love; hopelessly smitten. Wondering how on earth she was going to get through this, Alex ignored Richard's irate bangings on the door and succumbed to the misery of her impossible position.

*

Not two miles distant Nick was also subjected to bangings on the bathroom door, but this time the less frantic ones of Simon enquiring about his breakfast preferences. He shouted something back about a fry-up sounding just fine and carried on pounding his shoulders under the power shower, somehow hoping that the fierce spray might sluice away his misery. Twenty-four hours ago he had been doing much the same thing, only then he had been using the force of the water to pummel some sense into himself and to muffle the sounds of his hurried rehearsal. Just thinking about the moment when he had emerged from the shower to find her gone made him wince. A peculiar pain in his chest was giving him a great deal of grief and his concentration levels had dipped to an all-time low. Simon had had to ask him three times to reload the camera the previous day, something he should have done as a matter of course. Thank goodness they were merely trying out a few set-ups for the big shoot the following week: he dreaded to think what Simon would have had to say if he had screwed up so royally in front of a client. Simon, in fact, had been remarkably patient, tempering that famous tongue and merely shrugging when Nick had stammered out his apologies.

Come to think of it, he had been incredibly sweet-tempered recently. Maybe he and Sebastian were getting on a bit better: Nick had noticed a definite coolness in the air whenever the pair met but perhaps they had sorted out their differences. Still, he had enough romantic problems of his own without worrying about Simon's. He was going to have to work out how to play it very gently without seeming too cool about the whole thing. Let Alex know that he was still interested in a subtle sort of way whilst slowly weaning her off the Habitat lifestyle and into something far more meaningful. A tall order, but he was going to give it his best shot. And if that failed, he'd give it another one. And another. In fact, there was no way he was going to give up now, not after he had tasted what had hitherto seemed forbidden fruit and found it addictive. That was what he must be suffering from – withdrawal symptoms. He'd have to hurry up and do something before the shakes really set in and he found himself incapable of functioning, although he rather feared he was dangerously close to that point already.

Roughly drying his hair with a towel, Nick emerged from the bathroom and followed the enticing smell of bacon along the corridor. Simon seemed to have picked up Nick's love of a good fry-up on a Sunday morning and had even managed to start using good old lard in place of extra-virgin olive oil for the genuine greasy effect.

If truth be told, Simon had been pleasantly surprised by the results of this about-turn in his cooking habits but had to do extra guilt work on the running machine as a result. He had been watching and listening carefully and several other Nick influences had crept in to spice up his normally ascetic lifestyle. His latest idea was just such a reflection of his new flatmate's taste and interests and he couldn't wait to tell him all about it. In fact, he had started saving up things to tell Nick, snippets from those odd moments when they were not in each other's company at work or at home. This consideration of someone else's thoughts and feelings had never happened to Simon before, and he was finding it a frightening but liberating experience. Although so far he had made no physical progress he was content to proceed with the utmost caution, viewing this as a long-term, almost sacred thing. Had any of his usual circle, or indeed any of his previous lovers, been privy to his thoughts they would probably have tried to have him committed but Simon was not suffering from any delusional illness, or at least no more so than any other person who has fallen madly and totally in lust and mistaken it for love.

'Smells good.' Nick peered hungrily into the sizzling pan before plonking himself down at the kitchen table.

Simon smiled in response, and savoured that glow he felt whenever he managed to do something that pleased Nick. Really, this love business was quite a revelation and he basked in the image of himself as a born-again earth mother. Any second now he would be tying on the pinny and declaring himself a house-husband for the duration. He deftly scooped up the food and arranged it attractively on large white plates, then sat down at the kitchen table and poured the Kenyan mountain coffee he adored. They ate for a few moments in appreciative silence, Simon concentrating hard on his food to avoid the disturbing sight of Nick still clad in a pair of boxer shorts and little else.

Finally, having mopped up the last crispy bits with a deep sigh of satisfaction, Simon lit a cigarette and smiled benignly at Nick. 'I've got some news for you. I've arranged for an addition to the household.' He couldn't suppress his excitement any longer, sure that Nick would be thrilled with his announcement.

'Oh, yes?' Nick still seemed absorbed in his bacon and eggs. Old habits die hard, and Simon always ladled the larger portion onto Nick's plate, his generosity a mix of his desire to please and a morbid fear of letting his own lean figure go to fat.

Simon pressed on, watching Nick's face carefully to catch his reaction. 'I've decided to give myself an early birthday present. As of later today, we are the proud parents of an Abyssinian Mountain cat, or kitten I should say.' His expectant look was met with a rewarding grin.

'Great. I didn't know you were into pets, but that's wonderful. They're very beautiful creatures, you know.'

And they were not the only ones. Simon dragged his eyes back up to Nick's face and took a drag of his cigarette. It had worked: he seemed genuinely delighted. As evidenced by his pictures, Nick adored animals and Simon had deliberately gone for the wildest, most exotic variety he could find without entirely disrupting his lifestyle. Cats he could just about countenance – they had a certain style and would not make too many emotional demands on him. In fact, he thought that he and it would get on rather well, having a similar outlook on life.

'Good. Well, I have to pick it up at three. Want to come along for the ride?' He spoke casually, trying not to betray that he liked to keep tabs on Nick, who occasionally went out to meet up with one or other of the few friends he had in London. Simon had met most of them and considered them unthreatening. He was ultra-careful, however, not to frighten Nick off with any whiff of possessiveness, which he felt sure would induce instant flight in such a free spirit. Most of the time they socialized together, or occasionally with Alex, when she was not too caught up in the Richard fiasco. But, really, this kitten represented a present to Nick, a common interest to bond the two of them closer together.

'Sure. Want a hand with those?' Nick, as ever, offered to help clear up and Simon shook his head in his customary refusal. He had his own way of doing things and Nick's cheerful but imperfect efforts only irritated him.

'No, thanks, mate.' Tellingly, Nick's vocabulary was starting to creep into his own but he could get away with that one. 'Oh, one more thing. I thought I might also have some sort of gathering for my birthday. It's ages since I had a party and it would be nice to get everyone together. It is, after all, the big three-oh.'

In actual fact, Simon had never had a proper party in his pristine flat, restricting himself to select little dinner parties and once even a drinks do where he had been careful only to serve champagne to the chattering guests drifting over his precious pale rugs. He was sure, however, that a red wine ban and careful policing of the event should ensure that his soft furnishings survived unscathed and that no stilettos marked his hideously expensive wooden flooring. Simon was not exactly a party pooper but he might have been happier living in a different, more respectful age.

'Great. When is it exactly?'

'Three weeks yesterday. Third of June, conveniently a Saturday. Hopefully the weather should have warmed up a bit by then and we can open things out on to the roof terrace.'

Simon's mention of the weather conjured up the sight of Alex swathed in her ankle-length coat as he had opened the hotel room door to her. It had been unusually cold for May, allowing her to cover up her giveaway outfit with what was practically the call girl's uniform long coat. Nick remembered thinking how sweet she looked all wrapped up, then the impact of her emergence from its all-enveloping folds in a knockout dress, which had left little to the imagination and a lot to be thankful for. Hastily banishing that dangerous thought to the back of his mind he returned his attention to Simon, who was clearly expecting some input into his party plans.

'Terrace sounds great. We could even string up some fairy-lights out there or something.' That should make most of the guests feel right at home.

'Fabulous. You can be in charge of décor, I'll look after the food.' Simon's eyes sparkled: this was all going far better than he had anticipated. A party was the perfect opportunity to flirt wildly with Nick in the safety of numbers. He could just see the pair of them bonding over the arrangements with the stress of the whole thing drawing them closer together. He had read somewhere that strife tended to cement the most unlikely partnerships and he could think of no better opportunity than hosting a stylish bash to test Nick's mettle.

The weeks until the grand event passed in a daze of catering decisions and a hundred and one changes of mind before Simon declared himself happy with a colour scheme of white upon more white with the merest accent of silver, obviously a radical departure for him. Menus were perused and canapés sampled without much enthusiasm until his favourite fashion editor passed on, in great secrecy, the telephone number of the hottest new caterer in town, a woman who could do wondrous things with a couple of woks and an encyclopedic knowledge of the food of every country that could conceivably be called Pacific Rim. This decision was not a little influenced by her vegetable-carving skills, a gentle tribute to Nick's liking for all things Thai.

Candles were to be floated in great flat silver dishes, with the odd water-lily thrown in for romantic effect, and tiny lights were strung amongst the fig trees with which Simon had adorned the terrace. A pianist would tinkle away whilst the guests mingled, a Cowardian touch that would at least give the piano its first airing since Simon had installed it some two years before, having rescued it from a dusty corner of his parents' barn. He had undergone the usual round of lessons and half-hearted practice but, really, his perfectionist nature meant that unless he was at concert standard he would rather not play. It did, however, lend the sitting room a touch of culture and that feel of old money, which Simon was at such pains to convey. The DJ would be arriving later on and was under strict instructions to provide the sort of mix that would appeal to both the staider guests and those denizens of clubland who would be adorning the event. His personal taste veered strictly towards the conservative, with a secret adoration of Abba, but Simon had a cutting-edge reputation to maintain and a number of important contacts to impress.

As the hour approached and Mrs Ang arrived to set herself up amongst the fig trees, Simon noticed that his beloved Miu Miu was missing. Even the waiters were summoned to help in the search but to no avail. He was just contemplating the awful thought that all the noise and fuss might have pushed her into jumping off the roof terrace when Nick arrived back from a last-minute dash to the corner shop and located her cowering under his bed. He reflected that in a lot of ways the kitten reminded him of Alex, all prickles and fur raised at the possibility of an invasion of her space. He had seen her a couple of times since that fateful night and both times she had been in the company of the doleful Richard and he had been unable to get any further than polite, meaningless conversation. On one occasion he could have sworn that he had caught her off-guard and that the expression she had thrown him was one of naked longing, but he had told himself to stop living in the land of wishful thinking. The presence of her dreadful boyfriend was clue enough that she had made her choice and intended to abide by it, whatever the consequences. He had no doubt that very soon now she would be sporting a string of pearls and talking of tennis parties and he most insincerely hoped she enjoyed it. As for him, he intended to drink his way steadily through the evening and try very hard not to trip over the designer-shod feet that would be tiptoeing gaily through the party.

Whilst Nick was soothing the fractious Miu Miu, Simon was buzzing around the flat giving it a last inspection before the arrival of the first guests. Rugs received a last little tug, flowers were tweaked and hand towels rearranged on their wooden rail. It was during his final whirl through the bathroom that Simon noticed Nick's silver ring left on the side of the wash-basin. He scooped it up in his hand, then swept on through to his own bedroom, ostensibly a no-go area but likely to be inspected by the nosier of his acquaintances. Everything seemed in order and he was just about to get back to the supervision of the final catering details when the telephone rang beside his bed. It was one of those annoying last-minute queries, some friend of a friend of a friend whom Simon had been prevailed upon to invite and who obviously had little common sense and absolutely no sense of direction. Simon patiently explained how to get to his place at least twice before curtly suggesting that Claudio might like to call a cab and be done with it. Roundly cursing all Milanese handbag designers and any other idiots who might cross his path, he marched off back to his command post, forgetting that he had left Nick's favourite possession on his bedside table.

All too soon the early arrivals were making their appearance and things were quickly in full swing, Armani-clad waiters stalking with a certain catwalk chutzpah amongst the glossy throng whilst hoping desperately to be discovered. The pianist moved smoothly from boogie-woogie to Beethoven and back again, the candles flickered in the gathering dusk, and Mrs Ang's titbits were judged most favourably. Lurking in a corner with a half-empty glass in his hand, Nick kept one covert eye on the door as he pretended to be fascinated by a dramatically delivered discourse on the perils of the Manhattan singles scene. One half-cocked ear registered something about an unfortunate encounter involving a shower-head, a belt and an over-exuberant supply of foaming gel, but it didn't seem to make much sense. In fact, nothing was really registering except that Alex had not yet made her entrance.

Joining in the conspiratorial laughter that greeted the end of the disaster date story, Nick knocked back the rest of his drink and was just making his way across the room to fix himself another when she appeared not two feet away. Dressed in a slightly more modest but stunning black frock, with her hair loosely swept back, she lit up the room. No doubt she would have had a similarly illuminating effect for him dressed like a Carmelite nun, but she seemed to have acquired a new sort of glow. Nick could only hope that it wasn't regular sex with Doughboy that was responsible for the sheen on her skin and the blush in her cheeks. As if on cue, Richard hove into view and walked up to her with a drink in each hand. She took one without a word, then looked around, doubtless searching for Simon so that she could give him the present she was clutching under her arm. As her gaze swept the corners of the room and found nothing it came to rest on Nick and, more specifically, his eyes. She froze for a second, then dropped her stare, stuck momentarily to the spot until Richard nudged her and pointed to the roof terrace. For once throwing Richard a look of immense gratitude, she headed off to deliver her gift, leaving

Nick to fix himself one hell of a stiff drink and knock it back in one.

Emboldened by the bracing effects of a large whisky, he wandered out after them on to the terrace and joined a little group, at the centre of which stood Simon.

Everything had so far gone to plan, in fact almost too smoothly, and the occasional demanding flicker of his gaze betrayed Simon's determination to keep it that way. For the moment, however, he was prepared to relax and bask in the limelight. When Nick appeared at the edge of his little group it only added to the lustre of the evening and Simon pulled him over to introduce him, to the envious glances of more than one of his fashionable guests – from the way he was behaving Simon had obviously got himself a nice little domestic set-up and many a mental note was made to discuss and dissect at the first opportune moment.

Nick took advantage of the general introductions to turn to Alex. 'Hello,' was all he said but she returned his greeting with the same measure of distance with which she had behaved ever since their close encounter. Nick was beginning to wonder if he had imagined the whole thing. Looking at her leaning into Richard's expensive armpit, Nick suddenly decided that he was buggered if he was going to carry on making a fool of himself over someone who clearly valued stacks of cash over substance. His unusually eager intake of whisky unfortunately fuelled this uncharacteristic belligerence and he turned on his heel without another word.

Alex watched him go with a sense of acute despair, unable to run after him and beg him to listen to her yet dying to do so. No one else had noticed their stilted encounter, being self-absorbed or far too drunk to pay her much attention. Richard seemed to be conducting a one-man love affair with a champagne glass, while Simon was far too busy playing the hip young host to pick up on the sudden undercurrent of tension that had crackled between her and Nick. Weary of the bitchy repartee that flowed all around her, Alex muttered something about going to the loo and made a bolt for it.

Yet again she was behind a locked bathroom door, head pounding under the unbearable pressure of her situation. The trouble with hiding in the bathroom at parties is that, sooner or later, you have to emerge, either to face the music or to convince everyone else that you are not in there for nefarious purposes. Mercifully, no one had banged on the door and she managed to slip out without bumping into anyone. She couldn't, however, face going back to the main party yet and instead went into Simon's bedroom, knowing that it would be out of bounds to all but his closest friends. She sat on his bed for a moment or two and considered her dilemma. Here she was, stuck at a party where her supposed boyfriend was making heroic efforts to drink the champagne fountain dry, probably because she had only that evening come up with a new and even more inventive excuse for keeping him at bay, and all the while the man she was desperately in love with was laughing at the side of his landlord and probable lover. They had seemed very much a couple as Simon had proudly introduced him around and Alex had picked up on the interest it had generated. No doubt even now they were guessing at his prowess and casting discreet glances at his crotch to ascertain the extent of Simon's good fortune.

Alex could stand it no longer. She decided to call a cab and be done with it, slip off quietly and leave them all to their little games. Richard probably wouldn't even notice she'd gone, and as for Nick, she couldn't bear to spend another moment in his presence and not be in his arms. Really it was best all round that she leave and Alex turned to make her call, stopping dead in her tracks when she noticed the ring on the bedside table. Nick's ring, his precious silver band, beside Simon's bed. Alex almost gagged: it was bad enough having suspicions but having them so baldly confirmed broke down her last defences. For a good ten minutes she sobbed uncontrollably, not caring who came in or even what happened to her mascara. Then she pulled herself together, repaired the damage as best she could and strode back to the party, determined to go out in style. With the ring in her hand she marched straight up to Nick and dropped it into his palm: 'I think you mislaid this.' Not pausing to take in his astonished reaction, she then walked out on to the terrace and slap-bang into Richard, whose consumption of vintage bubbly had infiltrated his brain to the point where sentimentality had emerged to express itself in a most flamboyant fashion.

Grabbing Alex by the shoulders, he pulled her towards him and planted a slobbery kiss on her mouth before dragging her off to what he fondly imagined was a secluded section of the terrace. There he dropped to one wobbly knee and, in a voice filled with trembling emotion, begged Alex to become his wife. She stared at him in open-mouthed astonishment before asking him to repeat the question. He gasped out the words a second time, adding the immortal rider, 'I'll even make you a named party to my credit cards,' before gazing up at her with the expression of a hungry spaniel.

As she gaped down at him Alex discovered another truism: her life seemed not just to flash before her but to engulf her in a nightmare whirligig of lurid images and grinning faces. The seesaw finally subsided and she realized that the grinning face was still there at waist level, waiting hopefully for an affirmative answer. In fact, a ghastly expectant hush seemed to have fallen over the entire party as Alex teetered on the edge of certain disaster. She could still feel the imprint of the ring in her hand, burning her skin with what felt suspiciously like betrayal. With all the despair of a drowning woman she released her last clutch at hope and let herself slip under. She seemed to observe from a great and disinterested distance as her lips formed a three-letter word and Richard's red face suffused with drunken delight at her answer.

He staggered to his feet and engulfed her in a bone-crushing embrace. She wondered vaguely why she found his probing kiss quite so repulsive. A couple of partygoers were wiping away surreptitious tears, although whether of laughter or sentimentality Alex could not be sure. One erstwhile performance artist was so overcome that she abandoned her air of studied cool to hug them both spontaneously. Someone was clapping, and she knew that it just had to be one of the American contingent, truly in touch with their feelings and expressing them as openly as ever. Even the more cynical observers could bask in the warmth of knowing that there but for the grace of God and a severe lapse of taste they could have fallen.

A general cry went up for more champagne and an astonished Simon came back out from his networking to find out if it was true. On being assured that it was, he managed heroically to conceal his dismay and generously filled every glass in sight before proposing a toast to the happy couple, with only the merest hint of irony to warp his straight delivery. Richard basked in the congratulatory atmosphere, feeling like a hero and puffing out his chest with pride. Still in her disembodied state, Alex smiled hesitantly and avoided catching Simon's eye, uncomfortably aware that there would be a lot of explaining to do. As for Nick, well, that sense of defiance came flooding back. She couldn't see him anywhere and wondered if he had somehow missed the announcement.

He had, in fact, heard every word as if it were a death knell, and had proceeded to attack the whisky bottle with unprecedented ferocity. He couldn't bring himself to offer congratulations, even to look at her, for if he did he had an awful feeling that he might break down and beg, anything to stop her making the mistake of her life.

Swept along indoors in a mêlée of billing and cooing, Alex found herself dancing to a requested smoochy number whilst Richard alternately muttered endearments into her neck and grinned inanely at all and sundry. She decided to fix her gaze just above the tip of his right ear and to endure the grinding of his groin against hers with good grace. She supposed that she would have to give in now and break the run of celibacy, although the very thought filled her with a sort of virginal horror. Well, she'd done it now. Sold herself out completely, betrayed every dream and hope she'd ever had, and all because she had nothing left to lose. Except love. Or, rather, the misery of loving someone she could never have.

Still lurching around the dance floor in Richard's unsteady grasp, Alex's eyes filled. One or two of those dancing alongside were touched by her emotion and exchanged understanding smiles, wistfully wishing for a similar kind of true love story to touch their own empty little lives. Across the room the source of all her longing and despair watched sourly over his Scotch and prayed with all his heart for the stock market to crash spectacularly, taking every smug suit with it into financial Armageddon.

'Well, she's finally lost it.' Simon had sidled unnoticed up to Nick and was looking sorrowfully at the débâcle on the dance floor.

'She certainly has,' was his embittered and heartfelt response as he in turn observed the wrecked dream that was currently being manhandled around in a peculiarly unrhythmical way.

At last the mushy music ended and a relieved Alex freed herself from Richard's possessive arms and slipped back to a semblance of sanity in a corner of the room. She headed for the kitchen door, reasoning that a few moments away from the mayhem would be restorative. The catering staff were far too busy to notice the presence of one forlorn woman who had just made a horrendous mistake. She was hiding by the fridge and trying hard not to get in the way when Simon came in to have a word with Mrs Ang's back room team and found a much more worthy recipient of his wit and wisdom. With nowhere to run, Alex decided she might as well get it over with and hear what he had to say.

'Have you gone completely mad?' he demanded, diving straight in with not an atom of sensitivity, such was his horror at her actions.

'No,' she muttered, and concentrated hard on her nose, having heard somewhere that it was a foolproof way to stop yourself from crying. Whoever had written that particular article had obviously never been faced with a situation of such magnitude. Defiance was evidently the only option available to her and she thrust out her chin and prepared to justify herself. The best she could manage was a mad rictus grin and a level stare, before Simon shook his head in bewilderment, patted her gently on the arm, as if she were a deranged distant relative, and gently suggested that she might want to rejoin the party.

Wandering back through to the main room, Alex caught sight of a rather manic-looking Richard being embraced by an ageing but still beautiful portrait painter of dubious talent and melted back against the wall, intending to creep off in some other, less conspicuous direction. A handily placed Japanese screen presented itself and she slid behind it, certain that for a moment at least she was safe. Unfortunately, when she stepped back a pace in her kitten heels she was rewarded by a muttered oath. There was something awfully familiar about the figure slumped against the wall and her worst suspicions were confirmed when a hand reached out to grip her arm and a thousand volts of lust shot through her in dizzying recognition.

'Well, if it isn't the blushing bride. I suppose congratulations are in order.' He spoke quietly and with remarkable steadiness for a man on the brink of self-induced oblivion.

Despite the gloom, Alex could feel the force of his stare, and for long, agonizing seconds neither of them said anything. The hand on her arm tightened its grip as if to pull her closer and she involuntarily glanced down at it. There, glinting up at her mockingly, was the silver ring back in its rightful place. It brought it all back to her: the despair that had overwhelmed her in Simon's bedroom and that illogical but deeply felt sense of betrayal. Breaking free of his grasp, she forced her way back into the party.

The heaving mass seemed to swallow her up and Nick watched her go leadenly, his lips unable to form the words he wanted to scream after her. He would have done anything, offered up his soul for one more chance to beg her not to go through with it, but his body would not respond to his thoughts. Still clutching his bottle, Nick stared at the spot where she had last stood and tried hard not to cry.

SIX

Simon basked in the glory of his successful bash for at least a week, coincidentally about the same length of time it took for Nick's hangover to subside. A few silent days at work passed before he felt able to summon up more than a grunt in response to the simplest of questions and Simon was beginning to wonder if it was something he had said when the sun came out again and Nick cracked a smile.

No one had really believed his excuse of a hangover from hell and Simon hoped secretly that he had somehow managed to get a green-eyed response from his eternally placid flatmate. He could vaguely remember flirting rather wildly with one or two of the choicer specimens he had invited to the party, and it seemed more than coincidental that Nick's sudden descent into gloom had resulted from an occasion that had been such a resounding success, crowned by the gloriously ghastly announcement of Alex's sudden engagement. He could not have staged a better incident himself to ensure his lasting notoriety as the party-giver *par excellence*.

It did not occur to him that this might have been the trigger for Nick's decline. Once Simon had his blinkers in place it would have taken a cataclysmic event to shift them and he much preferred the surety of tunnel vision. He just needed to find some way to win Nick's trust, to convince him that he wasn't going to hurt him as the unnamed person obviously had out in the Far East. Perhaps it would help if they were both away from the gossipy city scene with its attendant onlookers. A trip to the country might encourage nature to take its course, as it were, and he knew just the right setting. For years his parents had maintained their tiny country cottage right on the edge of the moors, in the hope that their grandchildren might one day run outside in the tangled garden or play cowboys-and-Indians in the copse that formed the boundary of their land.

Simon had had to suffer many a meaningful comment from his mother, desperate for her romantic vision to be fulfilled, but now that the heat was off and his sister Helen had produced a dutiful one of each he could relax and play the doting uncle to perfection. It didn't silence his mother but it meant that she was more than happy to lend him the cottage for what he described as 'a weekend with a friend'. She might not have been quite so keen to hand over the keys had she known that the friend was more likely to shave his beard than his legs, but as long as she remained in blissful ignorance everyone was happy. It had been quite a while since he had had time to tear himself away from work, but suddenly the thought of the desolate silence of the moors seemed infinitely appealing. It would also afford him the opportunity to disappear mysteriously off the scene for a few days, giving rise to yet more titillating gossip and ensuring that his name remained on everyone's lips for a while longer. The dinner tables would be positively buzzing by the time he made his re-entrance and he would hopefully have something to justify their interest dangling on his arm, although Nick didn't really strike him as the accessorial type.

All in all it seemed like the perfect plan but it struck him that there was a missing element. If he had not succeeded when he was a mere six feet from Nick's bedroom door every single night there was no good reason why a simple shift of location would yield any better results. No, there had to be a reason for bonding closer, a shared sense of tension, and Simon thought he had just the answer. He would invite the happy couple along on the pretext of getting to know Richard better. Come to think of it, that in itself might reap dividends. He could fake a great interest in all Richard had to say whilst simultaneously searching for the inevitable Achilles heel that would facilitate his eventual toppling from the lovebirds' perch. It was plain enough that Nick could not bear to be in Richard's company but a jointly polite show, whilst ganging up behind his back, should ensure the sealing of the common bond that for ever binds together those who have survived a stressful experience. And there could be none more stressful than putting up with Richard's particular brand of humourlessness for an entire weekend.

Simon broached his idea over supper that same evening, smoothly elucidating all the reasons why they should make a joint show of support for Alex. 'After all, poor girl, she'll feel very isolated once she actually marries that idiot, if she ever does. Most of her friends hate the bastard but they're just too nice to tell her, and there's nothing worse than hitching up with a partner who no one else can stand. Instant social death. We shall just have to show our support and try to get to know him. There must be something there to like. A fondness for small animals or something.'

It takes one to know one, and for a mad moment Nick had a vision of hordes of weasels greeting Richard as a long-lost brother. He wondered if Simon had lost his marbles, condemning them all to a couple of days of unadulterated forced jollity, but he seemed to be in deadly earnest. Nick was not at all sure that he could endure it. However, it might turn out to be a godsend, affording him a snatched moment or two to win her back, or at least convince her to go for the longest engagement in human history. If he could just get through the weekend without luring Richard into firing range of a twelve bore then this might well turn out to be a productive experience. So he sipped his coffee and listened absently as Simon outlined his plans for country walks and enormous binges of wholesome pub grub, while he indulged in a vision of his own involving a back-to-nature experience of a different kind.

Alex's initial reaction to Simon's suggestion was one of suspicious surprise but he seemed genuinely to want to forge some kind of relationship with Richard and to accept their affianced status. In the main her engagement announcement had been greeted with stunned silence from all of her friends and family, unconvincingly covered up with the normal, and rather hollow, platitudes. Her parents had never met Richard and were rather miffed that he had not bothered to ask her father for her hand in marriage. Alex shuddered at the arcane thought and kept to herself the knowledge that he had been only too anxious to do so and that his eagerness to do the right thing betrayed his ongoing attempts at social mountaineering. She had to admit it: at times her snobbery shocked her but it was far superseded by the agonies of embarrassment she suffered whenever Richard used his pedantry to disguise his social ineptitude. She understood that it was a lack of basic self-confidence but she alternately hated and pitied him for it.

Since their engagement he had become much, much worse. The thrill of the chase had forced him into a charm offensive that precluded any form of possessiveness, but once the ring was on her finger it resembled nothing so much as a manacle. She sometimes thought that if he clamped a heavy arm around her one more time in that proprietorial manner she would die of claustrophobia. And she had noticed his disturbing new tendency to look critically at what she was wearing, as if a skirt above the knee was no longer permissible. But he was so obviously ecstatic at the thought of their impending joint merger that she hadn't the heart to confide that to her it felt more like a prospective life sentence. The shock of what she had done had worn off, to be replaced by the sure knowledge that she would rather face down a hundred bank managers than marry this man, although sheer cowardice, and a modicum of feeling for him, prevented her from speaking out. It would break his heart and she was not sure that she could be held responsible for the pall of despair and balance sheets into which he would plunge if she told him how she really felt.

At least she had a wonderful excuse for avoiding his attentions, citing a romantic desire to wait until their wedding day. Amazingly enough, he swallowed this largest lie of them all, probably because it tallied with his view of himself as a noble figure able to restrain himself for the woman who was to be the mother of his children. No man had ever suffered quite such a bad case of the virgin/whore complex and it could only be attributed to over-eager assimilation of the worst of popular culture with the influence of a background where appearance was everything. However, it made him all the keener to tie the knot with undue haste and he kept leaving glossy brochures lying around endorsing the virtues of a 'marriage in paradise'. Alex was not so sure that a canopy on a crowded beach and a local band playing bad cover versions constituted her idea of paradise and convinced him that her mother would be most upset if the wedding did not take place in her own village church. For once in her life she was grateful for the safety of in-built social constraints and thanked God aloud that her mother would give the most hardened of socialites a good run for their money when it came to organising things her way.

The following weekend, as she endured Richard's own particular form of road rage, Alex wished fervently that she had come up with an excuse to get out of the excursion. The journey to Devon was punctuated by his supposedly pithy observations interspersed with occasional explosions. Even Alex did not escape, as her navigational skills were roundly dismissed as worse than useless and a succession of startled locals were accosted for more accurate directions. These, of course, proved either incomprehensible or downright wrong and when Richard eventually switched off the ignition, some three and a half hours after they had set off, he snarled that he bloody well hoped somebody was in to greet them.

As if on cue the cottage door was flung open and Simon bustled forth, a welcoming smile firmly in place and a man-to-man hand extended. Luggage was scooped up and they were ushered into the low-beamed sitting room to be greeted briefly by Nick before being shown to their room, the only real bedroom in the place. Simon had nobly elected to camp out in the sitting room with Nick.

Alex silently cursed him for his thoughtfulness, although she was relieved that she and Richard would be sharing the one double bed rather than Simon and Nick. They dumped their bags on the bed and Alex backed swiftly out of the room, only too happy to find more congenial and less demanding company in the shape of Simon.

The sun had tried hard to beam through the constant drizzle that had accompanied them on their journey but it could hardly be called a beautiful summer's evening, and Simon had begun to wonder what they would do cooped up in the confines of the cottage. The original idea had been to throw an impromptu barbecue in the back garden and to lounge around on the grass with a glass of local cider to keep the conversation flowing. They would need some sort of lubricant for their tongues: Nick had reverted to keeping his own counsel and the lovebirds were communicating through decidedly gritted teeth. The unrelenting rain grew heavier, putting paid to any thought of an alfresco evening. The only thing for it was to decamp to the pub for one of Mrs Bridge's excellent meals.

Soon a sated but happier party sat contemplating a game of darts and admiring the great swirls of clotted cream that set their apple crumble off to perfection. Barely able to move with contentment, Alex wondered whether she could manage another mouthful. At first Nick's taciturn presence had inhibited her appetite but, as the meal had progressed and the warm atmosphere of the village pub had penetrated through the damp, she had begun almost to enjoy herself. Simon was on his best behaviour, asking Richard all sorts of intelligent questions about the markets and pretending to be fascinated by his answers or astounded by the breadth of his knowledge. Richard bloomed under all the attention and forgot himself so far as to drop his defensive arrogance. He actually laughed at one or two of the scurrilous stories Simon told about the secret lifestyles of a couple of the more prominent bankers. Their loyal wives would have been horrified to learn of their interest in pretty young things, none of whom were remotely female, and more than one expensive divorce lawyer would have given his sharkskin briefcase along with the keys to his brand-new BMW for concrete proof of such flagrant goings-on. It was in Richard's best interests, however, to maintain a loyal discretion whilst storing up the knowledge for future unspecified use, so he merely listened and let forth the odd bellicose chortle, a sound Alex knew she would grow to hate.

Simon reeled Richard in like the expert angler he was, a skill he had acquired at his father's side not a mile from where they sat during many a long and glorious summer break. Salmon was his speciality, and he privately thought that Richard rather resembled one, his greyish complexion betraying the many hours spent in front of a flickering screen or putting together complicated deals. Still, he had a vested interest in creating a close-knit atmosphere whilst subtly exposing Richard as the object of derision he hoped he would become. He progressed from his examination of the stock market to a discourse on blood sports and then on to solicit Richard's opinions on the use of conservation areas as prime building land. Out of the corner of his eye he could see Nick shift uncomfortably in his seat. As yet Nick had uttered no more than the odd syllable, seemingly absorbed in his food and then the concentrated dissection of a beer mat.

'Can't see what all the fuss is about myself. It's not as if the bloody birds and butterflies can't fly off and find somewhere else to perch. Don't you think, darling?'

Frankly, in his company, she tried not to, but Alex roused herself from her observation of Nick's growing mound of shredded paper to smile sweetly at her red-faced fiancé. 'Actually, I disagree entirely. If we all thought like that we'd be living in a concrete jungle where the only sign of wildlife would be the fat cats who built it all and are happily raking in the profits.' Richard snorted at her irrational female response and turned his attention back to Simon, who obviously appreciated a sane, logical argument.

'Well said.'

Nick's words were spoken softly but they lit up her heart instantly with their impact. It was the first nice thing he had said to her since their night together, and she was touched. Encouraged by the thaw, she decided to risk a conversational stab. 'So, how have things been?'

It was meant purely as a friendly question but Nick leaped immediately to the defensive. 'Fine,' he muttered.

'You been busy at work? Simon says things have been pretty hectic but that you're doing really well.'

Well at what she wasn't too sure, as Simon had a habit of hinting archly at a wider meaning.

Nick smiled bleakly and looked up at her properly for the first time that evening. 'As well as can be expected.' His eyes held hers fractionally.

Alex heard herself babbling nervously again. 'Oh, good, good, that's great. Really. I'm very pleased for you.'

'Shame I can't say the same.' His meaning was all too clear and Alex experienced one of her revelatory moments. It was so obvious, now that she thought about it. Just like Simon, Nick wanted to maintain the *status quo*, the happy little threesome who spent long evenings giggling together, all too often at Richard's expense. It was all right for those two selfish bastards: they had each other and clearly looked on her as some kind of mascot to entertain and amuse whilst reinforcing how good their relationship was when compared to her own. Well, stuff them. She would show them she could have a life of her own outside the stylish confines of their lives. She might have a dull job that was going nowhere and a fiancé who gave most politicians a good run for their money when it came to pomposity but Richard had a kind heart and was incredibly generous to her. The third finger on her left hand was weighed down by the diamonds that twinkled on their platinum band, and although she would have preferred a simple solitaire she was touched that Richard had chosen it all by himself and had presented it to her nervously only the previous evening. She stretched out her hand self-consciously to admire it and caught Nick staring at it with an unreadable expression on his face. No doubt both he and Simon would consider it vulgar but right now it made Alex feel secure, screaming its message that she belonged, she had been chosen by someone.

The light reflecting off the many facets caught Simon's attention and he stopped mid-sentence to grab her wrist and scrutinize it. 'My, my, that's quite something.' He had always been a master of ambiguity and Richard beamed proudly at what he assumed was outright admiration of his choice.

'Designed it myself along with this bloke in Hatton Garden. It's entirely unique, just like you, darling.'

Simon and Nick cringed in unison but Alex, riled by their insidious derision, snuggled dutifully up to Richard in a parody of every fifties movie she had ever seen and favoured them all with a coy smile.

'It certainly is. Unique.' Simon seemed hard put not to laugh but covered himself by coughing then offering to get everyone another drink.

'Let me help you.' Richard leaped to his feet before Alex could stop him and left her just where she didn't want to be. Alone with Nick.

'Must be quite tiring lugging that ring around all day,' was his laconic comment.

'Oh, I'll get used to it.'

'I'm sure you will.' This time she was the first to look away, his meaningful stare having made her feel distinctly uncomfortable. She was relieved when the other two returned with the drinks, followed soon after by last orders. The idea of sleep suddenly seemed immensely appealing. She had been encouraging Richard to hit the whisky all evening in the hope of overcoming his current fretful insomnia but so far with little result.

Thankfully, as soon as they were settled back in the sitting room Simon whipped out his trusty supply and waved aside all protests to pour Richard an enormous double. In truth he was still on the charm offensive and doing Alex a favour was just a by-product, but she was gratified when Richard knocked back the first and happily accepted another. With his weak head for spirits he should be snoring within thirty seconds of touch-down, leaving her in peace to lie awake and think about what might have been.

What might have been was, in fact, laying off the whisky for once. Alex watched him covertly from the depths of the squashy old armchair but he was engrossed in an inspection of the rug on which he sat and contributed to the conversation with only the occasional grunt or nod. Alex wondered if he was saving his breath for later and hoped fervently that the earplugs she had brought with her would do the trick. The old wooden doors in the cottage were not exactly sound-proof and as far as she could tell there had been no additions to the sitting-room furniture since her last visit. The sofa on which Simon and Richard currently sat also served as a double bed when unfolded. Great: a night spent next to Richard doing his best impression of a warthog whilst next door Simon got it on with the man she loved.

Richard stretched, yawned and pronounced himself whacked. Alex was sure that a flash of relief swept across Simon's face but he played the dutiful host to the end, half-heartedly insisting that the night was yet young and the bottle half full.

'No, really, thanks all the same. Must get our beauty sleep, eh, Alex?'

In his case, perhaps, but she was too dispirited to do anything but follow him into the low-ceilinged bedroom which, in any other circumstances, would have been irresistibly romantic. The gently faded colours in the patchwork coverlet glowed softly in the lamplight and the mounds of duck-down pillows looked all too inviting. Simon had thoughtfully placed fluffy white towels on the end of the bed and he bade them goodnight before closing the door. The click of the latch sounded like the clunk of a prison door closing to Alex, and she moved nervously around to the far side of the double bed before offering one of the towels to Richard and suggesting that he use the bathroom first. She took the opportunity in his brief absence to strip off hastily and don a large, baggy grey T-shirt that hung almost to her knees and did about as much for her figure as a shroud. The ghastly metaphor seemed only too accurate and she huddled beneath the covers until Richard's return before bolting past him to the bathroom and spending as long in there as she could, until she was fairly sure that he would have fallen asleep.

On her way back she tried her hardest to eavesdrop through the partially closed sitting-room door but could hear nothing other than a low murmur of conversation. In the bedroom, she was greeted by a wide-awake and purposeful-looking Richard. The fresh air and good food seemed to have had the opposite of their usual effect and the alcohol had only relaxed his recent self-control. As she climbed gingerly into bed, keeping as close to the far edge as possible, he reached across playfully and tweaked her bosom. Alex kicked his shin but he seemed to take this as an invitation to wrestle and within about thirty seconds she found herself pinioned under him whilst his mouth slid about her face searching for hers.

'Richard, bloody well get off!' She managed to get her knee between them and he rolled over with an aggrieved sigh.

'For Christ's sake, Alex, I can't keep up this frigid business much longer. Can't you see I'm bursting here?'

For a second she entertained a vision of him exploding before her eyes and solving all her problems. Life, unfortunately, was not so simple and she noticed with a flicker of remorse that he seemed genuinely upset. The softening on her part lasted a meagre few moments before Richard launched another unwise attack, this time thrusting a hand up her T-shirt whilst trying to insinuate one of his thighs between hers. This was too much and a sharp elbow gave her enough leverage to force him off for a second, enabling her to roll over and out of the bed and stand over him. 'If you can't behave yourself I shall go and sleep in the sitting room with the other two. You don't seem to understand that there is no such thing as conjugal bloody rights and when I say no I mean no.' Her furious words had an instantly chastening effect and Richard looked contrite. There was no need to tell him that she would rather bunk down in the woodshed than spend a night with a pillow over her ears in the same room as the boys. She had an uncomfortable feeling that Simon performed best in front of an audience.

'I'm sorry, darling, really I am. You're just so irresistible and it's been so long . . .'

Not long enough, as far as she was concerned, but Alex was tired and this was all becoming quite impossible. Having elicited a solemn promise from him to keep his hands to himself, along with his tongue and any other probing part he cared to think of, she clambered back into bed and spent most of the night wide awake, listening as hard as she could for any suspicious sounds from the sitting room. She was determined to be up at dawn so that she could clatter casually through the sitting room on the pretext of making coffee and discover for herself the awful truth. To make sure of this she had set her travel alarm clock and placed it under her pillow.

The faint ticking beneath her head seemed to mark off the minutes of her life, leading inexorably towards the manacles of marriage and a lifetime of gazing at the ceiling in one way or another.

Had she but known that Nick lay similarly sleepless on the sitting-room floor it might have offered some small crumb of comfort in the lonely hours before dawn, and it would definitely have cheered her up to discover that Simon was tucked up at a safe distance on the bed-settee, his generous offer to share having been gently but firmly rejected. Chastely zipped into his sleeping-bag, Nick was pretty sure that Simon meant no more than to be hospitable but he still did not relish the thought of lying beside him on the narrow pull-out bed.

They had chatted for an hour or so after the other two had departed for bed, when Simon had made some sarcastic allusion to the thinness of the walls and his foresight in bringing earplugs. He had offered Nick a pristine spare pair but this thoughtfulness had again been gracefully declined. Like a super-keen guard dog, Nick had every intention of staying awake throughout the night to gauge the state of play and wanted nothing to get between his keen hearing and the slightest sigh or snuffle from the bedroom. The softest squeak would have had him crouched by the keyhole in a flash.

By four o'clock he could bear it no longer. His back was screaming in protest, his head aching with a maelstrom of wild imaginings. Added to that, he had discovered that Simon had an irritating tendency to grind his teeth in his sleep in a way that reminded him of nothing so much as chalk screeching across some long-forgotten blackboard. Deciding that there was nothing else for it, he wriggled out of his tangled bedding and tiptoed into the sanctuary of the kitchen, hoping that a mug of cocoa might see him through the rest of this long, lonely night.

Breathing a sigh of relief that he had made it out of the sitting room without waking Simon, he eased open the door of the kitchen and slipped through, silently cursing its ancient squeaks of protest. He patted the wall to the left and then the right of the door, searching in vain for a light switch. Realizing that it was in some impossibly awkward position, he edged forward, doing his best not to bang into the furniture. His eyes were slowly adjusting to the almost complete darkness and he made out the dim shape of the kitchen table and the lighter square of the small window beyond. Nick hesitated a moment: something was wrong. Where the window should have been a clear, perfect square a corner was missing, obscured by something standing between him and it. Something that seemed to be breathing faintly but distinctly in the darkness.

'Alex?'

It was a statement more than a question. He would have known the faint smell of her perfume anywhere and could probably have traced her outline in his dreams. There was no response and he moved purposefully forward until they stood barely inches apart.

Like a deer at bay she stood rooted to the spot, barely controlling the sudden upsurge in her breathing. She had always wondered why people felt the need to pinch themselves to see whether they were awake or dreaming but in this instance only physical contact would have convinced her that she was indeed standing on the cool slate floor and not tucked up in bed beside a snuffling, grunting Richard. Serendipity, in the familiar shape of Nick, swung into action and proved her point.

Without pausing to think or utter another word he reached out and gently touched her cheek before pulling her to him in one graceful movement and kissing her so thoroughly that all of her senses spun and her sleep-deprived body began treacherously to beg for more. For what seemed an age they clung there together until somewhere in the house a door banged and they sprang guiltily apart. Not knowing whether she was more terrified of being caught by Richard or of lingering alone with Nick, Alex stepped out of his grasp and brushed past him towards the door, forgetting that the table stood solidly in her way. Not even the sudden and painful bruising her thigh received could diminish the way her body was still singing to his recent touch.

Confusedly aware that she was probably running from herself as much as anything else, Alex made it to the corridor and was swallowed in darkness, leaving Nick alone with his thoughts. He wondered for a second or two if it had really happened, so silent and swift had it been and so much a part of the strange tension of the night, then he went back to his makeshift bed and spent the rest of the night drifting in and out of consciousness, his restlessness heightened by the traces of her scent on his fingers and the renewed memory of the sweetness of her lips and the softness of her hair.

When her alarm went off next morning, Alex could not believe at first that she had fallen asleep. She definitely remembered hearing birdsong and seeing the darkness give way to a watery grey and had thought that she might well have to get through the next day on sheer adrenaline and will-power. She heard the alarm, acknowledged it and promptly turned over to fall straight back into a most disturbing dream where she was wrestling with an octopus whose sole intention seemed to be to crush and suffocate her to a horrible death. When she eventually prised apart her eyelids, it was to discover that her nightmare had come true and that the octopus was Richard. The resultant tussle left her red and cross. Having stridently convinced him that if he didn't stop it once and for all the engagement was off, Alex flung herself out of bed and cast about for the alarm clock. She eventually found it where she had flung it, across the room and under a small chest of drawers, and was horrified to discover that it was way past ten o'clock. Now she would never know if their kiss had been snatched whilst he had temporarily forsaken Simon's arms or whether he had spent the next few hours, as she had, in lonely contemplation before sleep treacherously overtook her.

Jeans and T-shirt were tugged on and she bolted out of the bedroom as if a hundred Richards were snapping at her heels. She managed to check herself enough to take a deep breath before strolling into the sitting room, only to find it deserted and suspiciously tidy. The bed-settee had been folded back, bedding stacked away, and not a shred of evidence remained to enlighten her on the goings-on, or otherwise, of the night before. A cheery shout came from the kitchen beyond and Alex wandered through to find an upbeat Simon and a tousled Nick, who was sitting silently nursing a large mug of coffee.

'Morning, sweetheart. Sleep well?'

Simon's manner was gently mocking: he knew full well that Richard snored like a steam engine and had guessed that connubial bliss had not been achieved.

That much was obvious from her jumpy pallor and reluctance to do anything other than accept the proffered mug and sit down at the table in a close imitation of Nick. Its reassuring solidity brought with it a flash of recognition and she surreptitiously touched her bruised thigh as if to convince herself of the reality of it all. She obviously wasn't discreet enough. Looking up, she caught Nick's eyes upon her. The expression in them was unfathomable. Flushing slightly, she shifted in her seat and addressed herself to her cup of coffee.

'Well, we are a pair of grumps this morning.'

Simon had slept remarkably well for a man prone to bouts of insomnia and his perkiness was due to nothing more than his caution with the whisky and great joy at having finally awoken in the same room as his beloved. He assumed, quite rightly, that Nick had not slept at all well but reassured himself that this was probably due to unrequited lust and secretly congratulated himself on his irresistibility. Another night like that and he would practically have to fend him off. Nick was obviously finding a way through his shyness and Simon was generously prepared to let him make a move in his own time. After all, he had a lot of demons to conquer and a lasting happiness to find and when it finally happened it was going to be absolutely right.

He put a plate piled high with toast in front of the silent pair, announcing gaily, 'Aga toast, best in the world,' before turning back to his frying-pan. The arrival of Richard saved the pair of them from elongating the excruciating silence over their mugs, although it bothered neither of them, exhausted as they both were. Poor Simon, however, was grateful for someone to talk to as he was getting a little tired of whistling tunelessly over his hot stove, all attempts at conversation having fallen on still apparently sleeping ears. Alex had always considered Richard's annoying ability to bounce around in the morning as the clearest indicator of their incompatibility but had half-heartedly hoped that he might somehow grow out of it or at least mellow with age.

Nevertheless, it served its purpose now, and he and Simon conducted a lively debate on the day's plans whilst Alex and Nick tucked silently into their breakfast. Alex wondered at what point Simon had progressed from a blend of banana, wheatgerm and spirulina to a fry-up but she was too tired to care.

Simon had planned a hearty walk over the moors, punctuated by a pub lunch and culminating in a cream tea. All very countrified and it should give him plenty of time to size up Richard and work out the best way of averting the disaster that would represent the marriage. Affable though undoubtedly he could be, he was clearly the wrong man for Alex and she was just too down on herself to see it. Somewhere in the depths of Simon's manipulative heart dwelt a firm core of decency, and he held Alex in the greatest affection. Lord only knew why she had allowed herself to get into this mess but he was quite sure there had to be a way to get her out of it. Alex was far too confused to stop herself from making a ghastly mistake, but Richard knew when he was on to a good thing. And therein, perhaps, lay the key. All Simon had to do was subtly dissuade him from that belief and somehow insinuate that things were not quite as they seemed with Alex. Perhaps he could hint at mental instability in the family or some dreadful secret that would prove horribly embarrassing if it ever came out.

He would have to tread carefully, of course. If Alex found out she would kill him, and Richard was bound to let the cat out of the bag. No, it would have to be something supposedly so hush-hush that even Alex knew nothing of it, some family secret he had stumbled across and kept from her all these years. Something dire enough to threaten Richard's precious career and turn him off for good. Well pleased with himself, Simon resolved to keep his plan strictly to himself. He knew that Nick would not approve, would probably insist on telling Alex, such was his unfortunate penchant for honesty and integrity. Well, sod that. A lot was at stake and, if not quite a knight in shining armour, Simon saw himself as the one to save Alex from herself – and indeed many an evening at some suburban golf club.

As soon as breakfast was over he charged into action, bundling them all into walking shoes and assigning useful items to each member of the party. He was nothing if not organized and had been tramping across the moors since early childhood. They were soon well equipped with chocolate, water, spare socks and wet-weather gear, this despite protests that summer was upon them and the sun shining outside. He brushed aside all their grumbles in a firmly adult fashion and they set off in one car, Richard's new convertible being deemed far too impractical to make it over the first cattle grid.

As they bumped along the tiny lanes Nick took the chance to make a few plans of his own. Squashed beside

Alex in the back, he refused to be defeated by her intense concentration on the scenery outside. Simon had organized the seating arrangements and had put Richard in the front, leaving the other two to their continuing silence in the back seat.

Alex rested her head against the window and allowed the blur of passing hedgerows to lull her into a semi-comatose state, which allowed her to ignore Nick's nerve-wracking nearness.

Nick took this calculated attempt to ignore him in much the same spirit as he took everything these days, with a certain dull defiance and a refusal to quit. Even in his most whisky-fuelled moments he never allowed himself to despair, not deep down. Somewhere in his gut he knew he could make it all right again, if only she would give him the chance. And if she wouldn't he would just have to take it, which was precisely what he intended to do during their ten-mile hike. If she wouldn't bare her soul to him then, with only the skylarks and the wild ponies to hear, she never would, but he had a feeling that the savage beauty of the open heath and the bleak majesty of the standing stones might encourage her to speak the truth.

All too soon for a soft city-dweller like Richard, they were parking in some remote spot and getting themselves together for their expedition. Richard had spent nearly all his life in some form of concrete surrounding and had a marked distrust and dislike of nature. He really did not want his brand-new Timberlands to be marked by mud or scuffed by twigs. A gentle stroll around Fulham was more than enough for him and the occasional weekend away was usually spent lapping up the luxury of some resort hotel or talking business in the guise of playing a round of golf. He had once endured the cold and horrors of a country-house party and had vowed never again to participate in the dreadful rituals that constituted the English upper class idea of fun. The greyish food had been inedible, the house freezing and the enforced jollity more than he could stomach.

This walk was going to be quite an experience and one he did not relish, not least because it had been at least six months since he had seen the inside of the corporate gym. The thought of showing himself up against the obviously fit Nick and Simon was not a welcome one. But there was no getting out of it. Simon seemed desperate to march them all over hill and dale, so he would just have to grit his teeth and get on with it. Alex might even be impressed by his efforts, possibly even reward him with slightly more than the odd peck somewhere near his mouth and a fat yawn to signal exhaustion. A man could live in hope.

The straggly party set off, Simon striding ahead, almost forcing Richard into a trot to keep up, with Nick and Alex trailing an increasing distance behind, the sound of their trudging footsteps the only noise save the occasional crack of a snapping twig or whistle of birdsong. The route that Simon had chosen was varied, leading up through trees to take them to a vantage-point from where they could see the river, beside which they had parked, then along an open stretch of moorland before descending again to the riverbank and past the rock pools where, if you knew where to fish, fine salmon could be caught. The hill led upwards in an increasingly steep gradient and Richard's thighs were soon aching and his calves complaining at the unaccustomed exercise. Simon kept up a stream of hearty chatter, impervious to the effort, but it was soon all Richard could do to puff out the occasional monosyllable in response, something in which Simon took a secret and malicious pleasure. He would soon have him softened up enough for stage two of his scheme. He kept up the punishing pace, not noticing that he was leaving Nick with Alex a considerable distance behind.

As they trailed up the hill behind the diminishing figures ahead, Alex hummed to herself, both to break the crushing silence and to keep up her spirits and strength. Her night without sleep had not been the best preparation for such an outing but she was getting used to keeping up a brave front and soldiered on gamely, pausing only when an untied shoelace forced her to stop. Somewhat to her surprise, given his demeanour that morning, Nick waited for her, a friendly gesture even if he did survey the horizon in the manner of a man whose thoughts were miles away and who wished his body could follow suit. Alex didn't know if she could take much more of this hot and cold behaviour. One second she was in his arms swooning with pleasure and the next he was acting as if she had contracted a dangerous disease. If that was the way he wanted it she was damned if she would be the one to show her feelings and lay herself on the line, but at the very least they could be civilized about things and hold some form of conversation. She decided to break the silence, which was rapidly becoming oppressive rather than companionable.

'Thanks for waiting.' She smiled encouragingly at him and he broke from his reverie to shrug in a not unfriendly manner.

'No problem.'

Then he was off again, trudging along the footpath with Alex keeping in step beside him. Glancing down at her striding along at his side, her pale face betraying her determination to keep up, Nick softened. The stolen kiss had unsettled him, and he had retreated into the safety of his protective shell. She seemed remarkably cool about it and he had to keep reminding himself that he hadn't imagined it, that she had indeed arched her body to meet his with a yearning that matched his own desire. Hastily bringing his thoughts back to the safer ground of the present, he noted that the other members of their little party were by now completely out of sight, not to mention hearing, and this might be the only opportunity he would get on his own with Alex. If there was to be any soul-baring, it was now or never. He cleared his throat as noiselessly as possible and tried to think of the best way to broach the subject. He couldn't very well attack Richard directly – after all, there was obviously something about him that she liked, such was the inexplicability of woman. No, he would have to keep the focus on the two of them and try to get her to speak the truth, let him know where he stood once and for all. And perhaps the best way of doing that was to open his mouth and tell her exactly how he felt about her, take that brave leap into the unknown and risk making a total tit of himself. All for love.

Fine in theory but he seemed to be having remarkable difficulty in formulating a sentence and getting the words out. This would never do: he would simply have to begin at the beginning and tell her how much he loved her. He just hoped that he could keep the pleading note out of his voice, take whatever she had to say manfully on the chin, even if it meant hearing the worst. And what could be the worst? Pretty horrendous stuff, he had to admit. She could tell him that it had all been a terrible mistake, that the kiss that still burned on his mouth had been yet another mistake and the night that he looked on as the purest expression of love he had ever encountered might have meant no more to her than the average one-night stand, and that she could never settle for a man who inevitably went into overdraft at the end of every month and still hadn't any career to speak of at the advanced age of twenty-nine.

This desperate wrestling with his thoughts passed unnoticed by Alex, who was concentrating too hard on the steep descent to the river valley below to spot the furrowed brow and sudden intense concentration of her companion. The pathway was slippery and treacherous, loose pebbles and stray tree roots making it hazardous, and once or twice her feet nearly skidded away from under her. Recent rain had made it worse than usual and she had to fling her arms back at one point to stop herself heading straight down the hill on her backside. A quick hand from Nick saved her from that indignity, and as he held her steady for a second she felt one of those peculiar flushes of regret tinged with another, much more painful emotion that she really would rather not entertain. For a wild second or two she hoped and dreaded that he might reprise his actions of the night before, but with a peculiar smile he dropped his grasp and the moment passed.

'Here, let me go first. Then I'll be there to catch you if it happens again.'

Oh, how she wished he was and always would be. Restraining herself to a smile of thanks was the safest option; she rather thought that anything she might have to say would only be of the deeply embarrassing variety. This friends thing was hard enough, without complicating matters by saying something she would instantly regret or by asking him a question to which she really did not want to hear the answer. Instead, she had to content herself with focusing longingly on his neat buttocks as they swung gracefully ahead of her down the pathway and towards safer ground.

As soon as they reached the bottom he would speak – that much he had promised himself after reluctantly letting go of her and taking the lead. Let them both get down safely and in one piece, and he would take a deep breath and get on with it. Strange how easy it was to take any sort of physical risk, save those that might have an adverse effect on the emotions. A broken ankle he could deal with any day; a broken heart was something else altogether. But much worse was carrying on not knowing if there was the faintest crumb of hope, if she ever wanted to be anything more to him than a lost opportunity and a source of desperate longing. The pain of not knowing was a lingering one, but if he got it over with, then it might be surgically swift, a sort of amputation that would let him get on with his own life. The cough medicine approach to love. Shut your eyes, open your mouth and swallow in one gulp. Instead of a gulp he was about to open his mouth and spill his guts, but the metaphor was good enough and the anticipation horribly familiar. Finally they were at the bottom and, true to his word, Nick helped her down the last little bit, over a treacherous tree stump, then simply forgot to let go. The seconds stretched into a minute and still they stood there, looking warily at one another with Nick's hand clamped gently around her upper arm. Well, here goes nothing, he thought, and opened his mouth to speak.

As he did so there was the most ear-shattering bellow and they both jumped out of their skins. Another shout followed the first and they could clearly make out Simon's voice calling something. All hopes of a heart-to-heart dashed, they set off along the river path, Nick plunging ahead to push the dense under-growth out of the way and Alex in hot pursuit. The two stragglers burst around a bend and stopped dead in their tracks. Up to his calves in muddy water was a clearly furious, soaking wet Richard, his hair plastered to his head in a singularly unattractive fashion. On the bank stood Simon, still immaculate and issuing frantic instructions to his less fortunate companion.

One look at the scene and it was obvious what had happened. The naturally athletic Simon had chosen to cross the river at this spot by leaping from a high boulder to the opposite bank and Richard had unwisely decided to follow suit, failing to make allowances for the lack of length in his legs and spring in his step. He had landed up to his thighs in the freezing cold water and was trying to slosh his way back to the bank despite the slipperiness of the river bottom and the clinging weight of his wet clothes. Simon had been trying to get him to come over to his side but Richard was having none of it and was making steadily for the original bank where Alex and Nick stood transfixed by the spectacle, their initial startled expressions giving way to helpless laughter. It was all too much for Richard, who swore viciously, promptly skidded and landed flat on his back, submitting himself to yet another unplanned dunking. By the time he had struggled up and ignored Nick's outstretched hand he was in a terrible state and even Alex had quelled her guffaws. He flapped his wet arms ineffectually in front of him and stood there, cursing, bedraggled and looking very, very sorry for himself.

'Shit! This muck stinks! Look at me! I'm soaked, absolutely soaked! I'll catch pneumonia at this rate. We really have to get back. I need to get dry. Right now. I get asthma, you know, and my chest feels all tight already.'

He did look awful and his teeth were chattering, despite the warmth in the summer air. Simon bounded back from the opposite bank and the foursome strode back to the car the quickest way possible, Richard squelching along with the pained air of a man whose every step spelled untold but bravely borne agony. All thoughts of a jolly pub lunch had dissolved along with Richard's sense of humour and he seemed determined to march along in self-pitying silence, which, apart from the odd meaningful look at each other, his companions had little choice but to respect. Alex thought privately that his dripping dignity would be suited to a *Monty Python* sketch but didn't think it the right time to say so. Best to leave him with some shred of self-importance.

The awkward silence continued throughout the car journey back to the cottage, Richard's suffering exacerbated by Simon's thoughtful placing of a couple of plastic bin bags beneath him. The rustle of plastic was thereafter the only sound above that of the engine, and all of them tried their best to ignore what could only be described as a curiously stagnant smell that increased in intensity as his clothes began to dry next to his skin. The second they parked in front of the cottage he was out of the car and waiting impatiently for Simon to unlock the front door before making a dash for the bathroom and a hot shower to wash away the mud and the pong of rotting river vegetation and to save him from imminent collapse. It did not seem to be his lucky day as the ancient boiler had already delivered the goods that morning, enabling him to experience the bracing effects of an ice-cold shower. It was an ominously taciturn Richard who emerged not long after and banged his way into the bedroom, causing everyone else to rattle their mugs of tea and start talking in unnaturally loud, animated voices for fear that he might suspect the truth and realize that yet again they had been laughing at him behind his back.

On his grim-faced reappearance, Simon clapped a comforting arm around his shoulder and declared jocularly, 'You city boys even think you can walk on water!'

After a martyred silence, during which his joke died of lack of appreciation, Simon dropped his hand and backed off towards the Aga. Richard sank into a nearby chair and gazed mournfully at the handkerchief he had balled into his hand. 'You could show a little more sympathy. I am absolutely frozen, I've pulled something in my leg and I'm sure that my chest is beginning to rattle.' He underlined this health bulletin with a pathetic little cough and a pained grimace.

'Oh dear. Yes, I did notice that you seemed to be limping. Where does it hurt?' Simon was already pulling evilly at the leg and Richard jumped away as if he had been scalded. 'Right there.'

'Oops, sorry. Well, how about a nice cup of tea? Alex, pour Richard a cup. There should be enough left in the pot.' She handed him a mug and they all watched as he sipped it cautiously.

'Bet you feel warmer already.' Simon was trying hard to re-establish the carefully nurtured sense of bonhomie but Richard was having none of it.

'Not really. Alex, I think we're going to have to go back to London. I haven't got my inhaler with me and I just know that an attack is coming on. Last time I got one I was in hospital for a week because I didn't have it with me and they said I should never let that happen again.'

Alex doubted the veracity of this assertion. She couldn't remember even seeing the wretched thing around the place and this was the first she had heard of Richard being asthmatic. It was much more likely that his shortness of breath resulted directly from a blow to his pride. It appeared that, yet again, he would succeed in snatching her away from her friends, and at a point when it seemed that Nick and she were on the verge of some crucial breakthrough. She had no idea what he had been about to say on the riverbank but she knew it was somehow vital. And he had said even more with the expression in his eyes. Volumes of information had been exchanged in that long, mutual stare and she was buggered if she was going to be dragged away just because Richard's precious pride had been half drowned.

'Surely you can try and manage without it. You don't even know if you're going to have one of your . . . attacks.' She tried to sound sympathetic but with a hint of resolution to indicate that for once she refused to pander to his self-pity.

'No, really, Alex. I feel worse by the minute. I simply have to get home and find it or . . .' This last statement ended in a sort of spluttered wheezing. Alex shrugged her shoulders and made a despairing face at Simon, who deliberately failed to pick up on its meaning.

'Of course you must, if it really is that serious. Will you be able to manage the drive back or is Alex insured for your new car?' Simon was all compassion and at that moment Alex seriously thought she hated him. Couldn't he see that Richard was milking the situation for all it was worth and conveniently forgetting that it was her weekend too? Obviously not. He was probably too busy rubbing his hands with glee at the thought of being left all alone in the romantic little cottage with Nick.

The thought of Alex being let loose on his precious

new convertible seemed to have a restorative effect on Richard. 'Ah, no. I should be fine to drive if we leave now. Any later and . . . Anyway, I am sorry about this, Simon. Hope you didn't have anything special planned for supper.'

'Er, no. Nothing special. I'm sorry you can't stay on but it's been great fun having you here.'

Richard had inadvertently played right into Simon's hands. To be left alone in the cottage with Nick for the evening was a godsend. He was pretty sure that the lamb he had intended for them all would go down a treat, accompanied perhaps by a well-chosen bottle from the cellar and a spot of Billie Holiday on the ancient record player. There was something about vinyl that was so evocative, reminiscent of a more open, less dangerous age. He was only disappointed that he had not had the chance to wind Richard up over some incipient madness lurking in Alex's genes.

He agreed that it would be dangerous to delay any longer and even helped them to load the car, ignoring Alex's hissed accusations of 'Traitor!' and eliciting a promise from them both to come again as soon as they could.

As Richard gunned the engine, impatient to get the hell out of there, Nick looked on with ill-concealed envy as the shiny new roadster sprang to life and they shot off in a squeal of tyres. Simon wanted to stay on at the cottage, but he knew where he would rather be. He would even sacrifice a weekend away from the oppressive city summer to carry on where he and Alex had left off by the riverbank or, even better, by the kitchen table. A sense of lost opportunity simmered in the air and he watched helplessly as the car disappeared down the lane, only following Simon inside when it had rounded the final bend and he could no longer see Alex's dark curls, although he carried with him a lasting impression of the final glance she had given him.

It gave him fresh hope and, much to Simon's chagrin, he spent the rest of the evening in distracted thought, barely noticing the ambience Simon had been at such pains to create. Candles and music went to waste and the lamb fell on muted tastebuds as the light at the end of the tunnel tantalized Nick with its possibilities. Simon was left with the distinct impression that, although some corner had been turned, it was not in the direction he had intended. Something had happened and he knew not what, but Nick was not the only one to feel the need to deal with unfinished business and it was in a remarkably similar state of mind that the two eventually bade each other goodnight and retired to their now separate sleeping quarters. Never had a sofa seemed so comfortable and Nick sank almost immediately into a deep and welcome sleep, his dreams keeping hope alive until morning came, and with it the chance to chase after whatever she had promised him with her lips and eyes.

SEVEN

'I just don't know what to do any more. I've tried everything and nothing seems to work. I give up, I really do.' Simon sounded as if he meant it but she had heard it all before, the long litany of despair followed by renewed energy as he felt unburdened enough to carry on precisely where he had left off.

'Um . . . what, exactly, have you tried?' Alex was not sure she really wanted to know this but the demands of friendship and some masochistic desire to hear the worst drove her on. Perhaps if she found out that there was an awful truth to be told it would extinguish the flame of hope that had been flickering ever since the disastrous weekend in Devon.

'Oh, you know, the usual. Dinner, candles, music, the works. I listen to what he has to say, I laugh at all his jokes. Actually, he has a lot more to say than you would think and I find most of it really rather profound.'

Oh, God, he had got it bad if he was using words like profound to describe conversations that usually centred around which lens to use or the latest amusing anecdote about the cat. Unabashed by this blatant clutching at straws, Simon ploughed on with his eulogy. 'He's so sensitive, so thoughtful. You know, he thinks a lot about all that environmental stuff. We even have recycled loo paper now and I have to keep separating all the rubbish into piles of different things.'

Things must be serious if Simon had sacrificed his precious supersoft luxury roll for the scratchy off-white stuff, and as for his admirable efforts at recycling, she could only imagine the effort it cost a man who had previously epitomized the throwaway society. Simon's idea of recycling was wearing the same shirt two days in a row, and then only if it was in dire emergency and he was coming home from a night spent catting about in some far-flung part of London. The thought of him carefully putting jars and paper into the appropriate containers was too ridiculous to entertain, and she would bet anything that the pile of empty champagne bottles far outweighed that of the organic food packaging.

'OK, so you talk and you divide up the rubbish together and then what?'

This fanciful stuff was all very well but she was desperate to get to the nitty-gritty, find out precisely what had gone on over the empty cornflake packets and used containers of ecologically sound washing powder.

'Well, nothing really. Oh, you know, the odd look and so on but nothing to speak of as such. I just wish there was.'

Her deep feeling of relief at these words surprised her with its intensity. She had thought that she had got things back under control but evidently not.

'Has he said anything to make you think he's interested?'

Excruciating though this might be to hear she pressed her point, praying all the while that Simon was reading much more into the most innocent of comments than was really there.

'Nothing specific, but I just know. You do, don't you? Well, I know how I feel about him. It's different this time, Alex. I really care about him. I really do want to make him happy.'

And you really, really do want to jump his bones. She kept that last thought to herself but she had her doubts about the purity of Simon's motives. Whoever said that thing about leopards and spots had obviously been an old and embittered acquaintance of his and she knew that, more than anything, the thrill of the chase kept Simon's interest alive. Plaintive though his voice had been, and there was no doubt he was convinced of the sincerity of his motives, Alex knew that Simon's emotional range extended as far as conquest and no further.

'I'm sure you do but you don't even know what he's into, if you know what I'm saying. I mean, have you ever seen him with another guy, in a romantic way?'

Simultaneously wincing and crossing her fingers, she waited for Simon to break the long pause that followed.

'Well, no, I haven't. Although I wondered if he might be seeing someone else, someone I don't know about. He does seem awfully quiet and distracted a lot of the time, as if he's got something to hide.'

'Does he?'

This time there was no suppressing that giveaway squeak in her voice but Simon was far too preoccupied with the tragedy of his own existence to notice Alex's sudden discomfiture.

'Then again, that might mean he's thinking about

me. You never know. He might be wondering what to do, how to make that first move.'

Somehow she doubted it but didn't have the heart or the nerve to burst Simon's bubble. Besides, this might get interesting.

'So, has he done or said anything that would convince you either way?'

'Well, no. But he is my flatmate and it's always tricky rocking the boat when you might ruin a good friendship. There is one thing I've noticed . . .'

'Yes?'

Practically on the edge of her seat, Alex forced herself to sound soothingly encouraging.

'Well, he did have a copy of that men on Mars and women on another planet book by his bed but that could mean anything. Could mean he's trying to work out his overall relationship with women. Has he ever seemed, you know, awkward in your company?'

Awkward was a pretty accurate description of the way they had been behaving with each other but she didn't really want to give Simon any cause for thought.

'No, no. Not that I've noticed, anyway. Maybe he doesn't know too much about women and is trying to find out. Maybe his, er, last experience has scarred him in some way and he needs to get his head straight. And you don't know for certain that this person was a man. He might just as easily have been in love with a woman out there. After all, you said yourself that you've never seen him in a clinch with a bloke and those boys you have around the place aren't exactly backward in coming forward. He's had plenty of opportunity.' Hadn't he just! Alex wondered just who she was trying to convince here.

'But that doesn't mean he's straight. I haven't seen him with a woman either.'

Simon's response was petulant. He absolutely hated to let go of one of his pet theories, especially if it would benefit him quite so spectacularly to have it proven right. Oh, if only he knew. If only they both did. Although Simon, true to form, seemed to think he had all the answers.

'Come on, sweetheart, you know me. Have I ever been wrong before? I knew that barrister bloke you were so crazy about swung both ways before you worked out his fascination with Gloria Gaynor, and as for that actor . . .'

'All right, all right!'

She really could do without her past mistakes being raked up to humiliate her. But at least there was one little piece of knowledge she could hug to herself, something that would blow Simon's theories right out of the sky if the truth were ever to be told. She knew from bittersweet experience that Nick was more than capable of making passionate love to a woman. There was always a chance that anything else came down to wishful thinking on Simon's part, despite his enviable track record as arbiter of sexual tastes, and that for once he was mistaken. A chink of light penetrated her dampened spirits and she almost began to feel optimistic again. Almost.

'Anyway, he has said that he wants to go away with me.'

There! She knew it. Her hopes dashed again in the

space of thirty seconds flat. The triumphant note in Simon's voice sang of 'I told you so' and she felt sick.

'Alex, are you still there?'

'Er . . . yes, yes. Sorry, just choked on my coffee.' She took a deep breath and swallowed hard, injecting a note of level normality into her voice before trusting herself to speak again. 'So, where are you planning on going?' Oscar-winning stuff. Even she couldn't believe the plausibly casual tone of her question although it was slightly ruined by the squeak on which it peaked.

'Photo shoot in Bali. We might even get to stay on for a few days afterwards, see the sights and that sort of thing.'

And quite some sights they would be, if Simon had anything to do with it. Alex flicked furiously at some imaginary speck of dust on her desk and briefly considered stabbing herself through the heart with her letter-opener. At least it would beat the slow suicide of having to watch and listen as Simon pulled his masterstrokes.

'Sounds great. When are you thinking of going?' Still casual, still calm. Thank God she had had only two cups of coffee that morning or Lord only knows what her response would have been.

'Couple of weeks' time. Actually, there's a big favour I wanted to ask you. I wondered if you'd mind looking after Miu Miu whilst we're away. I couldn't possibly put her in one of those cat homes. Poor little thing is so used to lots of love she'd positively pine away.'

Alex thought she knew exactly how the cat felt but agreed as charmingly as she could. At the very least she would have free access to the flat whilst they were away and could sit and do some pining of her own in Nick's bedroom. Better still, she might even stay over and share his sheets by proxy. After all, if she couldn't have the real thing she might as well be really sad and weep quietly into the pillow on which he regularly laid his gorgeous head.

Simon was delighted. 'Darling, that is so sweet of you. We shall bring you back something heavenly from Bali. How's about a beautiful local boy to liven up those dark nights?'

There really was only one beautiful boy who would do the trick but she giggled dutifully and promised to go round the weekend before to run through Miu Miu's routine. She replaced the receiver and sighed deeply, tapping thoughtfully at her keyboard. Lydia had left her with a mountain of work whilst she swanned off for a three-day jolly in some country-house hotel and Alex was working her way through it with great ill-will. At least once it was done she could turn her attention to her own stuff.

The one positive effect of this whole situation had been a growing desire to make something of her writing, if only to escape from an existence that resembled nothing so much as an incessant game of emotional ping-pong. She had been working away on a couple of pieces for a magazine competition and her self-confidence was growing daily. She had scribbled a few things before for Lydia, mainly when a looming deadline had meant that a puff piece or press release had been sacrificed to the constant whirl of lunching and entertaining. The results had been commented on favourably, although it galled her somewhat that more than once Lydia had passed off the work as her own. Still, it had given her the urge to explore her own ideas tentatively and to engage in something she had loved doing for as long as she could remember.

Since their aborted trip to Devon she had been swamped with the aftershock of her hasty engagement. Her mother had insisted on throwing a party for them, not least so that she could clap eyes on the man who had won her daughter's too-soft heart. Alex had so far managed to keep the two camps separate and, dreading the occasion, had been doing her best to downsize her mother's ideas. Neither had she been introduced to Richard's parents. He would have been quite happy to leave it until the big day and she suspected that his motives might rest in much the same place as hers, albeit for different reasons. She didn't give a hoot how or where he had been brought up and she despised his shame at his less than glamorous origins. His parents were probably perfectly nice people and he did himself no favours by keeping them so firmly tucked away. As for hers, she could only hope that the interrogation was kept brief and embarrassing revelations to a minimum. Persuading her mother to settle for dinner in neutral restaurant territory had been a masterstroke, although she rather suspected a need to impress had informed Richard's insistence on choosing the venue. All in all, the only thing that she could confidently predict was that it would be a memorable occasion.

Once the ring had slid inexorably into place on her finger Richard had gone into overdrive. As if afraid she would change her mind, he had been marching her around flats as if there was no time to lose. She had tried the one about living apart being far more romantic until the big day, but he was having none of it and insisted that now she was to be his wife she could stop living in Bohemian discomfort and accept his help for a change. Richard nearly always equated help with cash; emotional support would have frightened him silly. But he meant well and he seemed eager that she should be happy with their choice. She had to admit that it was rather fun swanning around with the estate agent, inspecting the sort of property she had hitherto seen in the back of those freebie glossies that plopped through the door to impress and depress in equal measure. She had enthused over oak kitchen units, fallen in love with expanses of polished wooden floor and entertained notions of spending many a long lunch break hunting out the perfect furniture to fill one of these suitably aspirational homes.

With so much to occupy her, a fortnight whizzed by alarmingly fast and the allotted Saturday afternoon found her knocking on Simon's door, nervously hoping that they would not be packing the sun-tan oil into one shared bag. Ever since the ring incident she had been wary of going into either of their rooms for fear of what she might find. More than once she had wondered if that was one of the things Nick had been about to explain that day on the riverbank. Well, it looked like this might be a golden opportunity to find out. There had to be something she could discover whilst the two of them were away and any guilt at snooping would be tempered by the knowledge that in her shoes Simon would do exactly the same.

'Hi.'

The door had been opened whilst she was still caught up in cloak-and-dagger thoughts and Nick stood in front of her looking irresistible in a black T-shirt and a pair of faded jeans, his bare feet surprisingly well kept for a man who paid so little attention to his appearance. She liked a man with well-kept feet: so many were afflicted with the sort of fungal infections usually only found on the stumps of fallen trees.

'Oh, hi.'

Strange how you could feel guilty without having done anything. Alex followed him into the flat and called out a greeting to Simon.

'He's in a bit of a state. Some problem with the stylist. Want a coffee?'

Nick seemed relaxed enough, in spite of the stream of abuse that could be heard from Simon's room as he rained curses down on the head of some unfortunate. She followed him into the kitchen and he favoured her with a conspiratorial grin.

'Let's hope they have plenty of Valium in Bali.' His wicked smile lit up his face but could not disguise the faint shadows under his eyes. She hoped that they were the result of overwork rather than anything more enjoyable and smothered her instinct to voice concern. He was old enough and ugly enough to look after himself, and it would not be alluring to cluck around him with her best mother-hen impression. Besides, he had Simon to do that. And she had better things to worry about than appearing alluring, including the welfare of the temperamental creature who was rubbing her head against Alex's ankles.

'Hello, Miu Miu. Have you been a good girl, then?'

'No, she bloody hasn't. Sodding cat tore up the middle of my duvet as revenge for staying out all night.' Nick's tart response brought her up short from tickling the cat's ears and her expression betrayed her sudden lurch of alarm.

'On a night shoot. For a car campaign.' He didn't really have to explain but somehow he seemed to think he should and she was grateful for it, although she could cheerfully have kicked herself for her transparency.

'Oh, right.'

Equilibrium re-established, she was tipped off balance again by the whirlwind that was Simon raging into the kitchen and ranting for a good ten minutes about the idiocy of someone called Serge. By the time he had calmed down she had ascertained that this exotic-sounding person was incompetent, indolent and a total idiot but still the hottest stylist in town. He was also a maniac and a spendthrift who had won over the client to his vision of a faithful re-creation of scenes from Hindu mythology as the perfect backdrop for the launch of a papaya liqueur, with thousands of extras and a baby elephant as essential components. And he would die if he couldn't get hold of them. Or at least disappear into a non-productive depression from which no one, least of all Simon, would be able to rouse him until his demands had been met.

If he wasn't quite so popular with magazine editors and advertising agencies Simon would have sacked him on the spot, but his hands were tied: the client had bought into the myth of the man and adored him and Simon had to admit that his previous work had been quite extraordinary, even if it had driven more than one art editor to unheard-of quantities of mind-altering substances. He had never met the man and already he harboured a faint loathing for him, tempered by a grudging respect. Finally Simon had come across someone as intransigent as he himself could be and his guts told him that this could be good, even award-winning.

By the time he had talked himself round to this point of view he had relaxed sufficiently to address the issue of Miu Miu's welfare and produced a neatly typed list of helpful hints, should Alex fail to take in any of the salient points.

'If she gets really lonely without us there's a packet of ham in the fridge. She adores that although you must only give her a little bit at a time and only as a real treat. Other than that, the tuna is all in here and her own tin opener here. She prefers her tuna to be chilled and usually has it first thing in the morning and then again at night.'

'Yeah, and the little sod has a habit of leaping on your chest at six in the morning to let you know it's time for breakfast,' Nick interjected ruefully, and Alex laughed dutifully. Was that just one chest or two, she wondered, and Simon hesitated as if a thought had struck him.

'Yes, she does like her breakfast early. In fact, you might want to stay over for the odd night, to make sure she doesn't get too lonely and to give her some continuity. Mrs J. will be popping in to give the place a dusting but Miu Miu is used to having us around most of the time. Aren't you, darling?' The little cat blinked up at her master and let out a squawk of agreement.

Alex agreed with alacrity. 'Sure. To tell you the truth, I could do with a few nights to myself. It's all been a bit hectic recently. Miu Miu and I can slob out in front of the telly and I'll even read her a bedtime story or two. Now, stop fussing, Simon. I know where everything is and you can leave me a number in case anything happens. Which it won't,' she added hastily, on seeing the worried look return.

Satisfied that his baby girl would survive his absence, Simon produced another bit of paper and a bunch of keys. 'Well, I think that's everything. I'll leave the number of the hotel beside the telephone and you can always call the studio if you can't get hold of me. Don't lose these keys. Mrs J. has her own set but she won't be here until Wednesday.'

Simon seemed anxious to get on with things and Alex took that as her cue to leave. They were catching a flight that evening and time was running short. He had planned it so that they would have Sunday to acclimatize and iron out last-minute hitches before work began at the crack of dawn on Monday. By then he would have rounded up his extras and procured a baby elephant. He only hoped that permission to use the sacred sites had been secured or they could be in for a frustratingly difficult time. Whoever this Serge was, he was going to make sure that they sat well apart on the long plane ride out there.

With exhortations to have a wonderful time, and promising to talk to as well as water the plants, Alex took her leave. As she let herself out of the front door she wished with all her heart that she was going too: that way she could at least patrol the hotel corridors at dead of night to make sure there was no tiptoeing around. She had already ascertained, by casting a casual eye over yet another neatly typed list, that they had separate rooms. Nick was in a bungalow whilst Simon got to lord it in the main house. The troublesome Serge had also been banished to a garden hut, no doubt as punishment for his diva-like behaviour. Simon famously never bothered himself with such trifling details as the organization of accommodation, that being the job of some lowly assistant such as Nick. She smiled to herself, wondering how Simon would react when he discovered that he had to traverse a lawn and feel his way through subtropical undergrowth to get to Nick's sleeping quarters. She set off for home with the smug feeling that this trip might be a little trickier than he had intended.

It seemed strange when, less than twenty-four hours later, she let herself back into the silent flat and found only a grateful Miu Miu there to greet her. The flat felt lonely without the boys there and she was glad that she had decided to stay over for the night and keep the cat company. The poor little thing was pathetically happy to see her, or at least the tin opener she was wielding. Alex wandered out on to the roof terrace to catch the late summer sun, a thick wad of Sunday papers under her arm, followed by Miu Miu, and the two passed a companionable afternoon in peace and quiet, save for the gentle purring that emanated from Alex's lap. It had taken the cat all of half an hour to decide this was her preferred perch and Alex felt mildly flattered by the attention. It had certainly been quite a while since anyone had curled up to her with such affection. She did not count Richard's attempts at physical contact as affectionate; desperate was more accurate. He had even had the nerve the other night to suggest it might be a good idea for her to visit a counsellor. He had evidently been reading one of her magazines, suggesting earnestly that the real prospect of marriage might be doing complicated things to her innermost psyche.

'Nothing more complicated than the fact that I just do not feel like it. And won't until the wedding night.' If then, she wanted to add. Instead she played her trump card and accused him of merely being interested in her body, which he denied hotly.

'In that case, prove it!' had been her response and he had retired, muttering darkly about the incomprehensibility of womankind in general and her in particular.

She had been rather pleased with that piece of gamesmanship but it was still only a temporary victory. The trouble was that things had gained an impetus all of their own and were gathering pace alarmingly. Her mother was pressing her to pick a date for this wretched dinner party, Richard had put in an offer on an admittedly gorgeous flat, and Alex felt trapped. It was all her own fault, she knew that without a shadow of doubt, but she could not see a way out without wreaking havoc on at least one person's life. Richard was not a bad person, he was just not her sort of person. She might never have known that, had she not met someone who was so right, even though the circumstances were so wrong. Perfection had rendered compromise impossible and there was no going back. Life was all about timing, and hers seemed singularly off. Oh, well, at least she had this bolt-hole for a week or so, where she could try to get her head together and hide from the rest of humanity. Taking a firm grip on herself, she turned her attention back to the most salacious of the Sunday tabloids and comforted herself with the knowledge that there were people out there whose lives were even more complex than her own.

A low rumble from her stomach signalled that it might be time to decamp inside in search of food and Miu Miu took this as a good opportunity to announce that it was time for her supper. Alex peered inside the fridge to find out what goodies had been left for her. Nick's influence ensured that alongside the salad and low-fat selection there would be some deliciously fattening treats and Alex came up with a combination that represented the melding of everybody's tastes. Oven chips, salad and cold poached salmon in dill sauce. Sheer heaven. Alerted by the smell of fish, Miu Miu came to watch her eat and pounced with delight when Alex tossed her a morsel. She had decided to make the most of the warm evenings whilst she could and had set up a tasteful little table for herself back out on the terrace. There they sat, the two of them, looking out over the rooftops and marvelling as the sky turned to red then gold and the sun set on another day without Nick.

She had deliberately avoided his room until that point, but a combination of the spectacular night sky and a couple of glasses of chilled Chablis had worked their magic, and she found herself standing beside his bed, searching for she knew not what. As people do when they are up to no good, Alex moved as quietly as she could, tiptoeing around and lifting things up before replacing them so that they looked undisturbed. She was just making her way guiltily over to the chest of drawers when she inadvertently stood on Miu Miu's tail and nearly leaped for cover at the resultant yowl of indignation. She reminded herself that no one else was there to either see or hear her and slid open the top drawer to find an innocuous jumble of socks and underwear. The other five drawers yielded similarly unspectacular results and Alex was beginning to wonder what she was doing.

In her heart of hearts she knew that she was searching for some form of incontrovertible proof one way or another, but quite what that would entail she was none too sure. There were no love tokens lying around, no notes to confirm her suspicions, no photographs to taunt her with images of a loving twosome. If Nick and Simon had indeed got it together then surely something would have given the game away. Everyone knows that in the early flush of romanticism that accompanies the beginning of a relationship there is almost always a flurry of little gifts or keepsakes to mark the fact. There was nothing. Nothing to signal even remotely that they were anything more than flatmates and colleagues. Everything seemed almost disappointingly above board.

Just to make sure she had a quick sweep through Simon's room and found exactly the same. Precisely nothing. Oh, there were the photos of previous encounters meaningful enough to have lasted a few rolls of

film. There was the beechwood frame that one
paramour had given him to display his own signed
photograph, which Simon had taken, and the beautifully simple mirror that another had given with
instructions to look into it each day to see the object of
his desire. Simon had to admit that it was a particularly
flattering gesture and always liked to tell that story,
although the lover concerned had long since departed
for the streets of Greenwich Village and the arms of an
art dealer of ill repute and considerable fortune. Even
the books beside his bed gave nothing away. Instead of
some inscribed volume of poetry she found a coffee-
table style bible and a biography of Oscar Wilde, from
which she deduced that if he was planning to deliver
orations of love it would be done as pithily as possible.
All in all, a disappointing haul and not a new trinket
in sight.

To her eternal shame she even drew back the bed-
covers to inspect his sheets. She could hardly bring
herself to look, such was her self-disgust, but look she
did and again found little, save evidence of the efficacy
of Simon's laundering and the faint smell of lavender.
A famously light sleeper, he tended to sprinkle his
pillows with the essential oil in the hope that it might
induce somnolence and she had once teased him that
his hair carried a faint, old-ladyish imprint of its smell.
A sudden thought occurred to her and, returning to
Nick's room, she swiftly pulled back the duvet and
stuck her nose into the pillows. Nothing, except what
she fancied was a delicious reminder of his skin and
hair. There was still a slight hollow in the pillow where
his head had been and she looked down at it for a

second, filled with longing. Bed making was obviously not his forte and, drawing back the covers further, she could trace an outline of where he had lain in the rumpled but pristine sheets. She tucked the duvet back into place and smoothed it abstractedly.

He had left a T-shirt slung over the chair beside his bed and she picked it up and stroked it through her fingers before raising it to her face. It smelt of soap and that peculiar musky tang that isn't quite sweat but still comes from hard physical work. Burying her face in it, Alex could imagine that he was there with her and felt so much closer to him than she had in a long, long time. Since that night in the cottage they had kept a careful distance that spoke volumes and meant that safe boundaries were in place. Now she was breaching those boundaries, doing the next best thing to touching and holding him and feeling as intimately connected as if they were in each other's arms. All she needed now was the flesh that had so recently been encased in the T-shirt, but the body in question was thousands of miles away and likely to remain so, in metaphor if not in fact. The tears welled in her eyes and she let them fall unchecked, soaking the T-shirt with all the pent-up pain, frustration and loneliness that had accompanied her through the last few months. Sitting on the edge of his bed she wept for everything she had lost and for the impossibility of what might have been. There was something immensely liberating about admitting to herself that she was still hopelessly and completely in love with Nick and probably always would be. It was also quite wonderful in a masochistic way to bite down on that pain as if it were a nagging toothache and to indulge herself for a few moments at least.

She sat there for quite some time, thinking long and hard about her situation. Scenes from the last few months flashed through her mind, some funny, some poignant and all of them containing a snapshot of Nick. That night together, an almost unbearably beautiful memory, the ghastliness of the morning after, the stiff embarrassment of seeing him week after week as she came to realize that to him she was probably nothing more than a reminder of something that had proved a point. And then the pain of finding that ring beside Simon's bed. She still could not come up with a satisfactory explanation for its presence there, but neither had she ever found anything else to substantiate the implication. Not then and not now. She often wondered what she would have heard if she had stayed to listen to Nick at the party. Well, it was too late now, just as it was too late to undo all the damage that had subsequently been done. But sitting there, with the tears drying on her cheeks, she could draw comfort from the fact that she had admitted to herself how she felt. Feeling far more cheerful than she had in some time, she decided to celebrate with a long, hot bath and an evening in front of the telly.

Alex could not bring herself to sleep in Nick's bed that night and instead tossed and turned between Simon's linen sheets. Miu Miu decided to abandon her suede bean bag for the night and keep her company, something that she was sure would have horrified Simon had he known – she would bet that his adoration of his little friend did not extend as far as cat hairs on the pillow. However, Alex found it enormously comforting to cuddle up to the furry body and eventually fall asleep to the rhythm of contented purring.

Miu Miu was vocal in her early-morning greetings. Peering blearily at the heavy weight on her chest, Alex remembered Nick's cheerful complaint and forgave Miu Miu her early-morning cat breath and raucous mewing. If this was what he awoke to every day she was only too delighted. Better a cat sitting on his chest than another type of friend demanding attention.

Thanks to Miu Miu's alarm system Alex was early for work and rattled through the morning with only the merest flicker of irritation when asked to rearrange a meeting four times to accommodate all the participants, most of whom had pressing engagements in the country on Friday and were reluctant to commit to anything that went beyond Thursday lunchtime. She was even able to handle a fraught phone call to the estate agent with unusual *sangfroid* and wondered if this was a new, grown-up Alex emerging. Even Lydia remarked on her unaccustomed cheerfulness, suggesting tartly that someone must have had her oats again for her mood to have shifted so radically. And all this because, even though she was missing Nick more than she could say, she could at last put a name to the numbness that had been affecting her.

She had even decided to resurrect the power of positive thinking and had taken the advice of some magazine guru to heart. She was going to write Nick a letter, and not just any old letter but one explaining her feelings for him in raw, excoriating detail, along with an unexpurgated account of her thoughts about

Richard. This would take a load off her mind as well as in some mysterious way bringing all of her hopes and dreams to pass.

She set to with her usual flair and, instead of bashing out yet another perky press release, produced a heart-stirring account of her innermost desires as well as a forthright list of a hundred and one reasons why she could never marry Richard. Reading it over, Alex could only be thankful that under no circumstances was she supposed to post this missive, merely to keep it safe and refer to it constantly until some miracle came to pass and her life fell into place. Safe in the knowledge that Lydia was still not back from some supposedly brief and vital meeting, she nipped off to the loo, leaving her efforts on top of the untidy stack of papers on her desk.

It should not have been too much of a surprise in Alex's topsy-turvy world to find a flushed and portly man reading that same exposition of her soul upon her return. And a complete stranger at that. Most of Lydia's visitors bore a remarkable resemblance to each other and this one was no exception to the rule of large belly and sagging features, but she was pretty certain she had never seen him before. Rigid with shock, embarrassment and anger, she took an uncertain step towards him and hoped that she could somehow pass the whole thing off as some innovative client strategy.

No such luck. To her frosty enquiry, 'Can I help you?' he turned and, with a benign smile, said, 'I don't think so,' followed by the accurate observation that someone somewhere was obviously in need of a great deal of help if she meant every word she had written.

Alex stared at him, unable to decide whether to snatch her letter back and berate him for invading her privacy or pray for divine intervention. Although the man was clearly somewhat inebriated, he seemed to recognize her dilemma. With a gentlemanly air, he handed back the letter and extended his right hand. 'Charles Beresford. Delighted to meet you?'

'Alex,' she supplied, her mind racing as she tried to remember where she had heard his name before.

'I like it. Very much indeed.' For a mad moment she thought he was referring to her name but he was indicating the pieces of paper she now clutched. Ignoring her confusion, he carried on, 'In fact, I like it so much I think you might be just the person I'm looking for.'

Now this was bewildering. Alex gaped at him and wondered what on earth he was going on about and, more importantly, where on earth this was leading.

Charles Beresford snorted impatiently and spoke as if explaining something to a particularly slow-witted subordinate.

'Y'know, for one of those opinion diary-type things. Young girl like you, just what we've been looking for. And someone new, not one of those tired old bags I have to put up with. Think they know it all just because they've written a couple of features on domestic violence and wittered on about the plight of the single gal today. Bollocks, all of it. What we want is someone like you, someone not afraid to speak her mind and tell it like it is. Fresh blood. A gal with balls. Great stuff, fabulous. How about it?'

His rheumy eyes fixed on her with a surprisingly

shrewd glint and Alex felt as if she had been hurtled into Wonderland. She was saved by the entrance of Lydia, who swept up to the bizarre Mr Beresford with a proprietorial air and tapped his arm in mock severity. 'Charles, you naughty thing! I turn my back for five minutes and here you are chatting up my assistant.'

'Trying to poach her, more like. This gal is bloody good. Have you seen some of the stuff she writes? Excellent! Knocks the spots off most of my sorry team. I can quite see why you've been keeping her to yourself, old girl, but share and share alike, that's what I say. Want to give her a column, one of those diary thingies. People love it. All the other majors have one. Been looking for the right person for ages, had the whole editorial team fighting over it. And here she is, hiding away with my old mate Lydia.'

Emitting a tinkling laugh, Lydia seemed unfazed by this startling stream of consciousness although Alex thought she detected a tightening around her jawline. Lydia, however, was nothing if not fair, a surprising quality in a habituée of her vacuous but tough world. 'Oh, Alex is extremely talented. Writes a lot of our client stuff, press releases and so on. I've been trying to encourage her to take it further for ages but she's far too modest, aren't you, darling?'

Far too bogged down in trivia, more like, but Alex smiled enthusiastically and hoped that someone would soon enlighten her. Thankfully, Lydia sprang to her rescue. 'Of course, you know that Charles is the editor-in-chief of the *Sunday Herald* and one of our dearest and most important friends. We've just been discussing a few old pals over lunch, haven't we, sweetie? Naughty boy sneaked ahead of me when I got waylaid by that dreadful little man from next door. No doubt wanted to check out my own set-up.'

She smirked coquettishly at him, aware that her beautifully appointed office more than matched up to his own seat of power. Charles twanged his red braces playfully and chortled before returning to the business in hand. Over forty years on Fleet Street had endowed him with a cast-iron liver and the ability to snap straight into frightening sobriety when profit was at stake.

'So, m'dear, think you could handle it? Pay you the usual rates, of course. Give my secretary a ring, set you up with a meeting with the team and away we go. More like this and the readers will lap it up – all that woman's-magazine type thing does go down so well. More's the pity. Can't beat hard news, if you ask me, but times have changed. All these bloody journalists bleating on about their thoughts and feelings . . . if you'll pardon me, m'dear, but it's true. Yep, call Serena and set up that appointment. That'll set the cat among the bloody pigeons, using a total unknown. Heh heh!'

Alex flicked a nervous glance at Lydia, who was nodding her head furiously, a smile firmly in place to belie the rapacious expression in her eyes. Alex's stock had risen quite suddenly and alarmingly and Lydia was already trying to compute the likely repercussions and whether or not they would be of any benefit to herself. Taking her cue, and realizing that she had no choice and that there was no room for discussion, Alex found herself agreeing to this unexpected offer, in a tiny voice. God knew where this ballsy female was to be found. Right now it was as much as she could do not to hug the man and promise him her undying subservience for this incredible opportunity.

Charles Beresford brushed off her thanks with another firm handshake and a stern admonishment to deliver the goods or she would be out on her pretty little ear. Alex stammered out her reassurances that she would do her best and he seemed satisfied with this. Then he and Lydia disappeared into the inner sanctum for the rest of the afternoon, spurning all offers of coffee in favour, no doubt, of a few tots of the fine cognac Lydia kept for her special guests.

As a first-time visitor to her office, despite their long and fruitful acquaintance, Charles Beresford was afforded the utmost hospitality, doubly so now that there was this new and strange alliance. Lydia was sure it could only work for her good and made a mental note to keep closer tabs on Alex. She had learned a long time ago that the cultivation of contacts was the name of the game, and who knew where the girl could go from here? Some of her best press relations had started off in stranger circumstances and Lydia was pragmatic enough to encourage those who, in the fullness of time, would remember the hand that had fed them. And she had absolutely no doubt that Alex would go far. Her talent was obvious and Lydia knew that she had been just a tad selfish in using it for her own purposes for so long. Now that it had been recognized by the wider world, she was determined to take her slice of the cake, in the most charming way, of course.

Finally able to sink back behind her desk and contemplate her good fortune, Alex spent the rest of the afternoon in a blur of excitement. So light were her spirits that she didn't even rise to the bait when Richard called and asked her to some company function. He rang off in shock, delighted but at the same time astonished by her co-operation and too taken aback to moan when she announced that she would be spending the whole of the next week looking after Miu Miu.

'Really, you all spoil that creature,' he had grumbled, but he agreed to wait until the weekend to see her. Anything to keep her happy, particularly now that the flat was going through and they would soon be shacked up in what he hoped would be connubial bliss. Surely she would consider them as good as married then and therefore allow for carnal contact. He bloody well hoped so, or he might soon have to consider alternative arrangements. She must know that a man had needs. Not that he would pay for it: God forbid that he would have to stoop that low. No, there was plenty of opportunity in the City and he was pretty certain that the new temp had been giving him the eye. He made a mental note to ask her out for a drink later in the week and turned his attention back to figures of a different sort. The thought of Samantha's mini-skirted bottom made him feel suddenly hot and distracted. That's what came of acting like a gentleman, something he was sure Alex did not appreciate. His restraint had been admirable but with the cat practically in the bag it was probably safe enough to play away and get improved secretarial services into the bargain.

Richard was the furthest thing from Alex's mind when she let herself into the flat that evening and found Miu Miu choking in a corner of the kitchen. Her helpless retching as she staggered around in a circle sent an immediate chill through Alex, who scooped up the cat and tried to find out what the problem was. But whatever she was choking on was obviously firmly lodged at the back of her throat and Alex grasped that the situation was serious. Grabbing the list of numbers Simon had left by the phone she located the vet's. By some miracle they were still open and the receptionist advised her to bring Miu Miu straight down there. Alex dashed out into the street and looked up and down frantically for a cab. As luck and the rush-hour would have it, there was none to be seen and she set off at an awkward jog, Miu Miu's gasps and frantic wriggles causing her to speed up as much as she could in her impractical heels.

The pair arrived similarly out of breath and burst through into the waiting room to be greeted by an old man with an equally grizzled dog at his feet and a girl clutching a cage. Ignoring their curious stares Alex staggered up to the reception desk, plonked an obviously distressed Miu Miu on top of it and declared to anyone who would listen, 'She's dying! You've got to help me – I called you – she can't breathe!'

The receptionist grabbed the cat and swept through a swing door with her, calling for Alex to follow. The professionals swung into action and a few moments later a forlorn but calmer cat shivered on the examining table as the vet brandished a serious-looking bone above her head.

'Salmon, I would say. I'm afraid she's a bit young to cope with a bone like that.'

Alex could not help but notice that he had the

kindest eyes set in a handsome face. Probably had some gorgeous girlfriend at home to serve up his roast lamb and wash his rugby shirts, which she personally felt signalled the beginning of the slide down that slippery domestic slope. To her great chagrin she felt herself blush and blurted out guiltily, 'It's all my fault!'

The vet smiled understandingly and patted her arm. 'Could happen to anyone. I expect the greedy little thing filched it out of the bin when you weren't looking. Anyway, she's fine now and there's no harm done. Give her lots of attention and I'm sure she'll have forgiven you by tomorrow. All right? You OK?'

He looked at her with a more than professional interest and she bit back the tears of relief as hard as she could. Old habits die hard and, besides, why shouldn't she try to keep her eyeballs from turning that unattractive pink in front of such a kind, attentive and, OK, she had to admit it, attractive man? She wasn't married yet and her ego was overdue for a boost. She thanked him profusely and asked for the bill to be sent for her attention to Simon's address, spelling out her name slowly and loudly. That at least should ensure that when Miu Miu came in for her next set of jabs he would remember Alex and might even mention her by name. She'd love to see Nick's face if that happened; it might even shake him into some action.

Grinning at her deviousness, Alex carried Miu Miu home cuddled up in her coat and treated her to the most minutely inspected bowl of flaked tuna and a large dish of milk. This was gratefully accepted and the tail-flicking gradually subsided, to be replaced by purrs and a little head rubbing vigorously against her ankles.

There was only one thing more to do, the most difficult task of all. She would have to call Simon and tell him she had nearly killed his cat but that everything was all right now and she would cover the cost. There was nothing to be gained by putting off the evil moment and she dialled the hotel number before nerves got the better of her.

So thrown was she by events that she quite forgot to take into account the time difference. An alert enough receptionist took the call, Alex gave Simon's room number and was put through, but it was a sleepy voice that answered the phone. More than that, it was the wrong voice. For a split second she considered hanging up but somehow found her voice and sputtered out something to the effect of 'Miu Miu's been to the vet but she's OK now, really. She didn't choke and it's all my fault but she's OK. OK? So, um, tell Simon, would you?'

There was a long, confused pause before Nick said, 'Alex?' and an even longer one after that before she finally squeaked out a frantic 'Yes', and an even more high-pitched 'Just tell him. Thanks', before slamming down the phone and backing away from it as if it was suddenly highly contagious. So much for her happy daydreams. Reality and despair hit in equal measure and she reeled into the kitchen where she collapsed into a chair and wailed aloud to a startled Miu Miu. 'Bastard! Bastard! God, I am so stupid. They're in the same fucking room, for God's sake. Probably laughing their heads off. Bastard!'

The rant went on for quite some time, only diminishing when she ran out of expletives and curses and had to fall back on muttering, 'Shit, shit, shit', as if it were some kind of mantra. The darkness closed in and still she sat there, twisting her fingers together ceaselessly. From her safe corner Miu Miu watched and listened, and probably empathized as much as she could, but Alex was utterly alone, abandoned once and for all. All thoughts of her new and glorious future were wiped out, superseded by the agonizing pain in her chest and the sense of numb despair in the pit of her belly. The one person with whom she had been dying to share her good news, and now the last person on earth she ever wanted to speak to. Alex could hardly breathe with the unfairness of it all.

Some few thousand miles away Nick sat up in bed and stared sleeplessly into the night. He had just about made sense of what Alex was saying and would tell Simon over breakfast, but right now the sound of her voice crackling down the long-distance line had rea-woken thoughts he reckoned to have left behind at the airport. The shoot so far had been frantic and much had gone wrong, not the least of which was the room allocation. He had taken one look at his luxurious accommodation and realized that there must have been some sort of cock-up. Simon's vociferous reaction to his vastly inferior room in the main house had confirmed his suspicions. It had all been amicably sorted, although no one had seen fit to inform the receptionist and now everyone was happy, including Simon's hyper new neighbour, Serge the superstylist. He and Simon seemed to be getting on famously after an initial stand-off and were probably even now calling to each other from their adjoining deluxe garden bungalows. Or perhaps even whispering into each other's ears from a somewhat closer distance. Nick had watched attitude turn to attraction with ill-concealed amusement but had so far been working too hard to feel more than a fleeting pang of longing for something similar. Until, that is, Alex had phoned and sent his senses soaring, his thoughts turning towards home.

He couldn't wait to see her again, to tell her all about the trip and to find some resolution to the whole crazy situation. It was amazing how distance could make your heart ache for someone ten times more than if they were close at hand. Stuffing the pillow more comfortably under his head, he tried to drift off to sleep on his thoughts but found that instead they compelled him to lie awake and remember every inch of her gorgeous body, every expression on her lovely face and even the sound of her voice, although he had heard it not so long before. The telephone line had distorted its natural timbre but the passion of feeling behind her words had been all Alex. He grinned to himself in the dark as he thought about her impulsiveness and occasional scattiness, which she would have hotly denied. Whatever had happened to the cat sounded par for the course but she had, of course, coped somehow. Only a few more days to go and then he could see her, touch her, and have that all-important talk with her. It was about time and he knew what he had to say.

Suddenly he couldn't wait for the shoot to be over, much as he was enjoying its chaotic creativity. Simon had been happy for him to shoot some background stuff, which would come in useful for both his portfolio and for touting around the picture libraries. He was learning a lot and making some great contacts but, frankly, that could wait. Nick was impatient to be home and nothing was going to delay him, not even demands for a baby elephant and the outrageous pretensions of a stylist who had plainly lost all sense of proportion quite some time previously. He would work day and night, do whatever it took, but they would finish on time and be on the plane on Saturday evening, or Nick would personally string Serge up by his bandanna until both he and Simon begged for mercy.

With that comforting thought and an anticipatory smile on his face he fell asleep for the hour or so before his alarm shrilled and he was back on the job with extra vigour and a renewed sense of purpose. Nick was going home to Alex and nothing and no one would stop him.

EIGHT

'Christ, what have you got in here? Did you bring back the bloody elephant?'

Nick was hauling the last of their luggage through the front door as Simon raced ahead to be the first to greet his beloved cat. The flurry of kisses and cuddles that followed would have done credit to a long-lost relative. Whilst the extravagant display took place, Nick looked around hopefully for Alex and his own version of a special welcome home, but the flat was devoid of her presence, save a cheery note she had left on the kitchen table: 'Welcome home. Hope it was everything you expected it to be. Call me when you've come back down to earth. Love, Alex.' He didn't know what she imagined a working trip to be but it had not been the celestial experience she implied in her note. Villagers had abandoned any pretence of time-keeping, religious leaders had thrown massive wobblies over the smallest of details and he had finally snapped over the baby elephant, informing Serge that the nearest one was in Sri Lanka and it would have to be a sacred cow or nothing. Arms had been twisted, strings pulled and, in due course, a baby elephant had arrived on a freight plane and had gone on to behave with the aplomb of a seasoned diva.

The other diva on the shoot, the redoubtable Serge,

had metamorphosed into a benign figure of positively Buddhist gentleness but it had not been the local influence that had transformed his spiky nature. That had been left to Simon, who had made full use of the fortuitous proximity of their deluxe bungalows to engage in late-night strategy meetings of a purely physical kind. Even now he bore the satisfied air of a man who has sown more oats in a week than a Midwestern farmer can hope for in a year. Nick was happy for him, and profoundly glad that the nocturnal activities had rubbed off the rougher edges of Simon's increasingly erratic temperament.

For his part, Simon felt like a man renewed, a generous sense of benevolence pervading his every action. The air of desperation had disappeared, replaced by the smugness of one to whom it had been proven that he was still a sex god of no mean prowess. He was even prepared to put his feelings for Nick on the back-burner, treating him with a kind of affectionate brotherliness mixed with a healthy dose of mentoring. The deeper feelings still lingered on in some inaccessible place and he had an idea that they might rise to the surface before long to transmute into something more comfortable and containable. Or become entirely superficial. It all depended on how things progressed with Serge.

Ah, Serge. Even the name sent a frisson of exoticism through Simon. The danger of his volatility and the foreignness of his passionate nature acted as a magnet to Simon's Anglo-Saxon sensibilities, and he became lamb-like in Serge's presence. As Simon confided to the makeup artist, he felt electrically alive for the first time in ages. She, sworn to secrecy, spread the word amongst the rest of the party and soon many a covert eye followed the unfolding of the daily dramas and speculated on its duration and emotional pitch. It had taken Simon and Serge all of two days to get it together and by the fourth day of the shoot bets were being taken as to which of them would emerge first for breakfast, the other following at what they thought was a discreet interval. By the sixth morning they had given up all notion of pretence and breakfasted together in Simon's bungalow, and by the time they all boarded the plane for home they were feeding each other grapes and cooing over their respective purchases. Balinese gift shops had been denuded as they both hunted out the ultimate gift for the other to remind them of such a special time in their lives. They had, of course, done their level best to outdo each other in the exclusivity and rare beauty of their choice, delighting the local shopkeepers with their orgy of overspending. It had been universally declared a draw but it was left to poor Nick to drag Simon's new toys up the stairs and through the front door.

It took Nick ten minutes to unpack his one bag whilst Simon disappeared into his own room for an age to unfold his clothes and fondle every item Serge had given him. Nick could hear him speaking excitedly on the phone, probably regaling all and sundry with his news, and itched to get on the blower himself. He wanted to wait, however, until he was sure that there would be no interruptions and, more importantly, no curious ears to listen in. And he wanted to arrange to meet. What he had to say was not the sort of thing to be dealt with via a curly plastic wire, and he needed more than anything to see the look on her face. He knew that if he could just gaze straight into her eyes he would be able to tell at once if she really cared for him and if he still had a chance. He had to be sure, once and for all.

Unfortunately for Nick's fraying nerves, he had to wait a week before making a successful attempt at communication. Simon and Alex played telephone tag: he left reports about Miu Miu's ongoing recovery and she responded with the news that they were terribly busy completing on the flat and she would get back to him when she could. Richard had decided to go for broke and was attempting the fastest purchase of a place on record. His libido and his pride could no longer accept separate living arrangements and his cash-flow dictated an unprecedented level of service from all parties concerned. If all went well they would have the keys by the weekend and could begin decorating and furnishing immediately. As he was departing on yet another business trip he had instructed that the keys should be handed to Alex if he was not around.

He had also suggested that she might like to engage the services of an interior decorator, at which she had snorted and announced that she would do it herself. She could not bear the thought of having to deal with one of those people and, besides, if she did it herself she could play for more time. As far as she was concerned, things worked very well just the way they were, with Richard accessible when she needed him and at arm's length when she didn't have the energy to live up to his exacting standards.

Richard had also decreed that the purchase of the apartment should coincide with the official announcement of their engagement and she had been too dispirited by her latest – and, as far as she was concerned, final – knockback to raise a murmur of protest. Her mother had made one last-ditch attempt to organize a full-scale party, a notion that Alex had again knocked mercilessly on the head. She was in no mood to act the loving couple in front of a roomful of relatives she hadn't seen since she last played with a Barbie doll, and the thought of involving herself in some farcical scenario with her friends was too ghastly to contemplate. Besides, since meeting Richard she had lost touch with all but the most stalwart and her erratic working hours had put paid to what remained of her social life. Now that her second job had officially taken its place in the closet she had a lot more time on her hands but somehow could not bring herself to take up with certain people again. She had moved on, grown away from frivolity. Sometimes she felt world weary, and at others as if she were too young to curl up her toes and retire to a living death, which was hardly the most appropriate thought on the eve of her engagement party.

She had been hoping that if she ignored the situation long enough it might go away of its own accord, but when it became clear that it would not she decided to go under as quietly and privately as possible. So, no overt flashing of her ring, no girlie discussions about designers and dresses and no mention of the big day. Richard was growing increasingly impatient with her refusal to name the day, but she had held firm to a sudden belief in long engagements leading to lasting marriages. If Richard had known her better he would have understood that the romance of an elopement was much more her style but, thankfully, his lack of perception blinded him to this, as it did to so much else. And while she could keep him fairly sweet and off her back, Alex could sit tight and wait for the miracle that was bound to happen. That, or knock on the door of the nearest nunnery. One thing she knew for certain: a wedding would only take place if and when every other option had been exhausted, including mysterious disappearances and possibly, in her wilder moments, even a declaration of latent lesbianism. She knew that Richard would never stand for the public humiliation of being dumped for another man. Perhaps it would be easier to swallow if it were a woman who swept her off her feet. Then again, and knowing her luck, it would probably only turn him on even more, if that were possible.

Reluctantly discarding all of these ideas as appealing but unrealistic, she concluded that the best thing to do was to keep everything as low key as possible. That way, if she did duck and run there was a fair chance that most people wouldn't even know she had been engaged in the first place, and particularly not to someone as inappropriate as Richard.

On the basis of all of that, and despite her mother's disappointment, she had stated that the engagement dinner was to be a family affair. Simon would be invited of course, being practically related by surrogacy, as would his parents. With any luck Simon's father would say something so appalling that the focus would shift from the supposedly happy couple to the plight of his mother, the hapless Vivienne. Although she did seem to cope remarkably well, to give her her due. Probably years of practice in ignoring everything he said. Alex wondered if she, too, would end up like that, preferring to occupy a parallel universe rather than acknowledge the embarrassing reality of her partner's bigotry and pomposity. Hell, half of the Home Counties survived on just such a system. If they could hack it, those denizens of the charity committees and stalwart supporters of some vaguely artistic cause, so could she. As for Nick, well, she supposed he had better come along too. Might as well let him witness her discomfiture at first hand. It could even give him a taste of what might have been. She stopped short on the edge of that one, reluctant to let her thoughts stray into forbidden territory, although she knew that if it were Nick's ring she was wearing it would be nothing so banal as a whacking great diamond. He would have whisked her off to some foreign shore and married her then and there, not caring to wait for the social niceties that usually preceded such an event. Of course, convention didn't play much part in his scheme of things. If it had she might not now be caught between the devil and the depths of suburban bliss.

Putting aside this brief attack of bitterness, she decided to bite the bullet and pop round to see them both. Might as well hear all about it and find out if they were both free. Simon was thrilled to speak to her and more than delighted that she would be dropping in to listen to all his gossip. 'I'm afraid I've been rather a naughty boy! Still, that can wait until you get here but, for goodness' sake, hurry. So much to tell you, darling!'

She was sure that he had. Triumph was one of his favourite feelings and he had a lot to crow about. She made sure that she looked good before she left the house. Might as well go out in style, with a slash of red lipstick to prove that there were no hard feelings, and that whilst the best man might have won she was still a force to be reckoned with. As she approached the front door she braced herself and had the smile firmly in place before it swung open. At least all those times she had knocked on anonymous hotel-room doors had taught her something. Bravado was not to be sniffed at: it had carried her through many an awkward situation and it was going to get her through this.

She swept in as if gracing a ballroom, and bestowed kisses on all and sundry, including the cat. Graciousness was a wonderful weapon and her benign smile encompassed all, including a tanned, healthy-looking Nick, who seemed pleased to see her if a little jumpy. As well he might be. She settled down in her favourite spot on the sofa, accepted her coffee with that same vague air of social condescension and chirped brightly, 'Well, come on, then. Tell all.'

There was a pause whilst Simon threw a sideways glance at Nick, who laughed and patted him on the back. 'I think I'll leave that to Simon,' was all he said before settling back to allow him centre stage.

Thrilled as ever to be the focus of attention, Simon had barely opened his mouth to speak when the door-bell rang. With far more chutzpah than Alex could ever hope to manage, in swept Serge, who bestowed upon her his most regal glance of appraisal before the façade cracked and he launched into an emotional account of how he had just escaped an attempted mugging at the corner of the street. 'There he was, tugging on one strap of my rucksack and I was hanging on to the other, screaming, screaming. And this man was huge, I can tell you. And mad, quite mad. Big, staring eyes and shouting something horrible at me. But there was no way I was going to let him have it. NO WAY! I bought that bag in Milan – it's one of a kind. The finest calfskin and full of all my things. And you know how important my things are to me, Simon, my whole life is in that bag. So I held on and on and eventually he lets go and runs off, bosh, just like that! Of course, I was shaking by then and so upset and this kind woman came over and told me she had seen everything but didn't want to get involved or anything but was I OK? Of course I wasn't OK! I was in bits, in pieces, I can tell you. But I knew that I had to get back here and that once I was here you would know what to do. Oh, I think the shock is beginning to hit me. I feel quite weak.' And with that he collapsed with theatrical grace on to the sofa beside Alex.

She couldn't help but notice that the most remarkable thing about his impassioned speech had been the steady descent of his accent from what was vaguely Eastern European to what was distinctly Estuary English. Well, he wouldn't be the first boy with beautiful bones but no breeding to become the ultimate fashion victim and adopt a swinging East European persona.

Simon, however, seemed not to notice a thing and,

distraught, rushed to Serge's side. 'You poor love! Look, take a few deep breaths. That's it. Nick, get a glass of water for him, would you?'

He was stroking Serge's forearm as he said this, trying to diminish the frantic half-sobs and hiccuping gasps for air. Serge had shut his eyes as if to blank out the horror and Alex, while sympathetic to his plight, had to hold back a giggle. He had evidently ringed his eyes in kohl or mascara to enhance the gypsy allure of his dark good looks and this was now dribbling down his face as the odd tear squeezed through his eyelids. Combined with the bandanna, which had slipped down over one eyebrow, the effect was curiously comical rather than effortlessly street.

Nick returned with the water and Simon held the glass up to Serge's lips, encouraging him to drink whilst keeping up his flow of soothing murmurs. Watching him, Alex wondered just what was going on here. Simon's friends were often flamboyantly demonstrative but this was something else. She caught Nick's eye and he dropped her a slow, meaningful wink. Curiouser and curiouser. Now Serge's eyes were fully open again and he was making contact with reality. 'Gotta get him, Sime. That bloke could've had a knife. Or worse.' A dramatic shudder underlined his words.

Simon nodded gravely. 'Absolutely. We must first get you checked over and then we shall call the police. Nick, where are the car keys?' Somewhat to Alex's astonishment at this sudden role-reversal, Nick didn't seem to mind being relegated to the role of errand boy. In fact, it didn't seem unfamiliar to him. Simon helped Serge up and silenced his protests. 'I know he didn't touch you but you've had a shock. I think we should at least get your shoulder looked at in case he dislocated it or something.'

This was going a bit far but Serge accepted Simon's solicitude as his due. Together they moved towards the front door – Serge seemed to have acquired a leg problem since his arrival.

'Nick, you drive. I'll keep Serge company in the back. Alex, love, I am sorry but, as you can see, he's had a terrible time.' Simon was practically buckling under the other man's not inconsiderable weight.

'Oh, don't worry about it. You go and I'll catch up with you later. I hope you feel better soon.' This to Serge, who inclined his head in thanks and let out a little moan. This spurred Simon on and they had soon bundled him out to the car and settled him, still groaning softly, in the back seat alongside a clearly anxious Simon. Alex watched as they drove off and raised a hand in answer to Nick's wave. Confused, and none the wiser, she set off for home.

This time it was her turn to wait for enlightenment as her messages went unanswered. Finally, Simon called her on Wednesday to say that of course they would love to come to her engagement dinner and that everything was OK. He was on his mobile and in the middle of what sounded like frenetic activity so she didn't get a chance to press him further but promised to leave the time and venue on his home answering-machine. This she did, along with the information that she would be up to her elbows in paint for the rest of the week, having taken a few days off to start work on the redecoration of the new flat. With the dreaded parental head-to-head looming she had decided that the best thing to do was immerse herself in mindless activity and hide away from the world at large and her mother in particular. It would also give her the chance to come up with some ideas for her new column. Alex always found mundane activity hugely inspirational – some of her best thoughts came to her in the most banal circumstances.

Thursday and Friday were spent scraping and priming, DIY handbook constantly open for easy referral and music pounding out from the radio. Occasionally she downed tools when something struck her as worthy enough to scribble down on a scrap of paper, but diligently took them up again the moment her imagination had been caught in some form of permanence. She sang along happily as she worked and shouted aloud to the interchangeable idiots who phoned up to opine or to request some tune or another laden no doubt with meaning for someone somewhere. More than once she yelled at some faceless person, 'Get a life!' before sternly telling herself that she could talk. She danced to the boppier stuff, shamelessly indulged her secret liking for soppy ballads and cheered aloud when someone on air proposed to someone called Michelle who worked in Accounts. Whoever Michelle was, she hoped that she would agree like a shot, or at least let him down gently if he was some spotty anorak with a hopeless crush. In fact, she hoped she would accept anyway and 'make him the happiest man in the world'. Then at least someone out there would have got what they wanted.

All in all, the couple of days she spent in hard

manual labour were enormously therapeutic, not to mention productive, and she let herself into the flat on Saturday morning with a sense of happy anticipation. Not even Richard could spoil her enjoyment – he was too far away and, in any case, far too inept, to interfere with her efforts. Now she poured herself a coffee out of her Thermos flask, and set to work again. With the hard, dull bits out of the way, she was ready to slosh her paint about and got to grips with the roller to the accompaniment of the breakfast show and some well-chosen dance music from the eighties. The roller glided over the wall in time to the beat and she ignored the fine spray of paint that spat back at her whenever she got too enthusiastic. She was having fun, certainly more so than she would be having that evening at the dread dinner, and she intended to enjoy the moment.

A couple of hours into her artistic efforts and her arms were beginning to ache but her singing was as raucous as ever, which was probably why she didn't hear the knocking at first. When she did, she had to stop and turn down the music a bit before realizing that it was coming from the front door. She put down her roller and guiltily went to open it, preparing an apology for whichever irate neighbour she had upset before they had even moved in. Thank goodness there was a peephole through which she could view the enemy and take stock before having to open the door. Peepholes always made her feel as if she should hold her breath and peer through unobtrusively, as if the other person could see her as clearly as she could see them. Of course, she knew this to be an impossibility but it didn't stop her feeling like some sort of Mata

Hari figure as she applied her eye to the tiny aperture as noiselessly as she could.

What confronted her on the doorstep proved more disturbing than any member of the residents' association and for a split second she seriously considered pretending not to be there. Her hair was all over the place, her face paint-spattered and the baggy old T-shirt and torn jeans she was wearing could most charitably be described as functional. She licked a finger, rubbed away at the crusty splodges of paint she could feel on her cheeks and ran frantic fingers through her hair. Once again she contemplated keeping still and hoping that he would go away but adult good sense, and the fact that her music was giving the game away, forced her into decisive action. She undid the locks and opened the door.

Nick smiled and she couldn't help but note the irony of the role reversal. All those months ago it had been she scuffling around on the threshold and now here he was, nervousness nearly masked by the grin and a hearty word of welcome.

'Nick! This is a surprise. Um . . . come on in. Dump your jacket somewhere. I'm afraid there's no furniture to speak of as yet but . . . yeah, on the floor will be fine. Good.' She picked away at the specks of paint on her face as she spoke, and led him through into the living room, turning down the music still further and holding a hand out as if to show off her artistic achievements. He had a couple of bags slung over his shoulder and these he dumped in the middle of the floor before he stood back to admire her efforts.

'I see. Ever done this before?' She thought she could

detect a twinkle in his eye but his voice sounded sincere enough.

'Evidently not.' She wasn't going to have her efforts belittled without getting in there first.

'Hey, it's not bad at all. Quite good, in fact. Well, very good. For a beginner.' He was still standing there, hands on hips, apparently fascinated by the paint drying on the wall in front of him.

A thought struck her and forced her to interrupt his efforts at admiration. 'Nick, how did you know I was here? In fact, how did you even get the address? I mean, no one has it apart from me and ... Richard.' She tailed off uncomfortably but Nick seemed at ease.

'From Simon. And he got it from Richard. He phoned the other day looking for you, said he couldn't get hold of you at home and that you'd taken time off work. When Richard told him what you were doing we wondered why he wasn't helping you out but he said that this was something you wanted to do on your own. I just thought you might be glad of some help with the heavier stuff. Simon did too and he'd be here now but ... er ... something came up. Anyway, thought I'd surprise you. I hope you don't mind or anything?'

For a second he looked a bit worried, as if he had just realized that what he had planned as a happy surprise might seem to her more like an intrusion.

'No, no. I— It's very sweet of you. I don't mind a bit. It was more Richard not wanting to get his hands dirty than me being precious about it. And I really could do with some help. As you can see, I'm not exactly an expert. Erm . . . I don't have another roller or anything, though.'

With a triumphant flourish, Nick delved into one of his bags and produced not only a roller but a spare paint tray and a couple of rags.

'*Voilà!*' He looked immensely pleased with himself, and she couldn't help but giggle.

'You seem to be very organized. Coffee?'

'Now who's organized? Thanks.'

He swigged it down in a couple of gulps and then, as if remembering why he had come, became disappointingly workmanlike. Paint was poured carefully into his tray, a handy roll of masking tape produced to neaten things up at the edges and they were away, rollers swishing almost in time and a not too uncomfortable silence punctuated by the odd comment.

'Oh, I love this song!'

Tina Turner had burst through their concentration with a well-loved howl of pain and anger. Alex skipped over to the radio and turned it up full blast. She sang along at the top of her voice as she worked and swayed her hips in time to the music. When the song finished she turned the sound down again and flopped on the floor with her back to an unpainted bit of wall. 'I'm knackered!' she gasped, as she reached for the water bottle she had also brought along.

'Wimp!' Nick teased but he, too, elected to take a break and gratefully accepted the proffered bottle, slugging back at least half its contents. 'Thirsty work, this. And hot.'

She looked up in agreement and was momentarily mesmerized by the sight of him tearing off his T-shirt as if to underline his words. Disconcerted by the sight of that perfect torso, she dropped her gaze and then leaped to her feet with a brisk, purposeful air. They painted on but the musical interlude had broken down some barrier between them and the conversation flowed more easily.

'So what's with Simon and that Serge bloke?'

Alex had been dying to ask ever since the mugging incident and now seemed the perfect opportunity with a half-naked Nick sweating away in a relaxed fashion not three feet away. He rolled his eyes in response, then shook his head and grinned infuriatingly.

'Come on, Nick! You know something, I can tell.' Playfully, she flicked paint at him and it landed with a satisfying splat right on the end of his nose. For a second he stood stock still and then rounded on her, paint tray held menacingly above her head.

'No! Don't you dare.'

She was backing away from him as fast as she could and he was following, the smile on his face belying the look of deadly intent in his eyes. She looked behind her to see where she was going, then back at him, just in time to see him trip over the spare dust sheets she had chucked in a careless pile in the middle of the room. As if in slow motion, the paint tipped out of his tray and all over her head, running thickly down her face and the back of her neck. She brought her hands swiftly to her face to protect her eyes and the paint oozed through her fingers, dripping down in dollops on to her feet. It was lucky that the tray had been half empty or her entire body might have been turned a tasteful shade of Basic Bamboo, but there was still enough to do considerable damage to both her hair and her self-esteem. They both froze for what seemed an age but must have been all of about three seconds before Alex wiped a thick layer away from her mouth and drawled, 'I suppose this is what you call being immortalized in paint.'

'Oh, my God. Alex, I am so, so sorry. I didn't mean to . . .'

Nick looked mortified but she waved an airy hand at him, and a sizeable splodge of paint landed on his chest. They started to laugh.

'You look like you've been iced or something,' he finally managed to blurt out.

'Oh, great! At last I'm good enough to eat.' She hadn't meant it to sound provocative but that was the way it came out and they both paused fractionally, awareness shooting tangibly between them.

'Well, I'd better get cleaned up.'

Alex broke the mood and walked towards the bath-room, trying hard not to drip across the unprotected part of the floor as she went. Luckily, the hot water was on and she had put a threadbare old towel in the bathroom as a cleaning rag. She climbed into the shower, all too aware that Nick was close at hand and that she was stark naked. She scrubbed away with her hands at the paint in her hair until it no longer felt like one sticky mess, although the absence of shampoo and soap did not make things any easier. Great; she was going to emerge with dripping hair, stinking of emulsion. At least her hair could be rescued later – she had booked an appointment to give herself a boost before the engagement dinner. It would give her hairdresser something new to talk about.

Rubbing herself with the inadequate towel, Alex wondered how she was going to get there. Her own top was sticky with wet paint and even her jeans had suffered under the onslaught. All she had was her underwear and the T-shirt Nick had gallantly handed her on her way to the bathroom. Slipping it over her head, she discovered that it was about three inches too short for decency, skimming as it did across the danger zone at the top of her thighs. But it was dry and would have to do. He would just have to avert his eyes if he found it offensive, not that it was anything he hadn't seen before. Feeling acutely self-conscious and scrubbed clean of any helpful artifice, she emerged from the bathroom, still rubbing her hair with the sad scrap of towelling.

'Well, at least I won't match the wall any more,' she attempted, and looked up to see how he was doing. He had, in fact, made good penitential progress and was taking a quick water break when she reappeared. He lowered the bottle from his mouth and stared at her, transfixed. Her self-consciousness rocketed alarmingly under his intent gaze and she fluttered a hand up first to her face and then her hair to check that no smear or streak marred what she had thought was a squeaky-clean appearance. Not for the first time she thought he could be most disconcerting at times, even downright rude. Just as she was about to open her mouth and fire out some withering retort to his unrelenting examination, he snapped, 'Don't move!' and reached into his other bag for the camera he had constantly to hand.

This was all becoming too bizarre for words and she couldn't think of anything clever enough to say.

Seizing that moment of hesitancy, Nick fired off a couple of shots before she had time to think, never mind adjust her expression. Through the lens she looked even lovelier, the heightened crispness capturing the glints of the water droplets that still ran down off the ends of her hair and snaked across the damp T-shirt. Where her skin was not quite dry it clung, outlining the promise hidden beneath the simple white cotton and suggesting far more than a deliberately sexy outfit ever could. The absence of makeup made her seem more fragile, and her uncertain expression only served to underline this rarely seen vulnerability. Nick thought he had never seen her look more desirable and was desperate to capture the moment before she became aware of how she looked and felt.

'What the hell do you ...' Half laughing, half embarrassed, Alex found her voice and confronted her tormentor as he walked to one side of her to capture a different angle.

'Shhh! Don't spoil it. This is perfect. Just turn to me a bit ... that's it ... shoulder down a fraction ... yessss! No, don't frown ... don't smile either. Just look at me ... look into the camera ...'

He was moving around her as smoothly as a dancer, encouraging and cajoling, forcing her to move with him as he kept clicking away. It was like some crazy snake dance and Alex found herself falling into his rhythm, hypnotized by his soft but constant voice and by the lens of the camera. Her lowered chin had been a defensive gesture but it worked beautifully as she

stared up at him from under her lashes, her slight frown
giving way to a wonderful neutrality of expression and
then to a mischievous glint as she began to play with
him. The dry mouth caused by her initial nervousness
forced her to lick her lips quite unselfconsciously, but
half-way through the gesture she realized what she was
doing and threw him a self-mocking but hungry stare.
Nick practically dropped his camera but kept his professional cool and constant motion, sometimes almost
caressing her with the lens as he stalked her with its
all-seeing eye. As he continued, without once taking the
camera away from his face, she found herself relaxing as
she had with him so long ago on that hotel-room sofa,
trusting him implicitly whilst wanting to give him the
best of herself. Which was really what he was doing,
making love to her through his lens, drawing her in
with his absolute focus until she was putty in his hands
once more.

And for him it was at the same time an erotic yet
tender experience, the camera lens a phallic symbol but
his purpose to capture the incredible openness of her
beauty and at the same time dig deeper and deeper
until he had exposed the truth in her eyes. With the
camera as a prop he could draw it out of her, make
her look right into him and reveal everything, without
being aware that she was doing so. The camera was the
safety value, the neutral third party to their feelings and
emotions, and the device that would record everything.
Permanently. Nick felt the rush of excitement he always
got when he knew something was going to be great:
his head was exploding with unexpressed thoughts

and his heart was thumping so wildly he had serious concerns about his shutter speed.

At last they were done. The film was finished and he had got what he wanted. He lowered the camera and put it carefully to one side whilst keeping his gaze firmly locked into hers. Without the camera he wondered if they could sustain the intensity or if she would again back off. She might as well have stripped naked for the amount of emotional exposure he had extracted and he felt as if he had just moved through an elaborate form of foreplay. Now all they had to do was bridge the physical gulf. Just a few feet separated them from the emotional abyss they should never have crawled out of in the first place. They both stood still, nervous of being the first to risk rejection and terrified of it all going wrong again. In the end Alex took the first step, placing one foot in front of the other as she braved the barriers and reached out for him.

When the bell rang they almost expected it, such was the familiarity of their frustration. The sudden sound made her turn her head towards the door.

'Alex . . . don't.'

The pleading note in his voice brought her eyes back to his but the damage had been done, she had had a second to think and Nick could see that there was no way he could stop her now, the danger was too great: it could be anyone at that door – a neighbour, a salesman or even an irate Richard who had forgotten his keys. She couldn't ignore it.

'I have to.'

Her tone was flat and Nick hoped that it wasn't relief that was making it so. She peered again through the peephole before opening the door and Nick could only surmise from her sharp little intake of breath that whoever it was, they were not going to be the easiest of visitors.

'Darling! What on earth are you doing dressed like that? All that decorating work up too much of a sweat for you?'

Simon didn't even notice Nick at first, intent as he was on bustling in to see the new apartment with a clutch of carrier-bags dangling from each arm. The second he did, however, the enquiring eyebrow shot up and he looked from one to the other with a bemused expression on his face. For once Simon was lost for words.

'Paint fight,' Alex offered, tugging desperately at the inadequate T-shirt she was wearing.

'My fault!' Nick interjected as his contribution. Simon recovered himself enough to sweep an appraising glance over her state of undress before drily commenting, 'I see.' Thankfully, he had more pressing matters to address than the perplexing situation in front of him and set off to stalk the new property, admiring her good fortune whilst throwing in the odd 'Fabulous!' and 'That has got to go!' Simon preferred to get back to more complex situations when he had had time to regroup. For the moment he was content to be both fascinated and repelled by someone else's taste in wallpaper and to offer his suggestions as and where he felt necessary.

'So much potential, though, darling. You could do wonders with this place.' They had come back full circle to the living room and he was looking thoughtfully at their joint painting efforts as he spoke. 'I'm sorry I couldn't be here to help but I had rather a lot of shopping to do. Which reminds me . . .' Happily, his attention was diverted again and he delved into one of the more impressive-looking bags and drew forth an item wrapped in tissue paper, handing it reverently to Alex.

'For you. A small engagement present and something for you to wow the wrinklies with tonight.'

Alex unwrapped the layers of tissue to expose a carefully folded rectangle of red silk satin. She shook it out gently and a divine cocktail dress slithered from its straps, its simplicity belying that, cut on the bias, it would mould itself around her body as it whispered of expensive sophistication. Alex didn't think she had ever seen anything so lovely and for a second or two was overwhelmed.

'Oh, Simon! It's gorgeous. Really, you shouldn't have . . .'

'Oh, but I should. At the very least those people will be able to see just how well you clean up . . .' She swiped him playfully as he smiled at her but couldn't rise to the bait. It was only the truth, after all.

'Seriously, sweetie, I knew as soon as I saw it that you'd look fabulous in it. And tonight of all nights you need to feel like a queen. I should know.' Always the witticism to offset any overdose of emotion, but Simon's expression was soft and she knew that the sentiment was genuine.

'Thanks.' She reached up and touched his cheek softly before rewrapping the dress and placing it in its chi-chi carrier-bag, noting the name of the store and surmising the small fortune Simon must have spent. He had even got it in the right size, a trick she guessed he must have picked up from all those years sweating over hot fashion shoots.

Until now Nick had stood by silently, too gutted to care what Simon thought and a sick feeling in his stomach where there had been a brief flare of hope. The damn engagement dinner was going ahead, and nothing he could say or do would avert it now. He had half hoped that, even at this late hour, she might see sense and cancel, but it would seem that, once again, the fates and a lousy sense of timing had conspired against him. He had a sudden desperate urge to be out of there and in the darkroom, developing his precious photographs of her so that he would know that it had really happened, that it had been there and that they had both felt it.

'I should get going . . .' They both seemed to have forgotten his presence and Alex started guiltily.

'Oh, my God, what's the time?'

Her watch was still sitting on the side of the washbasin, having been cleaned as thoroughly as possible with a wad of loo paper. A quick check revealed that it was far later than she had thought, unsurprising when she had spent the last forty minutes or so being comprehensively made love to through a lens. She had just about enough time to make it home to change and then to the hairdresser's, so long as Simon could give her the lift he promptly offered. The only problem was going to be getting her out of the building without offending half the neighbourhood: her jeans were unwearable and, the weather still being warm, none of them had bothered to wear a jacket or coat. They finally solved the dilemma by forming a protective little posse around her with the help of Simon's mound of carrier-bags and shuffled out of the building, only collapsing in fits of laughter when she was safely out of sight in the car with the bags in a pile on her lap.

Nick was hugging his precious camera in the front seat. As soon as he got home he intended to dive straight into the darkroom Simon had made out of the tiny boxroom and set to work. He was doubly excited about these pictures, praying that they would turn out as well as he hoped. Not only were they staggeringly emotionally revealing, they were also immensely powerful portraits and professional pride fuelled at least part of his anxiety. A conversation held many months before echoed in his head. Maybe in taking her picture he really had captured a part of her soul for himself, something that nobody could ever take from him and that would be his for ever. He fervently hoped so: if he really did have to watch her slowly slip away from him then he would grasp on to whatever he could for as long as he was able. These photographs were a part of that, and perhaps a whole lot more. In a few short hours he would be able to tell. Impatient now to get to work, he said a distracted goodbye to Alex as they dropped her off at her front door and declined Simon's invitation to meet up with Serge and himself for afternoon tea. He couldn't imagine anything worse than watching the two of them canoodling over cups of Lapsang Souchong and, besides, there was work to be done and little time in which to do it. If perhaps he could just show her the proof, hold up her naked desire for the world to see, then, maybe, she would know for herself how she really felt. Just a few hours until the engagement dinner, a few hours until she belonged publicly to someone else. With everything to play for, and with a gambler's reckless desperation, he set to work, determined not to let his sense of urgency override the necessary coolheadedness.

Once the developer was prepared to his satisfaction, he loaded the film on to the reels and placed it in the developing tank, adding his chemical brew before setting the timer and then making doubly sure that the lid was shut securely. Nick had done this a hundred and one times before and normally moved on automatic but this time he felt an obsessive need to check and recheck everything before moving on to the next crucial stage. The second developing time ended he poured away the liquid and immediately immersed his film in a stop-bath before rinsing and fixing, then rinsing again, finally removing it from the tank and hanging it up to dry. At this stage he often took a peek to get some idea of the final result, but this time he couldn't bear to do so, and instead busied himself setting up the enlarger and the next set of chemical trays. He silently thanked whoever was in charge up in the heavens for making him take a camera loaded with black and white film that morning. The stock had been left over from a particularly moody shoot for one of the edgier fashion mags and Nick had intended using it for his own work. He was building up his portfolio, with Simon's help and encouragement, and if these pictures came out the way he hoped he would be adding a whole new dimension to his collection. And very possibly his life.

He moved through the next part of the process with grim determination, feeling a twinge of nervousness as he held the contact sheet up and scrutinized the results in miniature. Pure dynamite. That click in his head had been right but, then, it had never failed him yet. He felt his shoulders sag in relief, but pressed on, loading his negatives carefully into their carrier before creating his test strip, then going on to expose the final prints. He had deliberately shot at a very fast speed and the resultant graininess added an old-fashioned quality to the prints.

As he laid them out to dry for the final time, he could see that he had achieved the real thing. A set of pictures that revealed their subject without sentimentality or artifice, which didn't need to rely on flattering light or tricksy camera angles to highlight the raw beauty they had captured. And, more than that, the raw emotion exposed in her eyes.

An exultant surge of triumph swept through him. Whatever she said from now on, whatever she did, he would know the truth and, what was more, could hold it up for the world to see. Not that he gave a fig for what the world thought: what he wanted, more than anything, was to see her face when confronted with the incontrovertible truth. She wanted him, that much was obvious. But it went far deeper than naked lust. Those shadows in her eyes spoke of far more than that, more perhaps than he had ever dreamed of, and he was going to make sure that she recognized it. If not for him, then at least for herself.

NINE

As Alex was conveyed to her seat by a *maître d'* whose nose seemed bedevilled by a permanent sniff, she understood why Richard had chosen this particular venue for the dreaded engagement summit. Everything from the obsequious staff to the *faux*-Parisian ambience and a menu that had practically to be decoded screamed ostentation and represented his idea of a classy joint. He was probably wetting himself over the sheer joy of having an entire football team of waiters to cater to his every whim whilst serving them food that combined maximum presentational impact with minimal regard for the stomachs of real people.

She was relieved to see that none of the parents had arrived. Instead, the table was occupied by a glowingly smug Richard who was engaged in earnest conversation with Simon whilst Nick picked glumly at a bread roll, the collar of his shirt evidently made even more uncomfortably tight by the unfamiliar presence of a tie. She was touched that he had made the effort on her behalf but couldn't help thinking he resembled nothing so much as an oven-ready chicken in that get-up. He seemed to think so too, looking as markedly unhappy as a man does when his familiar habit of jeans and casual top has been abandoned in favour of 'proper' clothes.

Her own outfit, however, made a far better impression. As she sashayed up to the table, the audible click of dropping jaws added an interesting syncopation to the otherwise execrable sound of the background muzak. Simon looked up and smiled in satisfaction. His taste, as always, had proved impeccable. The glorious deep red brought a corresponding blush of colour to her cheeks and lent her an unaccustomed sense of drama. She looked like some exotic, hot-blooded creature from a country where passion was something to be celebrated and life savoured to the full. As Simon had so cleverly intended, Richard paled into less than insignificance beside such a glorious vision, his unremarkable appearance drawn into unfavourable comparison against her vibrancy. The dress fitted perfectly, skimming over her body in a way that suggested rather than displayed, therefore highlighting her charms emphatically. Practically every man in the place would gladly have traded his platinum credit card to get his hands on the zipper that ran the length of her back, disappearing just as the dress flared out gently over the swell of her buttocks. Nick was as mesmerized as the rest of them but Alex missed his look of blatant admiration, intent as she was on avoiding eye-contact after the disturbing events of that afternoon. Even Simon felt a twinge of the erotic afterglow that accompanied her entrance. Predictably enough, Richard seemed about the only one who was not affected by the surge in testosterone that flowed in her wake, being far too busy working himself up to impress his future in-laws to notice that his wife-to-be had just sent every other male in the place off the hormonal Richter scale.

'You look stunning, Alex.' Simon patted the seat beside him and she side-stepped the waiter to sit next to him, not caring if it wrecked anyone's ideas of place-ment. A starched napkin was ceremoniously unfurled into her lap and a solicitous enquiry made as to what Madam would be drinking as an aperitif. Madam thought that she had always hated that word and wondered what on earth was wrong with offering someone a drink and being done with it.

'We're all on champagne cocktails, darling. Richard very generously insisted.'

Simon spoke without a discernible trace of malice but she got the picture. Richard was determined to display his largesse to the hilt and would no doubt insist that everyone went for broke when it came to the menu as well. She wished she could tell him that profligate flashing of cash was not the way to her parents' hearts but knew she would be wasting her time and energy. If he hadn't worked out by now that con-spicuous consumption did not necessarily equal style then she wasn't going to be the one to enlighten him.

When her cocktail arrived, complete with silver salver, Simon took it upon himself to propose the first toast of the evening. He was in a remarkably buoyant mood, delighted that his parents had been unable to come. Unsurprisingly, the golden opportunity of some backslapping business function had taken priority. He was, however, looking forward to seeing Alex's parents, her mother having done more in his eyes to deserve that title than his own ever could. He was, therefore, in a generous frame of mind and only too happy to imbue this stilted occasion with at least a smidgen of sparkle. Clearly, someone had to: Alex was shivering inside that dress like a nervous kitten and Nick, far from being a helpful ally, seemed to have drifted off into some uncommunicative parallel universe. As for the prospective bridegroom . . . Doing his best to keep his side going in the face of Richard's insufferably parvenu presence, he raised a glass. 'Cheers. Here's to the happy couple, of course.'

'Of course.'

Nick's tone bore traces of irony, which did not pass unnoticed by Alex, but she was too thrown by the sudden arrival of her parents at the table to allow it to impinge on her fragile equilibrium. Simon leaped to his feet in greeting and Alex smiled weakly at them both. Now they only had Richard's parents to come and the stiff little party would be complete. Alex could hardly wait.

'Mummy . . . Daddy. You know Simon, of course. And this is his, um, flatmate Nick. And this is Richard.' Her mother was determinedly exuding graciousness all round whilst her father beamed at everyone absently, as he always did.

'Richard, how nice to meet you at last. Simon, sweetheart, lovely to see you again. And what a . . . delightful restaurant. Don't think we've been here before, have we, Teddy? Sorry we're a little late but your father didn't want to use the car-park across the road. Said he knew of some little side-street where he could park and we ended up circling around for quite some time.'

She favoured them with a conspiratorial smile and both Alex and Simon smirked dutifully in response. Her father's one quarrel with convention manifested itself in a belligerent refusal to pay good money when he could park his car elsewhere for free, and many a simple outing had been extended by the resultant lengthy hike. He was in all other ways, however, an absolute dear, and Alex was delighted to see them both. Her mother was looking very pretty in an understatedly elegant way and even her father had changed out of his habitual cords and cardie into something a little smarter, bullied no doubt by his wife who viewed coming to town as a treat and insisted that they dress up. Alex wasn't too sure that this would turn out to be much of a treat for them but was touched that they had gone to such effort.

'Teddy, Diana, may I offer you a drink?' Effortlessly assuming the role of host, Simon ignored Richard's chagrin and summoned one of the supercilious waiters. 'A champagne cocktail, Diana? Teddy, I expect you'd prefer a whisky and water?'

The subtle implications were not lost on Richard, who seemed for once to be out of his depth. Something in Simon's tone and words had made it all too apparent that he did not belong and never would, but for the life of him he could not pinpoint exactly what it was. Uncomfortably aware that he was without reinforcements, his parents being uncharacteristically late, Richard glanced at his watch and tapped his fingers impatiently on the side of his glass. His insecurity overflowed into arrogance and he stopped the waiter in his tracks with a loudly insistent, 'Make sure it's vintage bubbly this time. Something half-way decent . . . Bolly or Dom Perignon would do.'

The waiter retreated obsequiously enough but his

contempt was all too thinly veiled. Alex wanted to sink under the damask tablecloth in shame but her mother managed valiantly to keep up her bright smile whilst clearly wondering quite what sort of man her daughter had saddled herself with. Not one she would have chosen, that was for sure.

Like all mothers she could somehow convey her true feelings on any subject without appearing to alter her outward expression. Alex was miserably aware that she disliked Richard on sight, not as a person perhaps, but most certainly where her daughter was concerned. Typically, however, she was not going to breathe a word of dissension until such time as Alex came to her senses and she could murmur something along the lines of how they had both never really thought he was for her. It had happened time and again, during her earliest experiments with some inarticulate members of the opposite sex, through those headily rebellious days of encounters with wannabe rock stars who tried hard to disguise their middle-class roots with a permanent sneer and a host of glottal stops, and thence to the painfully poetic phase.

Diana and Teddy had shown great forbearance in putting up with a stream of unpromising specimens. None of these, however, had come close to breaching the scary barrier of commitment but this creature looked to be the most unpromising of the lot. At least the others had been misguided, instead of plain mean with their emotions. Richard's tightly held mouth and transparent, although ineffectual, attempts to impress spoke volumes. Diana kept her counsel but her heart was heavy and she had to make an almost superhuman

effort to keep up the small talk whilst casting a discreetly critical eye at this person who was supposed to
have won her daughter's fragile heart.

Her all-seeing gaze swept around the table and
rested with affection on Simon, chatting to Teddy and
heroically keeping up the faltering flow of general conversation. His flatmate seemed nice, if a little quiet,
and Diana leaned across to speak.

'Nick, how is it that you and Simon know each
other?'

Her innocent question brought a beady look from
Alex but before he could answer Simon butted in. 'He
arrived one night on my doorstep like some refugee
and I took him in out of the goodness of my heart and
have been keeping him there ever since.'

The ambiguity of this statement did not go
unnoticed but Nick merely laughed. 'Our fathers are
good friends and when I needed a place to stay Simon
kindly offered to help out. I'd been travelling for a
while but now I want settle down and get my career
going and London is the place to be.'

'And what is it that you do?'

'I'm a photographer, like Simon. In fact, I'm currently working as his assistant and learning a great deal
from him.'

'I'm sure you are,' Diana remarked drily, casting an
astute glance in Simon's direction. He had, no doubt,
heard every word and she was sure it wasn't just his
knowledge of lighting and shutter speeds that he
intended to impart. To Nick, however, she warmed
instinctively. He had what she perceived as a genuine
kindness about him and, despite Simon's dramatic

account, looked as if he were quite capable of looking after himself and anyone else who needed his help. A reliable sort, yet extraordinarily attractive too. She marvelled at this almost unique combination and wondered what on earth her daughter was doing with the pallid reflection of manhood seated on the other side of the table when right here was that elusive creature, a real man. And straight as a die – she would have bet her grandmother's pearls on it. The outward appearance of classically English gentility belied Diana's core of inner steel, which she shared with most women of her ilk. Naïve she most certainly was not, and she had been well aware since his early teenage years that Simon's close friendships with members of his own sex had everything to do with his sexual inclinations. Wisely, she had kept this knowledge to herself, knowing full well what the reaction would be if his martinet of a father ever found out that his only son was every homophobe's nightmare come true. Her very astuteness now gave her pause for thought and she wondered what on earth Simon was up to.

She didn't have much time to ponder, however, as it was at this point that Richard's parents showed up, his father sweating and apologizing profusely, his mother glowering in silent martyrdom. It turned out that they had taken the wrong turning off the motorway and had spent the last forty minutes or so trying to extricate themselves from the wilder parts of north-east London.

'Oh, you poor things.'

Alex's mother was all sweetness and sympathy whilst her father tried to reassure them that they need not give it another thought, although there were clearly going to be words when Carol got Mike home. Worse was to follow when she discovered that he had left his reading glasses in the car and therefore could not make out one word of the menu. With a long-suffering sigh Carol took it upon herself to read it aloud to him, thereby transcribing what was already fairly insufferable description into something that sounded like a bad parody of a seventies sitcom maligning all things foreign and suspicious. It would have been hilarious if it weren't so painfully obvious that she considered herself a mistress of obscure pronunciation and Mike a dolt to whom things had to be explained loudly and slowly, as if he were one of those wretched foreigners who so inconveniently didn't speak a word of English.

Having endured her mangling of the menu for quite long enough, Richard snatched it out of her hand and advised his father to have the soup and what turned out basically to be roast lamb. His surfeit of business entertaining had at least taught him how to tiptoe his way around a tricky menu and he knew that his father would cope with what he had chosen without pushing it around his plate and prodding it as if it contained some vile and poisonous matter.

A man of simple taste, Mike Matthews had been quite happy to be guided by the superior knowledge of his wife but, after all, it was Richard's do and as long as he'd heard of it before then he was quite happy to tuck into anything that was put before him. He still remembered with a shudder the time Carol had taken up an evening class in Creative Cuisine. For weeks and weeks they had both come home to an increasingly frightening range of dishes and when either he or

Richard had tentatively mentioned that it would be nice to have something normal like egg and chips or even spaghetti Bolognese, she had fixed them with that withering look and doled out her latest creations.

Further torture had come in the form of her subsequent dinner parties and many an evening had been spent making stiff-necked conversation, munching away at some unrecognizable culinary masterpiece as Carol accepted the fulsome praise of those neighbours she considered worth cultivating. Mike would rather have sat in front of the telly and snoozed at the end of a long day teaching technical drawing to recalcitrant teenagers, but he knew better than to argue. It was all part of Carol's great plan to elevate them to a social stratum that would ensure young Richard absorbed the level of sophistication necessary to guarantee his rapid advancement in the world. Not for nothing had she kept up her part-time job and gone without to contribute to his school fees. And she had been right: it had all paid off. Her bright boy was making pots and pots of money, certainly more than Mike could ever hope to, and now here he was practically married to the sort of girl who knew instinctively how to behave and who would suit her ambitious son down to the tips of his handmade brogues. Ambition: the most important thing she had instilled in him, and Carol's driving force. What else could have taken a girl from the rougher end of Romford to an occasion such as this?

Not that she felt in any way inferior to either of the other ladies at the table. Goodness, no. Resplendent in her appliquéd blouse and diamanté, beside her Diana faded into insignificance in her quiet colours and discreet pearl studs. And as for what the bride-to-be was wearing, well, it was hardly what you would describe as suitable attire for a girl who was engaged to be married. Her eyes swept over the thin straps and low neckline, and came to rest somewhere above that dangerous cleavage area. She noted that something sparkly around her skinny neck might have added a bit of class, although at least Richard's ring did her proud, not so much twinkling on her finger as positively flashing 'Notice me.' Carol smiled in approval as she caught sight of it. Good taste was something else her boy had inherited from her, and there was the evidence to prove it.

She tore herself away from her close scrutiny to engage in ingratiating conversation, most of which seemed to centre around the merits of her perfect son.

Diana observed the undercurrents flowing dangerously around the table but decided to keep her head down, at least for the moment. Simon felt no similar compunction and enjoyed himself hugely, making all the right noises whilst happily allowing Carol to dig an ever deeper pit of pretension.

Of all of them, Carol was most at ease in the ghastly restaurant and it became more and more obvious throughout the first course that Richard, her pride and joy, took after her. Why else would he insist on a finger bowl for the one large langoustine that the kitchen thought fit to serve up as an *amuse gueule* and then go on to engage in a long discourse with the wine waiter over which wine would suit a selection of main courses that would have benefited hugely from a judicious amount of dumbing down. Alex tried hard not to cringe as he ostentatiously sniffed the cork of the first bottle before sending it back without so much as a fair tasting. She doubted that it was off, as did her father who had kept a good cellar for over thirty years and could tell a corked bottle at a hundred paces. Both, however, refrained from comment, although Alex caught her father's swift glance and shrivelled inside that bit more.

Their starters arrived and everyone bar Carol tucked in, grateful for the chance to turn their attention to something other than the noxious atmosphere around the dinner table. It took a couple of seconds before anyone realized that the source of most of this awkwardness was gazing in horror at the contents of her plate.

'Is anything the matter, Mother?' Richard's solicitation soon turned to acute embarrassment as she looked up and declared, 'I should say it is. These are raw. Look at them! Anyone can see they aren't cooked properly!' Creative Cuisine had obviously not extended to the exotic realms of shellfish.

'They're oysters, Mother, they're not supposed to be cooked. And that is what you asked for, isn't it?'

Anxious to display her sophistication, and determined to extract her full measure from the evening, Carol had ordered by price rather than preference. Hence her oysters on a bed of samphire accompanied by a champagne risotto, and the lobster Thermidor to come. Alex could only hope that she wouldn't shriek that some idiot had chucked cheese all over her shellfish when that, too, made its appearance. Right now, however, she was regarding her food with singular suspicion. At Richard's irritated urging she took a tentative mouthful, only to rise up immediately from the table with her napkin clamped to her lips and an expression of disgust on her face. Her precipitous departure in the direction of the powder room resulted in an agonizing silence at the table, broken only by a muffled snort that Simon tried in vain to stifle but which burst forth treacherously nonetheless.

'Do you think I should go and see if she's all right?' enquired Diana half-heartedly, as Carol's absence extended itself into a lengthy interlude filled only with the chinking sound of silverware against plates. Mike merely concentrated harder on his bowl of soup. Richard shook his head but the staccato tapping of his foot could be heard reaching a crescendo beneath the tablecloth and it was with some relief that they greeted Carol's reappearance. The general relief was, however, predictably short-lived.

'So, Richard, what is it exactly that you do?'

In a noble effort to restore some sort of congenial atmosphere, Alex's father had unfortunately hit upon Richard's favourite topic. Himself. He visibly expanded a good three inches in his seat as he assumed the expression Alex had come to dread, one that signalled a long, uninterruptable diatribe on the complexity of being Richard. How Very Important and Indispensable he was. And how he had to fight every day against the odds to remain so in a tightening market and a hostile world. The polite nods soon diminished but Richard droned on, his social skills clearly at odds with his self-proclaimed business acumen. Had he not been so patently a product of his mother's overweening ambition he would have been intensely dislikeable but something about Richard evoked pity rather than derision. That same quality, unfortunately, which had landed Alex in this unholy mess and condemned her to this farcical breaking of bread when what was really being broken at the table was at least one heart, possibly two.

'And, of course, even in this day and age one has to be incredibly careful about the choice of . . . er . . . partner. One has to go for someone who can grow with you, keep pace with your ambitions and tastes . . .' Richard threw an affectionate glance at Alex.

'One does indeed. But, then, we all make mistakes.'

Nick's deadpan delivery gave little away but he, too, looked straight at her as he spoke. Something beneath her belly button fluttered and she felt a slow flush spread upwards from the top of her low-cut dress to suffuse her cheeks with telltale colour. Bastard. They had exchanged barely a word all evening, he seemingly enraptured by her mother's tales of Alex's childhood escapades. She had been quite all right up until that point – or, at least, as well as could be expected, given the paroxysms of hideous embarrassment that threatened to engulf her every time Richard opened his mouth to speak. Not even the gleam of sympathy in her father's eye had derailed her and she had just begun to congratulate herself on her mature handling of the situation when somewhere out of left field one understated remark and a look loaded with intent had thrown her for six. Talk about hitting below the belt, she would bet anything Nick had not been a team player at school.

Strangely enough, it was the ghastly Carol who rescued them this time from the ensuing awkward pause. Barely disguising the malicious glint in her eye, she smiled thinly as she turned to Alex and enquired after her own doubtless unimpressive career plans and prospects. Alex heard the unspoken message that whatever she did was surely nothing more than an adjunct to Richard's own precipitous scramble up the ladder of success and for a second or two felt a familiar sense of helpless inadequacy. Only for a second or two, however, as it suddenly dawned on her that she had something to boast about after all, something she had been saving up to tell her parents. And what better moment than this?

Carol was still looking at her in a faintly derisory fashion as she threw back her shoulders, unconsciously creating even more intense interest in her impressive cleavage, and smiled gloriously at her tormentor.

'Well, as from next month I shall be contributing my own opinion column to the *Sunday Herald*. The thoughts of the modern urban girl, that sort of thing. Should be a lot of fun and I'm really looking forward to it.'

There was a collective gasp of astonishment, varying in its degrees of pleasure and generosity of spirit, and Alex beamed at them all, for the first time that evening truly delighted with herself. Her mother was the first to recover, her stunned expression giving way to a look of pure and gratifying delight. Alex had the feeling that for once in her life she had done absolutely the right thing.

'Oh, darling, that's wonderful. But why didn't you tell us before? And when did you find out? Alex has always been very good at writing, you know. Her

English teacher was always telling us that one day we would see her name in print.' Diana addressed the table at large, flushed with pride and pleasure and suddenly only too thrilled by Carol's tight-lipped presence. Richard's glittering prospects now seemed a little tarnished in comparison.

Alex butted in before her mother's excitement threatened to overwhelm them all. 'Mummy, please! I was getting around to telling you but it all happened so fast. One minute I'm in the office as usual and the next this top editor is asking me to write for him . . . I still can't believe it myself. I've got to come up with some great ideas for this editorial meeting next week and, if they like them, away we go.' Belatedly, Alex realized that she had somehow managed to keep this startling piece of news entirely to herself. Simon, her usual confidant, was looking at her in astounded admiration.

Luckily, he soon regained control of his vocal cords. 'So you're saying that this editor person just wandered into your office and offered you a top job on the basis of your undeniable charm and good looks?' He was goading her good-naturedly, but it was a good question, the answer to which both Richard and Nick seemed all too eager to hear.

'Don't be so bloody silly— Oops, sorry, Mummy. No, he read some of my stuff and liked it. Amazing though it might seem to you, he thinks I've got talent and "refreshingly strong opinions", as he puts it. And he's a mate of Lydia's and one of her top contacts to boot so he wasn't just some weirdo wandering around the office and I got this entirely on merit, you sexist pig, so there.'

Realizing that she had all but stuck her tongue out at him, Alex attempted to reclaim some sort of adult dignity by sitting poker straight and favouring Simon with her most condescending smile, which coincidentally bore a marked resemblance to that assumed by the clearly disapproving Carol sitting across from her. The questions then came thick and fast and, as Alex attempted to answer them, she discovered how little she knew about her new post other than that it would probably at first be only part-time but would no doubt lead to the most amazing opportunities if she handled herself well.

Alex had not been alone in observing Carol's acid-drop reaction to this upstaging of her precious baby boy. Her mother had shown remarkable forbearance in dealing with a woman who evidently considered her daughter to be barely an adequate consort for her marvellous son but enough was enough. Seizing the chance to twist the blade a little further, Diana smiled sweetly at her. 'My two girls were always so talented, in their different ways. Oh, darling, I nearly forgot. Sarah sent you this along with the latest letter. She wasn't too sure if you were still at the old address... My other daughter married an Australian,' she added, for the benefit of Richard's parents, glossing over the ructions that had occurred when Sarah announced her intention to marry the handsome locum doctor and remove herself to some godforsaken farmstead in the outback. Fortunately for everyone concerned, she had positively thrived out there in the boondocks and now Diana doted from afar on her three tiny grandchildren, the two eldest of whom had turned their talents to the decoration of the envelope she was now handing to Alex.

'Rosie and Jack obviously take after the artistic side of the family. Do you have any grandchildren, Carol?'

'Not as yet. Richard is an only child.'

'Oh, I see.' Diana looked at the other woman with just the right amount of smug sympathy, unfortunately confirming Carol's mounting suspicion that she was being patronized.

A purple glow of righteous anger crept across her cheeks and she spluttered, 'I thought it best to concentrate on just the one. I'm proud to say that Richard never came home to an empty house and he always had a hot tea on the table. Not like nowadays with these front-door-key kids, or whatever they call them, living off chips and suchlike. That's all wrong in my book, all these working mothers. Selfish, that's what I call it. A woman's place is in the home, as far as I am concerned, and you can call me old-fashioned but there it is. If more of them looked after their own kids we wouldn't have half the problems on the streets and it's all because they think they can have it all. It's just not dignified. A wife should support her husband, not go gallivanting about trying to act like a man. It's no wonder there's so many poofters about. Those young boys don't know any better. Haven't had any proper mothering. If you ask me it's a crime, that's what it is. And all because you young women don't know what it is to be proper ladies.'

This remarkable stream of invective ended on a high note of heartfelt outrage and a laser-like beam of pure

malevolence aimed at Alex. Much muttering and shuffling from both Richard and his father signalled their
familiarity with the thoughts of Chairman Carol but,
fortunately enough, the rest of those present had not
been numbed by such over-exposure. Out of the corner
of her eye Alex could see her father reach over and put
a restraining hand on her mother's arm, but Simon had
no such scruples. He looked coldly at Carol before
speaking, each and every word enunciated so clearly
that there was no necessity for him to raise his voice
to enable the entire restaurant to hear. 'And you'd know
all about that, of course. Being so ladylike yourself.'

Carol bristled as she stared back at him, her lips
twitching with the effort of trying to conceal her dislike.
'And what do you mean by that?'

But Simon merely shrugged, irritatingly unwilling
to be drawn into the slanging match she was so
obviously itching for. The waiter chose this juncture
to hover nervously, offering coffee or dessert to those
who cared to consult the separate gold-tasselled *carte*.
Strangely enough, most of the party appeared to have
lost their appetites although Carol insisted on a liqueur
to round off her gourmand experience. Nick rather
hoped that she would go for a flaming Sambuca and
expire in a merciful blast of spontaneous combustion,
but the wickedly overpriced cognac she ordered offered
no such possibility. He glanced around the table at the
wreckage of the evening and his heart went out to Alex,
sitting there making all the right noises whilst
so obviously dying on her feet. He would have given
anything to have given the old trout a piece of his
mind but politesse and a desperate loyalty to Alex

prevented him from doing anything to upset her or her parents any further. At least now a kind of tense peace was being kept.

Indeed, after toying with her coffee for a few moments and indulging in desultory small-talk, Diana judged it within the bounds of propriety to make an inconspicuous exit. Affecting a slight yawn and throwing a meaningful glance at her husband, she pushed her chair back slightly and smiled brightly at no one in particular.

'I think, perhaps, that we should be going. It's getting late and it's a long way to drive. No, darling, don't get up. Daddy and I will just slip off and leave you to your evening.'

She urged an immensely grateful husband to his feet and smiled graciously in the general direction of Richard and his family. 'So nice to meet you at last, Richard. And you, Mike. Carol.' This last with a steely little nod. 'Come along, Teddy. No, I shall drive. Simon, darling, big kiss. Alex, I'll call you tomorrow. Nick, lovely to meet you – come and stay sometime. We'd love to have you. 'Bye-bye, darlings. 'Bye.' And with that she was gone, leaving her daughter to bring the evening to as graceful a conclusion as she could manage under the circumstances.

'You've got quite a drive as well, haven't you, Mother?'

Even Richard was anxious now to bring things to a close. The event he had looked forward to as his chance to polish up his ego and shine even brighter than before had crumbled into something that left a dry, bitter taste in his mouth. He swallowed nervously and peered at

Carol, hoping for some show of support, anything to let him know that in her eyes he was still the golden boy. He felt cheated, robbed of his moment in the sun, and he blamed Simon fairly and squarely for that. At the very least his own mother could show her gratitude for his lavish hospitality, as well as approval for the girl he had chosen as the most suitable of brides. Her folk might be rather backward in coming forward but he knew that his mother only spoke her mind for the best. Or, at any rate, for Richard's best. Besides, he secretly shared each and every one of her opinions and intended to make that abundantly clear to Alex the moment that wretched wedding ring was on her finger. And the first person off the Christmas-card list would be that mincing nancy-boy, poisoning her mind with his warped ideas and even more twisted morals. You could never be too careful with poofters. If nothing else, he would never be able to leave Simon with any child of his. God only knows what would happen to the poor little bugger, left to such perverted devices.

Carol noticed Richard's doe-eyed looks in her direction but chose to ignore him a little longer. If there was one thing she loved to have it was the final word and she didn't feel that she had yet extracted her due. The fine cognac warmed her bones and loosened any inhibitions that might have been lingering in her narrow mind. Taking a last, audible sip, she turned her attention again to Alex and raked her over made-up eyes over the offensive cleavage that had been bothering her since the evening began its doomed descent. Sniffing through pinched nostrils, she averted her gaze and pronounced, 'In my day men preferred mystery.

Don't you think you should cover yourself up a bit, dear?'

To her horror, Alex could feel herself going bright red and her eyes well with tears. This really was the final straw and she didn't quite know where to look or what to say. She needn't have worried.

'What did you say?'

Unbelievably, this time it was Nick who had come to her rescue, his beautiful eyes two chips of ice as he glared daggers at the gorgon. Cowardly as all bullies, Carol immediately began to back down but Nick was having none of it.

'I think you owe Alex an apology, don't you? God knows when your day was but as far as I and I'm sure everyone else here is concerned she looks absolutely gorgeous tonight. Far more so than every other so-called lady in this room.'

On this last comment he raised his voice slightly, intending it not just for Carol's benefit but for all of those women who had twittered and bitched behind their handbags since the moment Alex had lit up the restaurant. The odd gasp and disgruntled murmur could be heard from adjoining tables but Nick was undeterred. Still grimly staring the old bat down, he paused for a well-considered beat before demanding, 'Well?' in the tones of one who would brook no argument.

Thrilled and aghast all at the same time, Alex attempted a gracious smile as Carol turned to her and muttered the barest minimum of an apology. The effect was rather ruined, however, when she added, 'But I still stand by every word I said. My boy needs someone to take care of him, give him babies and a stable home, and from what I can see, that is not what you want at all.'

'And who can blame her not wanting to stick her toes into *that* gene pool?'

Simon's sarcasm was a little too clever for Carol but she got the gist of it. With a great huff of indignation she gathered herself together and rose unsteadily to her feet, at the same time announcing, 'Right! That's it! Mike, we're off.'

Mike looked somewhat baffled by the speed of events but Carol ignored his dithering, diamanté flashing magnificently in the light as she flung her parting shot at Simon. 'Young man, I'm sure I don't know what you're talking about,' she sneered, before once again turning her attention to her hapless husband.

'I'm equally sure you don't,' he replied, before adding in an almost innocuously conversational way, 'It's pretty obvious that Richard did not inherit his admittedly rather limited intelligence from you.'

Nick wanted to cheer but contented himself with shifting closer to Alex and placing a comforting arm around her shoulder. Alex was grateful for his touch. It was as if they were bracing themselves for the wave of fury that was about to break over their heads, and in the moment of deathly calm before the storm she was aware of the warmth of his touch and the faint, familiar smell of his skin. Carol was standing stock still, her gaze fixed unflinchingly on an apparently uncaring Simon and her throat working as she struggled to find adequate words for this latest and greatest insult.

'Mother, please. Simon didn't mean it. Simon, tell her you're sorry.'

Richard was tugging placatingly at her sleeve and Alex leaned ever harder against Nick, a peculiar kind of excited dread transfixing them both. Carol was still gobbling away like an angry turkey, her mind working as fast as it could as she tried to think of some way to make them all pay for this. One thing was sure, they wouldn't hear the end of it for decades to come.

Mercifully saving at least two of those present from years of grovelling, Simon looked up at her as if astonished that she was still there before commanding, 'Well, bugger off, then. If you're going, go. And by the way, I'm not sorry. I said it and I meant it. Every last syllable. So you can stick that wherever your ladylike sun doesn't shine.'

'Now, steady on . . .'

Mike's protest was obviously too little too late. Both Nick and Alex watched in mounting alarm as Carol's colour changed from pink to deathly white. Even her lips had turned a pale blue and Nick really thought they might disappear entirely inside her head, so tightly were they pulled together. Unable to utter another word, she fumbled for her bag, at the same time practically pulling Mike up and out of his seat. Richard did his best but there was no stopping her marching out of the restaurant, a sheepish Mike in tow and Richard scurrying after, trying in vain to convince her that Simon hadn't meant a word of it and clearly wasn't in his right mind.

'Never felt saner in my life,' drawled Simon, watching the departing trio with impressive cool before raising his glass in silent toast to their departed companions. Alex looked around the empty table in a daze, not knowing whether to laugh, cry or run after Richard and show the proper amount of concern.

'Sorry, sweetheart. For ruining your evening, I mean. But I'm afraid the old trout had it coming to her. It's about time someone told her to bugger off and mind her own business.'

Simon's contrition was genuine and, besides, Alex was none too sure there was anything to forgive. She had a sneaky suspicion she owed them both rather a lot and, summoning one of the ever-hovering waiters, she ordered large whiskies for the three of them.

Clinking her glass against theirs, she smiled wearily and declared, 'Well, there's nothing else for it. The sooner I forget all about this evening the happier I shall be.'

'The sooner you forget all about that idiot the happier you'll be . . .' Nick's self-control had slipped enough again for him to articulate his private thoughts but, apart from shooting him a warning glance, she didn't disagree.

'Don't look now but here comes Mother's Pride and Joy. Hello, Richard, old son. Glass of whisky to wet the whistle?' Simon's best young-fogey impression missed its target by a mile. Richard was far too furious to notice anything as subtle as satire.

'Well, I hope you're happy.'

Standing right over him in his Thomas Pink shirt and knotted Asprey cufflinks, Richard drew himself up to his full five foot ten and three-quarter inches and glared down at Simon, his self-righteous manner oddly reminiscent of his mother in full flood. He had never quite forgiven Simon for the river dunking and now all his rage and mortification were directed at him in equal, if unfair, measure.

Simon, however, was impervious to his ire. 'Ecstatic, now that we are no longer subject to the wit and wisdom of the delightful Carol. Has your mother always been so astute in her assessments?'

'Well, at least she's sharp enough to spot an interfering old poof when she sees one.'

Seemingly impervious to the gasps of outrage from both Nick and Alex, Simon smiled thinly before retorting, 'I'd rather be a scheming queen than the sort of pretentious prat who thinks he can buy himself credibility. And less of the old, please. I, at least, still have a nice healthy head of hair.'

Richard flinched at this final reference to the small but noticeable increase in the height of his own forehead but, to his credit, held his ground. Fighting to keep his voice level, he resolutely maintained eye-contact whilst reaching out a hand towards Alex. 'Come on, Alex. We're leaving.'

Flouncing out was obviously the theme of the evening but Alex was having none of it. She had had enough.

'You can. I'm not.'

This deviation from form flummoxed him for a moment, but only for a moment.

'You'll come with me now or—'

'Or what?'

Coolly, she surveyed him from across the table, enjoying the fact that for once she had wrongfooted him. It felt great, this defiance thing, and she was aware that both Nick and Simon were looking at her in astonishment and not a little admiration.

'No, you go on home, Richard. Frankly I have had enough for one evening.'

Deciding that the only thing to do was occupy the high moral ground, Richard looked down at them all much as a nursery-school teacher would when confronted with a particularly rowdy class of infants.

'Well, I hope you're satisfied. This evening has been an unmitigated disaster. God only knows what will happen at the wedding itself if that's the way you're going to carry on.'

'There isn't going to be a wedding.'

Had he paid closer attention to her over the time they had been together, Richard might have realized that the flatness of Alex's tone meant business. As it was, he mistook this pronouncement for yet another of what he thought of as her displays of temperament.

'Oh, for goodness' sake, pull yourself together. I'm getting sick and tired of all this childish stuff. Look, we'll go home and when you've calmed down we can discuss this like the adults we supposedly are.'

'I am calm. Perfectly calm. And I am not going anywhere with you.'

They faced each other down, a look of panic creeping across Richard's face as he saw that her expression was immutable. He tried again, his tone a little less hectoring. 'Now, come on, sweetheart. Stop all this nonsense and let's get out of here.'

'No.'

Alex had hit her wall of tolerance and the balance

of power began to tilt relentlessly into her lap. Simon and Nick had melted into the background, two silent but fascinated observers.

Privately, Simon put his money on Alex. Once she had made up her mind there was no stopping her and he was silently cheering her on to the finish line. It was better than sex, watching the smug bastard begin to crawl.

'Alex, please, stop this. Look, you're tired, it's been a long evening . . .'

'Oh, but I'm just getting started. Simon, Nick, another drink?'

She looked over at a waiter and waved her empty glass at him meaningfully. She then stared up at Richard with an expression of unbrookable defiance. His shoulders slumped, as if he knew when to admit defeat, but he pressed his point when to retreat would have been much the most sensible option. 'Alex, I don't understand. What have I done?'

Richard was begging now and even Nick cringed, his innate sense of compassion fighting hard with a strong desire to kick his rival further down than he had already fallen, if that were possible. Simon had no such compunction and was enjoying this spectacle just as much as the earlier entertainment.

'Nothing, Richard. And that is precisely the problem. You never do, not for me, anyway. Not really.'

'That is hardly fair. I have just entertained not only your friends but . . .'

This with a furious look at Simon, who responded by extracting his wallet from his pocket and throwing his credit card on the table, at the same time summoning a waiter with a glance.

'Allow me.'

His smooth munificence was designed to infuriate and it hit the spot. Richard snatched up the card and thrust it back at him, before slapping his own on top of the bill without so much as glancing at the total. They eyeballed each other like a couple of prize-fighters before Simon conceded. 'Very kind of you, Richard. Or, should I say, very kind of your firm?'

That really was below the belt: Richard's saving grace was his generosity and he was far too pedestrian a person to fiddle his expenses. He signed the slip without a word, sliding his wallet back into his jacket pocket with elaborate care before turning to Alex once more. 'I will ask you one last time, Alex. Are you coming with me or not?'

She raised her eyes to meet his and her expression of mute defiance said it all. He got the point. Summoning his last vestiges of self-control, he delivered his parting shot. 'Fine. I shall talk to you when you've calmed down and then perhaps you can tell me what all this is about.'

His dignity was painful to behold but Alex wasn't finished yet. She was still smarting from her mauling at the hands of his execrable mother and every atom of her body ached to extract a final revenge. It might not be fair to visit the sins of the mother on the son but it sure as hell felt good.

'There is one thing before you go.'

The hope that flared in Richard's eyes died the second they rested on the ring she was holding out to him on her outstretched palm. He shook his head and backed away. Without another word he marched out, leaving Simon to mutter, 'Pompous prick!' in his wake. The poignancy of his exit was somewhat marred by his equally brisk return to the table to pick up his forgotten briefcase, which was chained to his side even at weekends and which represented an incalculable part of his self-esteem. The three watched in silence as he strode off again, having thrown one last despairing look at Alex. This she missed, being apparently entranced by the label on the whisky bottle. The minute the restaurant doors banged after him for the last time she looked up at them both, smiled shakily and declared, 'I, for one, am going to get absolutely slaughtered,' before reaching for the latest in a long line of rapidly emptying glasses and proceeding to do just that.

TEN

The second she opened her eyes she knew it was a major mistake. Overnight, the world had acquired a technicolour hue and her eyes smarted from the effort of being kept open. Added to that, she seemed to be having difficulty in breathing and something small and hard was digging into her back. She wriggled, trying to dislodge whatever it was, and the pressure on her chest eased dramatically as Miu Miu hurled herself to the floor with a yowl of protest. Parts of the jigsaw began to fall into place, her disorientation replaced by a growing realization of her whereabouts. She was on Simon's sofa, that much was clear. It was obviously daylight, as could be ascertained from the light filtering through the expensive silk hangings that acted as curtains. Her dry mouth, protesting stomach and pounding head would seem to indicate either the onset of some mysterious illness or, far more likely, a hangover of epic proportions and her memory, although momentarily blank, would no doubt soon start obligingly to fill in the cringe-making details. Until that time, she thought it might be best to lie as still as possible and pray for early deliverance.

Her prayers might well have been answered had, in the normal course of events, the whole household stayed moaning into their respective pillows. Simon, however, had an annoying habit of bounding out of bed at some unearthly hour in spite or perhaps because of alcohol-inflicted damage. Having been awake since seven he had rapidly grown bored with waiting for the other two to surface. By nine o'clock his fit of nervous energy induced him to get up, slug back an unhealthy amount of coffee and tiptoe past the still unconscious Alex into his tiny darkroom. Once in there he thought he might as well give the place a good clear-out. He hadn't used the space himself in ages and there might be pictures lurking around that could be useful library stuff. In any case, he couldn't bear clutter and the place certainly looked as if it could do with a good going-over.

He started off by scooping odds and ends of debris into one pile and stacking up empty trays before lifting the lid of the developing tank. It was empty, although by the smell of it someone had put it to recent use. Since that someone could only be Nick he wondered what he had been up to and cast around to see if the results of his endeavours were somewhere close by. Simon felt a vicarious pride in Nick's work and in the building of his portfolio. He was always interested to see his new pictures and to provide constructive comment, relishing his role as mentor even if his other interest was fading in the wake of Serge's arrival in his life and bed. By the dim glow of the red lamp he could see that three or four prints were still hanging up to dry. He unclipped them before adding them to the small stack on the bench, which he presumed were part of the same batch. Curious to get a good look at them in proper light, he stepped out into the sitting room and began to look through the pile by the daylight streaming through the diaphanous curtains. What he saw brought such an audible reaction that Alex sat bold upright from her nest on the sofa and looked around wildly for the source of what had sounded remarkably like a howl of outrage.

Squinting in the general, and rather painful, direction of the window, Alex made out Simon's silhouette and what looked to be a bundle of cards in his hands. As her eyes grew accustomed to the light, she saw that he was flicking rapidly through a bunch of ten-by-eights, pausing every now and then to mutter another expletive as he turned the offending photograph this way and that. She wondered what on earth they contained to elicit such a dramatic reaction and tried hard to think of some sensible question she could ask in her current addled state. Thankfully, or perhaps not, the action of her sitting up had caught Simon's eye and he whirled around, still obviously in a state of shock at whatever ghastly images had confronted him. His eyes raked over Alex searchingly before they returned to the prints in his hand, then back to her as if in some inexplicable act of comparison. She frowned at him and opened her mouth to ask him what the hell he was playing at when a cold beam of clarity stabbed through the fog of confusion and she abruptly shut it again, followed swiftly by her eyes as she tried to blank out what was to come.

'What on earth . . . ?' Nick's voice from the doorway brought them flying open again and she cleared her throat noisily, intending perhaps to croak out a warning, although she wasn't sure what it was she wanted to say.

'I could ask you the same thing.'

Simon's face was grim as he advanced on Nick, coming to a halt in front of the sofa where Alex cowered and waving the offending prints practically under his nose. Wordlessly, Nick took them and went through them with equal but far more measured concentration before tapping them together and looking directly at a still twitching Simon.

'Well, it's obvious, isn't it? I mean, you can see that these are photos of Alex, can't you? I don't see what the problem is.' A shade disingenuous but he was, at least, correct. From her safe haven under the spare duvet Alex conceded the first point to Nick.

'Oh, give me a break. Of course I can see that they're photos but . . . these . . . well, they're practically pornographic!' Simon declared, on an entirely inappropriate note of triumph.

Now it was Nick's turn to snort in disbelief, a noise Alex didn't recall either of them ever making before. 'Pornographic my arse! If that's your idea of porn then you've been leading a far more sheltered life than you'd like us to believe.'

Simon snatched the topmost print off the pile and waved it menacingly in Nick's face. 'Look at this. I mean, she's practically naked. And as for the look on her face, well, Alex, I'm surprised at you.' Now that was unbelievably unfair but Alex shrank still further under the protective covers and bit her lip in shame and growing annoyance.

Nick, however, was having none of it. 'How dare you! There is absolutely nothing for Alex to be ashamed of here. Nothing!'

They both looked at him in surprise, unaccustomed to him losing his cool. Alex could see that Nick was practically spitting tacks and secretly felt a warm glow of maidenly gratitude at his defence. He snatched the print from Simon and carried on. 'In my opinion these are not only some of the best pictures I've ever taken but they're also some of the most honest I've ever seen, and if you don't like them, that, as far as I'm concerned, is just too bad. You don't own Alex and you don't control me, so just back off, Simon, OK?'

'I think you're forgetting that you work for me, you pay me rent and it's in my bloody darkroom that you developed those precious pictures of yours. And I can say what I bloody like about them. What I'd like to know is just when you set this little session up. Tough, was it, sneaking around behind my back like that?'

Now stridently sanctimonious, there was no way Simon was going to give an inch before he got to the bottom of things. Voices and tempers were rising by the second and Alex thought it wise to remain as inconspicuous as possible, not difficult given that they both seemed to have forgotten that the person around whom the whole argument pivoted was crouched under a pile of bedclothes not two feet beneath their noses.

'Nothing was "set up" as you so sneeringly put it. It happened by chance. She came out of the bathroom and I looked at her and I just knew I had to get all of that on film before I lost it. You have no right to belittle those pictures. Or to question their circumstances. Yes, I pay you rent and, yes, I work for you, but that still doesn't mean you own me. Or her. And you obviously have absolutely no idea how I feel about these or about her so just back off, Simon. Back off!'

He was breathing so fast and so hard that he was almost panting and for the first time Simon looked unsure of himself. Before he could even formulate some kind of comeback, Nick began again to speak, this time in a much calmer and steadier voice. 'Frankly, mate, I don't really care what you think. I know what I think. These are fabulous pictures, she's one of the most beautiful women I have ever met and I love her so much I can't breathe when I look at her so you can take all your smutty ideas and sordid thoughts and shove them . . . wherever . . .'

They were all shaking now, Nick with emotion, Simon with shock and Alex with, well, she wasn't absolutely sure. But, whatever it was, it was responsible for the most glorious feeling in the pit of her stomach and for the ridiculous grin that was suffusing her face with utter delight. She knew that the shit was about to hit the fan, that Simon would never forgive them both, but for now, right now, everything was perfect in her world. She couldn't bear to look at Nick, although she could faintly hear his still ragged breathing, and she didn't dare raise her eyes to Simon's. She supposed that this must be how people felt at the eye of a storm, strangely calm in those few seconds before all hell broke loose and ferocious winds tore everything away. She had even started to count the seconds until Simon's wrath broke over them both like some demented typhoon before she realized that the other sound she could hear was laughter. Simon's laughter.

'And I thought I'd finally lost my touch,' he sput-

tered, before subsiding again into uncontrollable
guffaws. From their bewildered expressions he grasped
that he owed them both an explanation. Simon took a
couple of deep breaths. 'Alex, sweetheart, let me tell
you about me and Nick . . .'

To the complete astonishment of both men, her
instantaneous reaction was to fling up a hand as if to
ward off whatever was coming next and to gasp. 'No,
no, I really don't want to hear any more, no, no, no, no,
no . . .' before she shut her eyes and held her breath,
as if that would somehow stop the freight train of truth
from bearing down on her.

What seemed like aeons passed, although by all the
laws of nature it could only have been a couple of
minutes, before she peeked through her lashes and saw
that they were both looking at her as if she had lost
the plot.

'Alex! Calm down, woman! I don't know what on
earth you think I'm about to tell you but whatever it
is . . . Look, just listen to me for a second. All that stuff
I told you, all those things, none of them ever came
true. Not one. Nothing, *nada*, do you understand?'

Simon had plonked himself down beside her on the
sofa and was shaking her arm as if that might shake
the truth of his words into her. She could see Nick
standing behind him, looking confused. Hardly surprising as she herself was having trouble assimilating
what he was trying to tell her. 'You mean . . .?'

Simon looked both shamefaced and regretful as he
nodded in answer to her unspoken question and Alex
gave him a long, hard stare before joyfully concluding
that he was telling her the truth. Nothing had

happened, nothing. All those moments of doubt, all those sleepless nights trying hard not to think of what they might be getting up to together, those months and months of sheer torture . . .

'But what about the ring by your bed? And when I called your room in Bali and Nick answered? And – and—' and a hundred and one other occasions where, fuelled by Simon's fantasies and an awful lot of innuendo, she had come to what now seemed to have been an entirely erroneous conclusion.

The ball of confusion was passed on, this time to land in Simon's lap. Now he really did look at her as if she had taken leave of her senses. 'I don't know what you're going on about. What ring by my bed? Whose ring? Really, Alex, you do talk in riddles sometimes.'

'Nick's ring. By your bed. I found it at your party and . . .'

A soft groan from Nick indicated that the penny had finally and painfully dropped.

'Oh, that. I put it there when I was tidying up the bathroom. Come to think of it, I did wonder where it had got to but, to be honest, it wasn't the most important thing on my mind at the time.' No, its owner had been the possessor of that honour, although Simon was loath to admit it. Especially now.

'Ah.' She looked distinctly nonplussed, her detective work clearly not as thorough as she had thought.

'Yes, ah, anything else? And what's all this about some phone call in Bali?'

'I think I can explain that one.' That penny was rapidly joined by a cascade of its copper cousins as everything in Nick's mind fell into place. 'When Alex called about the cat and I spoke to her, I never thought to explain that we'd changed rooms. Well, she did wake me up and everything and, you know, I just never thought . . . Oh, shit, I think it's all making sense.'

'Well, I'm glad one of us has some idea of what's going on!'

Simon's tone was tart but he was desperately trying to deflect too much blame from himself. He hated to admit it, even to himself, but some of the things he had said to Alex might just have been a teensy weensy bit misleading, given the circumstances. Although, by the look on Nick's face, he wasn't too far behind him when it came to final comprehension.

Sitting on the armrest on the other side of Alex so that she was now sandwiched between them, Nick looked at her. 'Now let me get this straight. You thought that Simon and I were . . . oh, shit!' The look on her face was confirmation enough and Nick banged his fist on his forehead as if to knock the last bits of the truth jigsaw into place. 'I do not believe it . . . I – I mean, how could you think that?' She winced at his flabbergasted expression, then looked to Simon for support or explanation.

Seeing that she was completely stuck for words, and even more importantly terrified of what she might say once she did find her tongue, Simon intervened as smoothly as he could.

'What Alex is trying to tell you is that she misread certain, er, situations. Oh, all right, we both did,' he added hastily, as she looked ominously as if she might find her voice in time to scream in outrage at his obfuscating. Realizing that there was nothing else for it but to come clean, loath though he was to break the habit of a lifetime, Simon dived in at the deep end. 'The thing is, I thought that you and I might, well, become closer over time . . .'

Nick's look of frank disbelief would have quashed the lingering hopes of a diehard optimist but Simon hurried on, determined if nothing else to save face.

'But I quickly saw that you and I were . . . batting for different teams, as you might say. And, OK, I did maybe lead Alex to believe perhaps a little more than the absolute gospel truth but, really, can you blame me? If you think about it, it's been obvious from the start that you two are crazy about each other and, well, I guess I was a bit jealous, if you must know. All that avoiding each other deliberately and those sneaky little glances when you thought no one else was looking. Really!'

He gazed reprovingly at them, as if they were nothing so much as two nine-year-olds caught red-handed with the cookie jar and smiled in sweet satisfaction at their mutual embarrassment.

'What amazes me is that you thought no one would notice. Not even each other.'

His air of knowing superiority would have been insufferable had it not been for the twinkle lurking behind his words and, more importantly, the sheer relief of knowing that he wasn't going to kill them both.

'You mean, you're not angry?'

Alex was finding his forbearance very hard to believe, having been the unwilling recipient of so many of his thoughts and dreams concerning Nick. God, she'd even tried to cheer him on, so deluded had she been about the entire situation and her own feelings in particular. But Simon had wanted him so badly and she knew from experience how tenacious he could be.

'Angry? No. Disappointed, maybe. Although, you know, if anyone had to win then only my very best friend would do. But mostly I'm just relieved that it's nothing to do with me. You know, for a while there I thought my charisma was fading. Perish the thought!'

He shuddered in mock horror but underneath the theatricality lay a large grain of truth. Simon was beginning to understand that what he had with Serge was far more akin to true love than anything he had ever imagined he felt for Nick, and it was far easier to be magnanimous with that to shore him up. Feeling positively saintly, he eased himself off the sofa, looked benevolently at them both and suggested coffee all round as if they had been discussing nothing so much as the weather. 'And I think you two should have a little chat whilst I'm in the kitchen, don't you? I'm sure you have plenty to talk about.' He was practically polishing his halo, so pleased was he with this new version of himself. Neither of them was fooled for a minute.

'I'm sure we'll manage,' was Nick's dry retort, and Simon tripped off, congratulating himself all the way. At the door he paused and, with consummate sincerity, announced, 'Nick, I didn't mean it about the pics. They're fabulous, really,' before gliding off around the corner in close imitation of a self-satisfied Mother Superior.

Left alone, they were both suddenly shy. There seemed such an awful lot to say and so many things to explain and neither was quite sure where to begin. Eventually picking up the pile of prints, Nick thought he might kick things off by letting actions speak far louder than words ever could. He held them out to her and watched her face as she went through them all, pausing over one or two longer than others and going back and forth to take another look. They were extraordinary photographs, capturing her naked emotion so tenderly that even the most obtuse observer would instantly have realized upon looking at them that there existed between photographer and subject much more than just a working relationship.

Like most people, Alex hated to look at pictures of herself but even she had to admit that these, whilst honest, were also flattering. The upside, she supposed, of the photographer being madly in love with you. The very thought made the tips of her ears turn pink and Nick must have sensed what was going through her mind because he chose that moment to take them from her. 'I think it's time we had a talk,' he said.

She cringed. 'You have no idea how much I hate it when people say that.'

'Yeah, me too. But there are obviously a couple of things we need to get straight . . .' It was a promising beginning and she looked at him expectantly, happy for him to lay his cards on the table first. This seemed to be more difficult than he had anticipated and she could see that, although there were a million and one unanswered questions, he was going to take the male line of least resistance and fumble around until she helpfully supplied the words he had locked inside his head. Sometimes the inarticulacy of the average male drove her, and the rest of the female population, to hair-tearing distraction and this was evidently going to be yet another of those occasions. She wondered if it was sheer cowardice or a genuine inability to string a sentence together that contained a fully formed emotion. Whatever it was, she had yet to come across a man who did not resort to boyish helplessness or even dumb terror when faced with the prospect of opening his heart along with his mouth.

'And what do you think those things are? That we need to get straight?' There, that should lead him helpfully up to the water, although whether he would drink or not was still open to debate.

'Um . . . well, you know, things . . .' Those waters were obviously a little too deep and muddy for him. She restrained herself from seizing him by the shoulders and giving him a damn good shake and tried again.

'Things like . . . ?' She opened her eyes wide to encourage the sharing of confidences and coax him along as best she could without imploding.

'Ah, well, you know . . .'

'No, I don't know, so why don't you tell me?'

She abandoned all hope of unknotting his tongue with the indirect approach and cut to the chase, recalling dimly that men were supposed to be far better at responding to direct commands than they were at mind-reading. This seemed momentarily to work. His face cleared somewhat and he took a deep breath as if he were about to launch into an impressive outpouring of emotional honesty before nerves, or prudence, got the better of him. He dried right on the edge and shrugged helplessly.

This was obviously getting them nowhere and, reluctant as she was to be the one to do so, Alex realized that she was going to have to lay her innermost self on the line if they were ever to progress beyond gaping at each other in an agony of emotional rectitude. Feeling thoroughly outmanoeuvred, and thinking that perhaps she had underestimated his native cunning, she threw all caution to the wind and did the first thing that came into her head. She leaned forward, took his face in her hands and kissed him thoroughly until actions had most definitely spoken louder than could any of the words he had temporarily mislaid.

When they came up for air she was stunned to see that Nick had tears in his eyes. There was nothing that made her stomach twist more than to see a grown man cry. It made her feel helpless, even if she had read all those articles that pronounced that it was a perfectly New Man thing to do. So it might be, but it reduced her to a quivering wreck. For want of anything better to do, she patted his arm and wondered if it was a good idea to fling her arms around him or if that would send him off at the deep end. After a couple of minutes of sustained concentration on the coffee table in front of him, Nick felt able to take a deep breath and blurt it all out.

'I can't stand this, you know. Watching you and that jerk . . . You might think he can give you everything you need, but he can't. Otherwise you wouldn't be messing me around.'

For a second there she was brought up short. 'That's not fair. I am not "messing you around" at all. It's the other way round if you ask me.'

The hollow laugh that greeted this statement left her in no doubt as to how heartily he disagreed with her. She couldn't believe her ears. Here was the man who had led her a merry dance for months, blowing hot and cold faster than the average British summer, and he was trying to tell her that she was the one at fault. Men. There was obviously no limit to their capacity for self-delusion, not to mention self-pity. Of course, had she been privy to his thoughts she would have found that they bore a remarkable resemblance to her own, but if things were that simple all the agony would go out of the ecstasy and sales of gin would slump. So they glared at each other in mutual misunderstanding and felt quite justified in feeling betrayed, bewildered and downright pissed off.

This might have gone on for quite some time had Simon not grown bored of hanging around in the kitchen and come bustling back in with the coffee to see how things were progressing. He had taken the opportunity to call Serge and indulge in a long and fruitful dialogue, but once that was done with he could not bear the suspense any longer. Any hurt he might have felt on having his unacknowledged suspicions confirmed was superseded by a desire to play matchmaker. After all, now that he was happy he could afford to be generous with his feelings and, besides, this new-found saintly aspect made him feel good about himself. Serge was always going on about being in touch with the spiritual and Simon knew that it wasn't whisky he was referring to.

Ever the chameleon, he was fully prepared to spread his love around and make the world a better place as long as his own nest was suitably feathered. He liked to think of it as a form of designer spirituality, a sort of Nichiren Soshu Buddhism for those who couldn't be bothered to chant but quite liked the idea of having it all. Karma he could deal with: back in Bali, many a long evening had been spent listening to Serge earnestly explain its meaning and consequences and ever since Simon had been looking for the perfect opportunity to make up for what he could see was lost ground on his part.

So, eager beaver that he was, he poured each of them a cup, then sat down expectantly, ready and willing to have his heart warmed and his ability to forgive and forget stretched in a most satisfying fashion. One look at their faces, however, and he knew that gratification might be a long time in coming.

'Milk, anyone?'

They wordlessly accepted the jug he passed around, Alex putting it on the table in front of her rather than risk bodily contact by handing it on to Nick. Funny how you could suddenly loathe someone who, only hours before, had made your flesh crawl in quite a different manner. Surmising that the situation was serious, Simon played for time by giving his coffee an extra long and thoughtful stare before again looking brightly from one to the other.

'I've got some croissants on the go as well, if anyone is interested.'

The marked lack of enthusiasm with which this was greeted only reinforced the sinking feeling that told him that he was going to have to be the one to broker some sort of peace deal here or suffer the two of them dripping around for many more months to come, a prospect that turned his guts to lead. Really, they wanted their heads banging together but, as ever, he preferred a more subtle approach.

'Well, looking at the pair of you, I'd get more meaningful conversation out of the cat.'

'Well, at least she keeps her opinions to herself.' Alex's *sotto voce* mutterings were not quite *sotto* enough and Nick rose to the bait.

'And what is that supposed to mean?'

'You know perfectly well what I mean. Unless, that is, you think I'm just messing around as usual.'

There was nothing like biting sarcasm to bring a flush of anger to a man's cheeks and Nick's duly obliged. He was still digging deep for that perfect retort when Simon decided it was time to referee before things got ugly.

'Children, children, please. What on earth has got into the pair of you? I left you alone to talk, not hurl insults at each other like a pair of drag queens fighting over a lipstick.'

'He started it, telling me I'd been messing him around. *Me*, messing *him* around. What a joke!'

Alex's lower lip wobbled mutinously and she resembled nothing so much as a recalcitrant six-year-old. Simon sighed gustily and held up a placating hand before Nick could leap in and trash her statement with an equally inflammatory assertion of his own. 'Wait, wait, wait. Now, as far as I can tell you two have not been so much messing each other around as missing the point.'

'That's exactly what I've been trying to tell her but

she just doesn't get it.' Now it was Nick's turn to re-enter the playground.

'Get what, precisely?'

There it was, the dignified tilt of the chin. Nick managed to betray all his New Man credentials by reflecting that she looked gorgeous when she was angry before hastily re-entering the fray. Wisely, he kept his thoughts to himself.

'The point. The point being that actions speak louder than words and you still have that – that *thing* stuck on the end of your finger like some sort of trophy or something. I suppose it makes sense, really, doesn't it? I mean, who in their right mind would walk away from that kind of dough? Eh? You might have made a big show of it to frighten him but if you were really serious about what you said you'd have taken it off by now. And you haven't. So, as far as I see it, you are still engaged to be married to that – that . . . walking wallet and you're still selling out on yourself and everything you believe in. And me,' he finished rather lamely.

'Judging by last night's performance I'm not so sure that is entirely the case. Well, Alex?'

God, but he was good at this. Simon had always secretly thought he might make a good barrister and only the thought of all those hours spent poring over very unsexy books had prevented him from taking his fantasies further. Besides, he wasn't too sure that the wig would suit the shape of his face, fond as he was of razor-sharp cuts that displayed his elegant cheekbones to best effect.

'I . . . erm . . .'

Alex twisted the offensive ring around her finger

and seemed lost for words. Nick seized his chance to bounce up and down and shout triumphantly, 'You see? You see!'

Ignoring this lapse of fair play, Simon looked at her levelly until finally she found her voice and quietly but distinctly stated her case. 'I wouldn't marry that man if you handcuffed me to his precious company car and threatened to beat me to death with his briefcase. The very thought of fifty years spent watching him do the *Telegraph* crossword in his stripy shirts makes me want to dye my hair purple and get my nipples pierced and as for his mother . . .'

They all shuddered, united by conspiratorial empathy and the still far too fresh memory of the night before. Having taken a moment to let that image pass, she carried on, her voice softening so that Nick had to strain to hear what she was saying. 'And most of all, I wouldn't marry him because I couldn't bear not to be with you. I mean, I know I'm not with you at the moment but there was always hope and if I married him that would be it. For ever. Or at least until I could get a good lawyer.'

Nick was so touched by this that he even forgave her the get-out clause cunningly disguised as wit. Simon had a lump in his throat so big he couldn't speak and the three of them sat there, grinning awkwardly at each other until the familiar but unwelcome sound of the doorbell rudely disturbed their golden moment. They might have ignored it but whoever it was was not prepared to wait and began to make a concerted effort to hammer the door down.

'Oh, God, that's probably Richard,' Alex whimpered, and shrank against Nick.

'Well, you're going to have to face him sometime. And that might as well be now.'

In truth, Nick was itching to see the look on that fatuous face when he heard what Alex had to say. It would make up for all those months of pure agony watching and wondering exactly what they had been getting up to together. The thought of those pale hands touching her warm flesh was more than he could bear, and sent his stomach into a tightly coiled knot of jealous fury. This moment was going to be sweet and he intended to savour every second of his rival's public humiliation.

Simon was a little more circumspect in his feelings, concerned more that Richard would burst through the heavy oak door before Alex stopped dithering and gave him permission to open it. Not that he needed permission to open his own front door but he understood that she might need to compose herself before dealing with her pinstriped nemesis who, for a wimp, was proving remarkably physical in his approach.

'Alex ?'

Simon's voice had taken on that adult inflection and she fought down her mounting panic, helped along by Nick's firm hand squeezing her own shakier one.

'OK, OK . . . No, wait! I mean, look at me, I have to put some clothes on. I can't face him like this!' Looking at her mussed-up hair and the old T-shirt he had lent her to sleep in, Simon had to admit she did have a point. He would have noticed it himself, had it not been for the rapid and dramatic pace of events and the fact that she had looked heartbreakingly cute back there, baring her soul without for once fussing over the streaks of mascara under her eyes and the state of her hairdo. It really must be love. Nick was no use at noticing these things as, in his eyes at least, she never looked less than perfect. The thought of Richard seeing her like that, though, made him feel ludicrously proprietorial.

'Here, take these. We'll keep him talking until you're ready. And remember, act normal! We don't want any more trouble than is absolutely necessary.'

Bundling her clothes into her arms, Nick threw the bedding together and chucked it over the back of the sofa whilst Simon made for the door, prudently sliding the chain across before opening it just in case it did turn out to be a mad axe-murderer instead of an irate banker. He opened the door a crack and peered out, to ascertain that the person staring belligerently back at him was indeed the scourge of the trading floor.

'What took you so bloody long?'

The careful veneer of manners had disappeared, replaced by a note of petulant fury and a look of murderous intent. At least, that's how Simon saw it. Loving every second, he closed the door again to release the chain but played for time, rattling away as he called through to Richard that the wretched thing seemed to be stuck. Correctly judging that he might well have pushed things as far as they could go, he finally flung it open only to be brushed aside as Richard stalked past him, looking wildly about him as he went.

'Do come in,' Simon murmured after him, and hastily followed, anxious to steer him away from the sitting room in case Nick had not yet had a chance to put things in order but failing miserably. After a cursory glance down the corridor, it was the first place Richard headed, Simon coming up short behind him as he stopped dead at the sight of Nick still clad in boxer shorts and a T-shirt, pretending to read the paper whilst sipping a cup of coffee. Fortunately, Richard was far too het up to notice that it was yesterday's paper and the coffee was stone cold, not a wisp of steam rising invitingly from it.

Nick looked up at him, assuming an expression of mild surprise as if it were an everyday occurrence to half break down a door on a Sunday morning. 'Morning, Richard,' was all he said.

Richard did not bother to reply. He stood there, clad in his needlecord trousers and weekend shirt, tapping his fingers against his thigh, his eyes darting to every corner of the room in turn.

'Where is she?' he demanded.

Nick knew it was useless to dissemble, and in any case he was anxious to get the whole thing over with. He met Simon's warning look before replying as graciously as he possibly could, 'Alex? She's in the shower at the moment. Did you want a cup of coffee or something?'

Behind Richard's back, Simon had been making frantic hand signals, trying to pass on the message that Nick should use whatever delaying tactics he could. Peeking out from the bathroom door, Alex was rolling her eyes, sliding behind it again when Richard suddenly turned to see what on earth Simon was up to. He was rewarded with the most innocent smile Simon could dredge up, which was replaced by a look of panic as he sniffed the air and ran off to the kitchen, screaming, 'Oh, my God, the croissants!' leaving Richard with Nick.

They sat for a few moments in fairly fraught silence before Simon reappeared, bearing fresh coffee and a plate of croissants with crispy edges and large chunks hacked out of them where they had turned to charcoal. Alex made her entrance just as the pouring ritual had been completed, looking a shade overdressed in her glorious red frock. Its incongruity did little for her self-confidence but at least the colour signalled some sort of fighting spirit. In the bathroom she had taken the time to consider the options and had come to the conclusion that attack was probably her only line of defence when faced with an intractable fiancé. Exuding as much breezy confidence as she could muster, she reassumed her position on the sofa and greeted him with a cool and fairly calm, 'Hello, Richard.'

This was wasted on him as he seemed curiously distracted by something on the coffee table in front of him. Too late, Nick remembered that he had forgotten to hide the photographs and leaned forward to grab them just as Richard snatched them up and began to go through them, gazing at each in turn as if he couldn't believe his eyes. Not one of them dared move a muscle and instead sat transfixed as the tension mounted, the only sound being Richard's rapid breathing and the swishing noise he made as he turned over one photograph to be confronted by another equally as offensive. Finally, he looked straight at Alex as if she had sprouted the regalia of a fully fledged harpy. 'You slut,' was all he said, but it was enough to bring Nick instantly to his feet with an air of quiet but total menace.

'Say that again and I'll break your neck.'

His height and build added to the impact of his words and none of them was in any doubt that this was no empty threat. Richard sneered as best he could but Alex could see that his knees were knocking. Nick leaned forward and, in one swift movement, took the photographs from Richard and placed them safely out of reach before turning back to him and stating baldly, 'I think it's time you left.'

Gathering the tiny vestiges of courage he had somewhere, Richard folded his arms mutinously and retorted, 'Not before I've sorted a few things out.'

Alex could well imagine what this would entail and tried to pre-empt any nastiness by taking off her ring and holding it out to him.

Richard recoiled as if he had been socked on the jaw. He looked at her hand, and then her face, with extreme loathing tinged by betrayal. The breath rasped in his throat and he seemed to have some trouble articulating his thoughts, but eventually the words broke through, fuelled by an angry surge of spite. Clearly, Carol's genetic gift was about to stand him in very good stead. 'You little bitch. So this is what you were up to whilst I was out there, slaving away so that we could have a beautiful home and you could indulge yourself in that pathetic little hobby of yours.'

Alex winced. There was nothing more guaranteed to undermine her than referring to her stories and articles as if they were no more than scribblings. Nick, too, had flinched at his words but it was more in an effort of self-control as he clenched his fists and took a step closer to the armchair in which Richard sat. Richard blanched but maintained both his composure and his curled lip, still staring at Alex as if she were something not entirely wholesome.

'I waited up all night for you to come to my place. I was worried about you. I kept calling and getting your damn answerphone and then I realized that, of course, you'd come back here to be with your cronies.'

Simon wasn't too sure that he liked his choice of vocabulary but there was no stopping Richard once he had the bit of self-justification between those expensively capped teeth.

'I felt sure once you'd had time to calm down and become less hysterical you'd see sense and be able to discuss things like any normal person.'

There it was, the unattractive whine that entered his voice whenever he felt hard done by. Alex made as if to respond but he carried on, caught up in his tide of reproach.

'I don't know what it is you think I've done to you to deserve this but to be confronted with pictures of my fiancée in a state of undress . . . That filth is no better than the stuff you see on page three. I suppose you took them. At least you won't have wanted to grope the goods.' He directed this last jibe at Simon, who ignored it with rather more dignity than it deserved.

Nick smiled coolly at him, barely bothering to hide his contempt. 'Actually, it was me. And if you really think those are filthy then you need to get out more. Or at least get some sort of a life. You could always start by finding yourself someone else to marry. Someone with a lot less to lose than Alex here.'

At this, all the colour drained from Richard's face and he sat as if turned to stone. He looked imploringly at Alex and whispered, 'I didn't think you were serious.'

Her resolve almost broke but she nodded in assent. Almost, that is, until he added two and two together and made his usual five.

Then Richard looked first at Alex, then at Nick, before spitting out, 'Oh, I get it now,' with such impressive venom that all sympathy she might have felt vanished along with the last vestiges of guilt. He had the disconcerting ability to look at people as if they were gnats on the face of his superior universe, a skill that must have been well honed in his time at the top of the corporate tree. Pushing himself out of the armchair, Richard thrust out his jaw and waggled a warning finger in Nick's face.

'You think you're so fucking clever, sucking up to her when I'm not around, shifting between her and your boyfriend over there. God only knows what kind of diseases you people have passed on to me, with all your arty-farty crap and your lack of morals. Well, you take her, mate, and good riddance. You deserve each other, all three of you. You're sick, that's what you are. Probably getting up to all kinds of kinky stuff with your cosy little threesome . . . You make me want to puke. Just you wait until I inform your parents what you've been up to – and I'm sure the tabloids will be very interested to hear about this as well. And if I've caught anything at all, I'll sue. I'll have you up in court before you can find some bent barrister to get you all off. As for you pretending that it was all romantic to wait until our wedding night – I can't believe I swallowed all that crap! You weren't exactly shy before. Yeah, well, it all makes sense now. Whilst you were shagging each other silly you were probably laughing all over your faces at how gullible I was – you slag!'

All his hurt and fury were being directed straight at Alex, who sat there whilst his verbal blows rained down on her head and prayed that he would stop before she dissolved into the tears she didn't want him to have the satisfaction of seeing.

Luckily for her, both Nick and Simon reached boiling point at precisely the same moment. Moving in concert, Simon yelled, 'Shut the fuck up!' just as Nick stepped forward and grabbed him by the throat. Richard thrashed around for a couple of minutes like a landed mackerel before conceding that there was no escaping from Nick's vicelike grip. He glared at him, his hands tearing ineffectually at those around his throat, whence strange mewling noises came. Just to make sure that no vicious elbow could find its target, Simon pinned his flailing arms to his sides in a brutal bearhug, enjoying Richard's panic. 'I shouldn't worry, mate, you're not my type,' he said.

Nick, too, enjoyed the feel of the enemy within his grasp before speaking to Simon over Richard's slumped shoulder. 'I think Richard was just leaving, don't you?'

'Without a doubt.'

As tall as Nick, although slighter, Simon formed the other half of a highly effective intimidatory sandwich as they manoeuvred the hapless Richard out of the sitting room and towards the front door. The unrelenting hand around his throat precluded any form of protest, which was probably just as well. One more word from him and Nick might well have carried out his earlier threat. Alex watched from her perch on the sofa, not knowing whether to offer up some form of feeble protest or cheer them on. She plumped for a version of the latter, reasoning that it wasn't every day she could bask in the glory of having two hulking great men defend her honour. Politically incorrect it might be, but she would bet anything that within every woman lurked that same gleeful response whenever a dragon was slain for her. The fact that one of her saviours just happened to be the gorgeous hunk with whom she was madly and passionately in love only added to the excitement.

It was such a glorious relief to be able to bask in the joy of it all without fear of crushing disappointment that she almost missed the final, inglorious moments of Richard's downfall. Luckily, she arrived just in time to see Nick hold him against the wall whilst Simon opened the front door with a flourish. Seeing her there, Nick relinquished one hand and held it out to her, demanding, 'Alex, give me your ring,' whilst keeping a squirming, kicking Richard pinioned firmly to the wall. She took one last look at her sparkler and handed it over with only the tiniest hesitation, her sense of fair play battling royally with a perfectly natural desire to hang on to a big shiny diamond for as long as she could.

'There you go, mate. Hope it keeps you warm at night,' said Nick solicitously, as he tucked the ring into

Richard's top pocket. Then, with one final shove he was out of the front door and it was firmly slammed in his face. Just before it closed on him he looked at Alex and rasped, 'You're making a big mistake,' before solid oak cut him off. Through it they could hear him shouting all kinds of threats and dire warnings but these soon died off, to be replaced by the sound of his car starting and the tyres squealing as he drove off at impressive speed, hopefully to be stopped in due course by the kind of traffic policeman who looked on over-paid City types as fair and welcome game on a slow Sunday.

For a moment or two Alex felt completely bereft. It wasn't so much that Richard was finally out of her life – that in itself was a relief – but he had been part of a solid plan for the future and now everything was up in the air and as scary as hell.

The other two were too busy howling with laughter to notice her silence at first, but a pause in the general backslapping and guffawing gave Nick the opportunity to look to her for approving gratitude. What he saw instead brought him up short and he instantly sobered and nudged Simon to do likewise. Her face was riddled with self-doubt and apprehension and, seeing that, he put a comforting arm around her and drew her to him, murmuring at her as if she were a small, frightened child, 'Hey, hey, come on, Alex. It'll be OK, you'll see.'

She tried to smile bravely at him but fear of the wide-open future, and the crescendo of tension that had built up through the last few months, came crashing down on her and she lowered her face into his chest before he could see the tears. It was all very well for him to say that things were going to be all right, but he wasn't the one who would have to sort out this unholy mess. It was all fine and good chucking Richard out on his arse, but there were still a million and one practical details to be dealt with and she was the one who would have to do it.

Her shaking shoulders alerted him to the fact that all was most definitely not well. Stroking her hair and uttering soothing noises, he exchanged a helpless look with Simon, who judged this a perfect moment to disappear and leave Nick to sort things out. A desperate shake of the head and a swift kick to the ankle told him that this was not a good move so he dutifully shuffled back into the sitting room with them, Nick half dragging Alex in some bizarre three-legged race. There, they both hovered whilst she gulped and hiccuped, her sobs preventing coherent speech.

'Look, Alex, if you're worried about the things Richard said, don't. He's all talk and no trousers. There's no way in hell he'd dare do any of those things . . .' Simon tried his best to instil some sense of logic into proceedings that seemed to be getting dangerously out of hand.

Alex lifted her face from the safety of Nick's chest to shake her head and gasp, ''S'not that,' between frantic gulps of air.

'Well, what is it, then?'

Nick felt a growing sense of alarm. Surely she couldn't have been in love with that jerk? Oh, please, God, no. A small, sure voice deep inside him scoffed at his fears but there was still the off-chance that all his instincts could be wrong. After all, they had led him a merry dance until now.

Calming sufficiently to blow her nose, she took a few deep breaths and in a plaintive little wail put him out of his misery. 'What on earth am I supposed to do now? I've handed in my notice for my flat because I was supposed to be moving into the new place and now I've got to go and tell everyone that it's all off. They're all going to laugh at me. And I'll have tell them at work. They gave me a lovely vase as an engagement present and now I'll have to hand that back and everything. And what about my poor parents? Mummy had already started talking to the vicar about dates and things and . . . Oh, God, I can't cope! I really can't!'

Once again she dropped her head forward to make despairing contact with Nick's sternum. He and Simon exchanged a glance before Simon stepped in with some brotherly words of wisdom. 'For Christ's sake, Alex, pull yourself together. No one's going to laugh at you. In fact, they'll probably pat you on the back and ask you what took you so long. And I can guarantee you that your parents will be amongst the first to offer their congratulations and tell you that they never really liked him anyway. As for the flat, you know you can always stay here. I'm sure there's room in Nick's bed if you ask him nicely.'

Alex gulped again, this time more in surprise than hysterics, before another thought struck her and she dissolved again into uncertainty. 'Thanks. But I'm sure you won't want us squashing in with you for ever – or me, at least . . .' She trailed off, not wanting to presume too much. She needn't have worried.

'That's really good of you, Simon, and I'm sure we'll look for our own place just as soon as . . . um . . . funds permit.' Nick, too, faltered, hating himself for even having to mention the stagnant state of his cash-flow.

'Oh, I shouldn't worry too much about that. Serge mentioned a while back that one of the majors is launching a new publication, some glossy lifestyle mag concentrating on exotic travel. He just happens to have very good contacts there and he showed them your stuff. You remember those Balinese pics he raved over? Well, when he told me about it I lent him your port-folio to back it up and he told me just this morning that they're very, very interested. They particularly like the fact that you've done so much travelling already and could fit in anywhere at a moment's notice. Serge is setting up a meeting but he thinks it's a mere for-mality. It's a great break and one I think you deserve. It'd give you a chance to do the sort of stuff you really love and you could still freelance for me when you're not trotting the globe on fabulous, well-paid assign-ments. What do you think?'

Simon resembled nothing so much as a conjuror flourishing a rabbit he had just pulled out of a hat. And a very glamorous rabbit at that.

'I – I don't know what to say. That's just amazing!'

It seemed that in his role as mentor Simon was always going to be able to reduce Nick to stuttering gratitude. As a broad grin broke across Nick's face, Simon basked in his moment of beneficence. There seemed little point in telling Nick that he had known about the possibility for weeks and had been waiting for just the right moment to break the news. Simon was no dummy and although the star-crossed lovers might have thought their true feelings for each other were undetectable he had found the prolonged silences and physical avoidance painfully transparent. The pair of them had almost driven him to distraction with their ditherings over each other.

Besides, he and Serge were coming to that stage where they needed to spend long evenings alone together, cosying up over some divine titbits whilst Serge extolled the virtues of his latest New Age discovery or bitched happily about some mutual acquaintance. Of course, he kept that piece of information strictly to himself, rationalizing that it would be best as always to operate on a strictly need-to-know basis.

Alex's flat tone interrupted his domestic fantasies. 'Well, that sounds great. I'm very happy for you.'

Try as she might to dredge up some generosity of spirit, she could not keep the hollow note out of her voice. Just as she had got her dream man it would seem that he was to be snatched out of her grasp, sent off round the world to become a rich, famous photographer and no doubt meet lots of gorgeous, dusky maidens along the way. She could cheerfully have throttled Simon.

Belatedly realizing the same thing himself, Nick looked from Alex to Simon, not knowing quite what to say. To have the perfect job offered to him on a plate was nothing short of a miracle, but then so was getting the woman to match. There had to be a way to make it work, but the rapidity of events had overtaken him and he was clean out of ideas. His mounting dilemma showed on his face but Simon raised a preemptive hand before he could say anything stupid.

'Now, come on, Alex. You didn't seriously think I'd leave you out of the equation, did you? There's no reason why you can't write that column of yours from anywhere in the world. I'm sure your opinions will travel only too well and I am also sure that once your name is on that masthead you'll be inundated with other freelance offers. God knows, you'll probably end up being our social arbiter in Beijing or something. So stop pouting, sweetie, and get ready to pack your bags!'

She had to concede he had a point. Finally beginning to believe that she had a major part to play in this particular fairy-tale, Alex hugged Simon and smiled up into his familiar face, now almost teary with the impact of his own generosity.

'Thanks. For everything.'

'You're welcome. Oh, I nearly forgot. Serge sent a little something for your suitcase.'

Reaching behind him, Simon produced a bikini of such divine sexiness that it brought tears to Nick's eyes. Flourishing it like a trophy, he presented it to her with mock gravity, adding cheekily, 'Actually, he nicked it from a shoot. Said the moment he saw it he knew it was meant for you.'

Alex regarded the minuscule confection with some suspicion. 'Very kind of him.'

'Yes it is, isn't it?' was all he would say and she wasn't fooled for a moment.

'And terribly perspicacious of Serge. One would almost think he had a vested interest in seeing us off in style.'

'One might.' Satisfied with himself, Simon beamed benevolently and continued, 'In fact, I'm just off to tell him the good news. I'm sure he'll be delighted to set up an early meeting for you, Nick,' and sauntered out, looking for all the world as if he were a prime candidate for instant canonization.

Left alone, the two looked at each other as if Christmas and a lottery win had come all at the same time. Then Nick let out a whoop of triumph and joy and flung his arms around Alex. 'I think this has to be the best day of my life!'

'Yeah, well, I reckon it can get even better.' She smiled cheekily up at him, tugging playfully at his belt.

'Now, just wait a second there. We're not doing anything like that until you make me a solemn promise.' His voice was light but his expression deadly serious.

'And what's that?'

'That you'll marry me. Straight away. Before you can get cold feet or start to panic that my shirts aren't stripy enough.'

Alex thought she was about to go into shock overload. She knew that she was crazy about him, of course, and thought that he probably felt the same about her. But this, coming so soon after the Richard fiasco . . . Making up her mind, she looked him squarely in the eye and announced her terms and conditions. 'I'll give you an answer if you give me a straight one.'

'No problem. Ask me anything.'

'That night at the hotel. What did it really mean to you?'

There was a long pause, so pregnant with implication that Alex thought he might be about to tell her some awful truth. Then he said, 'It meant absolutely every-thing to me. I, um . . . I have a confession to make.'

'Go on.' She was superficially calm but her heart was racing faster than a Ferrari.

'When I opened the door to you, it wasn't the total shock I pretended it to be.'

She furrowed her brow in puzzlement. 'I don't understand.'

'Well, you see, there was no mini-cab or anything. I made that bit up. I did find a card but you must have dropped it out of your bag or something. It was lying on the bathroom floor and I knew it had to belong to you because you'd just been in there putting on your face before we all went out to some bar or other. I couldn't believe it at first but curiosity got the better of me. And, OK, the fact that even then I was pretty smitten. So I called up the number and when that woman answered I described exactly what I was looking for. And she sent you along.'

'Oh, my God.' Alex was mortified, staring at him in an agony of embarrassment.

'I wanted to find out . . . I dunno. I suppose I wanted to know if it could really be true, if you would do that. And then when you told me all about your little scam, well, at first I couldn't believe my ears but then we made love, and it was so special, and, well, then I knew . . .'

'Knew what?' she asked softly, never taking her eyes from his face for a second.

'Knew that all that mattered was that you were in my arms and I was falling in love with you. And nothing that's happened since has done anything to change my opinion.'

His sincerity was so patent and so touching that she had to fight an urge to cry all over again. Never in her life had she felt so accepted. She knew then that whatever she did, wherever they went and whatever happened, he would always love her for herself. She wrapped her arms around his neck and, through blissfully half-closed eyes, whispered, 'In that case, the answer to your question is yes. Although now that my career is taking off I'm not so sure . . .'

He silenced the almost inevitable teasing with a kiss so intense that she felt as if he had stripped her naked right there and then. And, held tight against him in happy anticipation of what was to come, she kissed him right back.

A half-regretful smile stole across her face as she thought back over the months dangling from a great and tantalizing emotional height. The agony had only served to underline the ecstasy but she was only too delighted to give that up for the deep peace of a marital bed. Although, feeling Nick pressing urgently against her, she realized that any thoughts of rest and relaxation were a tad premature. For once, she'd let the future take care of itself, sure that, at some not too distant juncture, they would be tucked up sharing domestic thoughts under a warm duvet. Until then, she was going to be true to herself, true to them both and ravish him with every melting bone in her body.